THE SUNSET GATE

Grace Livingston Hill

L I B R A R Y

THE
SUNSET
GATE

ISABELLA ALDEN

LIVING BOOKS®
Tyndale House Publishers, Inc.
Wheaton, Illinois

Living Books is a registered trademark of Tyndale House
Publishers, Inc.

Library of Congress Catalog Card Number 94-61526
ISBN 0-8423-3175-1

Printed in the United States of America

99	98	97	96	95	
6	5	4	3	2	1

CONTENTS

WELCOME

by Grace Livingston Hill

As long ago as I can remember, there was always a radiant being who was next to my mother and father in my heart, and who seemed to me to be a combination of fairy godmother, heroine, and saint. I thought her the most beautiful, wise, and wonderful person in my world, outside of my home. I treasured her smiles, copied her ways, and listened breathlessly to all she had to say, sitting at her feet worshipfully whenever she was near; ready to run any errand for her, no matter how far.

I measured other people by her principles and opinions, and always felt that her word was final. I am afraid I even corrected my beloved parents sometimes when they failed to state some principle or opinion as she had done.

When she came on a visit, the house seemed glorified because of her presence; while she remained, life was one long holiday; when she went away, it seemed as if a blight had fallen.

She was young, gracious, and very good to be with.

This radiant creature was known to me by the name of Auntie Belle, though my mother and my grandmother called her Isabella! Just like that! Even sharply sometimes when they disagreed with her: *"Isabella!"* I wondered that they dared.

Later I found that others had still other names for her. To the congregation of which her husband was pastor she was known as Mrs. Alden. And there was another world in which she moved and had her being when she went away from us from time to time; or when at certain hours in the day she shut herself within a room that was sacredly known as a Study, and wrote for a long time, while we all tried to keep still; and in this other world of hers she was known as Pansy. It was a world that loved and honored her, a world that gave her homage and wrote her letters by the hundreds each week.

As I grew older and learned to read, I devoured her stories chapter by chapter. Even sometimes page by page as they came hot from the typewriter; occasionally stealing in for an instant when she left the study, to snatch the latest page and see what had happened next; or to accost her as her morning's work was done, with: "Oh, have you finished another chapter?"

Often the whole family would crowd around when the word went around that the last chapter of something was finished and going to be read aloud. And now we listened, breathless, as she read, and made her characters live before us.

The letters that poured in at every mail were overwhelming. Asking for her autograph and her photograph; begging for pieces of her best dress to sew into patchwork; begging for advice how to become a great author; begging for advice on every possible subject. And she answered them all!

Sometimes I look back upon her long and busy life, and marvel at what she has accomplished. She was a marvelous housekeeper; knowing every dainty detail of her home to perfection. And a marvelous pastor's wife! The real old-fashioned kind, who made calls with her husband, knew every member intimately, cared for the sick, gathered the young people into her home, and loved them all as if they had been her brothers and sisters. She was beloved, almost adored, by all the members. And she was a tender, vigilant, wonderful mother, such a mother as few are privileged to have, giving without stint of her time, her strength, her love, and her companionship. She was a speaker and teacher, too.

All these things she did, and *yet wrote books!* Stories out of real life that struck home and showed us to ourselves as God saw us; and sent us to our knees to talk with him.

And so, in her name I greet you all, and commend this story to you.

Grace Livingston Hill

(This is a condensed version of the foreword Mrs. Hill wrote for her aunt's final book, *An Interrupted Night*.)

FOREWORD

by Robert Munce,
grandson of Grace Livingston Hill and author of
The Grace Livingston Hill Story

TALES OF ISABELLA ALDEN:
THE MEANING BEHIND THE STORY

Not only was Isabella Alden the author of more than one hundred books, she was the beloved aunt and mentor of Grace Livingston Hill, who herself became a much-loved author of more than one hundred wholesome romance novels! So whether you have come here because you love the books of Grace Livingston Hill, or just because you love a good story, you have come to the right spot. Now, here you sit, book in hand, only a few pages from the threshold of one of Isabella Alden's lovely stories.

Just a moment ago I was watching TV, looking in vain for beauty and reason, joy and gladness. Instead, I found violence, chaos, and crude mirth. Finally, I went to the shelf and there, next to my set of Grace Livingston Hill books, was my collection of titles by Isabella Alden. Here, I knew, I would learn even as I was beautifully entertained. Here I would find value, pleasure, and solace at the end of the day.

Isabella, or Pansy as her readers called her, was the sister of Marcia MacDonald Livingston, the mother of Grace Livingston Hill. Though a wide age gap existed between the young Grace and her aunt, they developed a deep and lasting friendship. Certainly they had a lot in common. Both were great observers of the people around them and of the settings where they found themselves. They were both great story-tellers and could put their observations on paper in story form. Always coloring their novels were their strong opinions on what made people truly success-ful and happy.

These ladies saw themselves as evangelists and men-tors of the young. They always tried to get across the message that true success would only come by pleas-ing God, and to explain in their stories how that can be accomplished. Their godly influence has changed the lives of many.

May you find and enjoy that influence as you read this story.

Robert L. Munce
June 1994

1

"I DON'T KNOW!"

WONA!" The name echoed through the otherwise still forest. The hush of a late August day was on all nature; the very leaves seemed to be listening. The call came again, ringing through the stillness. After a moment of silence a syllable was added: "Wee*wo*na!" with the second one prolonged, so that the "wo" seemed to roll at her through the trees.

The girl crouching at the foot of one of the great sequoias started—having felt, rather than heard the call—listened, and when the name came again more prolonged, more penetrative than before, came to an upright posture and made answer with a curious note, half cry, half whistle, caught from a forest bird and appropriated to her own use.

"Whee, whee, whee-*ah!*" with a penetrating swell of the final *a*.

She waited a moment to see if the call was answered, then arose and shook dried leaves and twigs from herself, much as a dog might have done, her short skirt revealing bare brown feet and ankles. Shook herself and stretched up her brown arms, from which the scant sleeves fell away until the flesh was bared to the shoulders.

There was a kind of wild appeal in the upstretched arms that repeated itself in the single word: "Oh!" long drawn out, and presently added to in a sort of wail: "I don't know! I don't *know!*"

It was but an exclamation; not a hint of prayer in the words, and yet it was as distinct a cry for help as human lips could form. A moment she waited, clasping her hands together in mute appeal, an eager longing in her great, hungry brown eyes—that most pathetic of all longings—after something that she did not sufficiently understand to intelligently long for.

The girl had come, that day, face-to-face with a mystery so great, so solemn, so terrible, that she believed the shadow of it would lie about her forever.

For the second time in her life she had looked upon death. The first time was long ago, and the victim was her mother. The girl remembered it vividly enough, though she had been less than six, and now was sixteen. They had walked and walked and *walked*. Later, when she found out what the word meant, she was sure that they had come many miles. She was *so* tired, she remembered; so was her mother, too tired to heed even the crying of the little girl who tugged at her skirts; and always before she had noticed tears. Then suddenly, all unexpectedly, they had come to the cabin in the woods and had found Pete; Pete and his mother.

All that her mother said to the startled man and woman she put into three words that had always been terrible to the child: "We are lost!" She had heard them before; they had been spoken many times during that long, long walk, and always they had made the child cry; but this time there was a difference in the tone, and the mother had dropped as she spoke, a miserable heap among weeds and brush; and though the child had tugged violently at her skirts and called her name and wept bitterly, she took no notice at all. Then Pete had spoken, not crossly:

"Don't do that. Poor soul! She is dead."

The child had not understood what he meant, but something in his voice had made her not afraid of him, and she had turned suddenly and clung to him. Then the woman had bent over her mother, and after a moment had said those same strange words:

"Yes, she is dead."

And Pete lifted the child in his arms and carried her into the cabin. His arms were strong, and he was kind, and the child was not afraid.

Later, they had dug a deep hole in the ground and put her mother in it. Weewona saw her after she was laid there. Her hair had been smoothed, and a white cloth was pinned around her shoulders, and her hands were folded, and she did not look scared; but the child felt afraid of her and drew back and hid her face in Pete's neck.

"Is she lost now?" she had asked him, sobbing, and he had said, very kindly:

"No, she isn't lost anymore."

They had talked before her, Pete and his mother, quite as though she could not hear.

"I wouldn't let her look at her," Pete's mother had said. "It ain't no use and it will just scare her."

But Pete, with the child in his arms, had spoken firmly:

"Yes, she must see her. She may remember it afterward; anyhow, it's her right, and it's all we can do."

So the child had looked, and then hid her face and cried. She remembered that, after a little, she had told

Pete imperiously to wake her mother up, right away! that she did not want her to be asleep. But he had not done it; he had told her that he would if he could, but that she did not want to wake up; and Weewona had never seen her mother anymore.

With regard to the days and weeks that immediately followed this vivid experience the girl's memory was hazy enough. Certain things stood out plainly from the mass of vagueness. One was a conversation about herself. She was in Pete's mother's bed, and was thought to be asleep; but she heard Pete say, in the tone that she found out afterward was always obeyed:

"We've got to keep her, Mother; there isn't anything else that can be done." The girl remembered that the little child, lying on the bed made of dried sequoia, was glad that nothing else could be done. But the woman had said:

"I might take her away down the trail real early in the morning and leave her there; somebody would be sure to find her; she would naturally wander along down the path, if she was once put on it." Then the child shivered with fear. She did not want to be taken anywhere and left to wander along down. She told herself that Pete's mother was bad, and she did not love her. But Pete had spoken positively.

"No; I wouldn't leave so much as a dog alone on the trail in this wild place. Some beast would be the most likely to find her. There ain't enough people on the trail to make it safe to try such a thing. If there were, it wouldn't be a safe place for us."

Then the mother: "But we oughtn't to keep her here. How can we? She may have folks, and they may be looking for her; it will lessen your chances, Pete."

Then Pete had shrugged his big shoulders and said:

"That can't be helped. We didn't go after her; but

she's here, and the mother is dead without a word, and there's nothing for it but to take our chances. We can keep her from starving; and for the rest, if she's got folks and they find her, why—we've got to take that chance, too."

And they had taken it. Much of the talk the child had not understood, but she had remembered. She knew that the "folks" never came. She had lived on in that odd little two-roomed cabin that she came to know, afterward, Pete and his mother had built with their own hands. She shared Pete's mother's bed, and had her full share of the game and fish and vegetables which Pete's skill and industry produced. In the course of time she became helpful, especially to Pete; helping to plant and tend and, presently, to harvest beans and berries and corn and potatoes. As the years passed, she took her full share of the work, being out of doors with Pete whenever possible, and accepting indoor tasks with resignation as a part of life that must be borne, and that, if quickly done, would give her longer time outside with Pete. Always she felt cramped and choked in the little cabin; always she looked upon the woman who reigned there as Pete's mother, and, aside from him, of very little consequence in the world. She herself belonged to him, lived for his sake, and followed him about wherever possible, much as a faithful dog might have done.

Meantime, she learned some lessons besides those that field and forest taught her. Such crude cooking and housekeeping as the limited resources afforded she became skillful in; at first, as has already been said, because prompt attention to business there released her sooner to follow Pete, and afterward because Pete showed an interest in her work and praised the dishes she made for him. She early showed a taste for decorating the poor bare room that interested Pete and troubled his mother. This instinct grew upon her with her years, and the cabin blossomed under her touch with all the treasures of field and forest. She was skillful in finding wildwood blossoms that neither Pete nor his mother had suspected were their neighbors, and her disposal of a spray of feathery fern, or wild cucumber vine, or the graceful branches of the young madrones was a never-ceasing source of wonder and pleasure to Pete.

"Where does she get it all?" he thought aloud, rather than asked the question, one evening as he sat gazing at a bush with some of the leaves aflame that glorified the space between the two small windows—or, rather, the two small holes that let in light and air, but were guiltless of sash or glass.

"Get what?" His mother asked the question quickly, then her eyes followed his, and she spoke the thought:

"She ought to be named Weewona."

The moment she had said the words she would have given much to recall them. At first, Pete winced almost as if a blow had struck him; then, after a silence, he asked:

"What made you say that?"

"I don't know." Then, speaking doggedly, as one who felt that having said so much she might as well go on:

"I think it so often, I s'pose is the reason. She makes me think of her all the time."

Pete was still for so long after that that his mother, glancing occasionally at his face, wished again that her tongue had not made that wild slip. At last he spoke.

"We'll name her that, then. She is getting too old to be called just 'the child.' She couldn't have a name that would suit me better; and it is true, as you say, that it fits her. I wonder I had not thought of it before."

Then the mother was dismayed almost beyond the power of words. But the long silence had been broken and she resolved to go on.

"I should think that was the last name you would want her to use, or hear used. It ruined your life. The least you can do is to forget it."

"You are mistaken. I don't want to forget it. I couldn't if I would, and I wouldn't if I could. It didn't ruin my life. All the joy I ever got out of life came through her. I'll call the child Weewona, and be glad to."

It was in this way that the stray child came by her name. Some talk had passed between the woman and herself about a name; in truth, Pete also had questioned her carefully at first, but beyond the statement that she was Darling and Pet and Mamma's Baby, she had no name to offer save the diminutive Wissie, which Pete's mother said was no name at all. So they had contented themselves, the mother with saying "you" and "her," and the son by gravely speaking of her as "the child" whenever he had occasion to call her anything; and as there were no others to know her, she had gone thus far without even a name. Neither of the two with whom she now had to do could have framed their lips to call her Darling. Pet names were not in the mother's nature; as for Pete, he had used that word for one person in his life; it could never belong to another.

The child liked her new name. Her lips lingered over its syllables as if they were music, and so strange was the fierce little nature hidden behind a quiet surface that she liked it better for the discovery that Pete's mother evidently disliked its sound, and used it only when she had to. It was Pete's choice then; she was his Weewona. In truth, she had good reason to believe so. He had always been kind to the poor little waif; but from the hour of his naming her, his manner took on an added tenderness and care. He taught her all he knew, which was not a great deal; and had even begun to plan ways to secure books and writing materials for her.

"Girls of her age go to school," he once said to the mother, looking doubtfully after Weewona as she sped through the clearing toward the deeper woods. He knew she was in search of red and yellow leaves with which to hide the ugliness of the rough-hewn table. She had discovered a cloth that almost covered it, and this she daily washed and pressed, so that at each dinnertime it was as dainty as her fingers could make it. The girl's instinct for cleanliness could not but be approved by Pete's mother; she had the same herself; but daintiness, such as the careful pressing of the clean cloth and laying about its edges bright-colored leaves, or on its center a bouquet of wild flowers so skillfully disposed as to almost hide the ugly tin can that held them, Pete's mother openly scorned. Not so Pete; he liked it all, and discovering this, the child was more than indifferent to the woman's scoffing.

Clothing for the three was scarce and of the poorest. Each garment was made to last as long as needle and thread and many patches would admit. Pete's mother was skillful with her needle and early taught all that she knew to the girl who had been thrust on her care.

At first, sewing was utterly distasteful to Weewona, but one happy day she was set to patching Pete's shirt sleeve. Here was an object worthy of effort. She did her best, with such success that Pete's clothes were soon afterward put in her care, and royal care did they receive.

Three or four times a year came a gala day in their lives. On these occasions, elaborate preparations having been under way for days before, Pete's mother tied about her waist with strong cords great coarse bags heavy enough for a beast of burden. These were carefully packed with dried fruits, dried sweet corn, choice potatoes, and, in short, any and all of the products of industry and skill that had been gathered through the months. When all was ready, she seized her stout stick and tramped away; away off, down the trail; down and down, into the great, dangerous, unknown, wonderful world. This was all that Weewona knew about these journeys. Somewhere in that great world a place had been found where the contents of the bags could be exchanged for other much-needed things. Always there was brought back a few yards of some kind of cloth to be made into garments, Weewona coming in for her full share and always having "something red" brought to her by Pete's express direction. Weewona delighted in red, and Pete delighted in seeing it on her; and the mother could hardly repress her dislike of it all.

Always these pilgrimages were times of excitement. They had about them an element of danger. What it was the girl did not understand, though she questioned Pete closely.

Was he afraid his mother would get hurt?

No, not hurt. There was nothing to hurt her, but she might be followed.

Who would follow her, and what hurt would it do if someone did? Why didn't they go with her down to that mysterious world where many people stayed? Why did they live up here alone? She wanted to go down there and see people and things. When would he take her?

He put her off as long as he could. One day he told her, speaking very gravely, that he could never take her down the mountain; that he himself had gone away from the world forever, but that she was growing into a big girl now, and he had no right to keep her up there. She could go if she wished, with his mother, down to where people were, and find a place to work, and, perhaps, go to school and grow into a wise woman. But when that time came she must never come back anymore—never try to see him again.

She had turned white over the suggestion, and then had set firm lips and told him not to speak to her about the hateful world again. She would never go away from him, never, never. She did not want to see people, nor things. She wanted her dear, sweet, beautiful forest, and her dear, dear Pete, and nothing else in all the world.

2

"I'M A PILGRIM GOING HOME"

DELIGHTFUL holidays those excursions of the mother became to the two left behind. First, there was the dinner for Weewona to prepare all by herself, with no one to restrain her lavish hand.

On those days Pete must have just what he liked best; and the cloth must be smooth and shining, and the table and room gay with forest treasures. And they lingered over the meal and talked as Pete seldom had time for on other days. He helped her, too, with the work, and asked queer questions as to how things were done; and as the day waned, they went together through the thickest part of the wood almost out to the trail to meet and help homeward the burdened woman; and in many ways the day was set apart and looked forward to, on Weewona's part as schoolgirls look forward to vacations, or birthdays, or special holidays. In these simple, monotonous, and yet most unusual ways, the days and years passed, until the girl of six was the maiden of sixteen; and nothing happened to break the order of the strange life she lived. Occasionally, in her dreamy moods, the girl would speculate over, and in a crude way try to forecast, her future. She had learned many things of Pete, besides those that he laboriously tried to teach her. For instance, by dint of careful questioning of both him and his mother, she had come to understand that the appointed end of all living things was death; that people, especially, were the marked subjects of this strange foe; that sooner or later they would certainly die. At first she fought in blind but fierce rebellion over this discovery as applied to Pete. His mother might die, sometime, if she must; when she was old, oh, *very* old, and could not work anymore, nor go down the mountain, and had nothing to do, why—she must die, she supposed; and she, the girl? Well, yes, she was willing. She would have to be willing; but never for Pete! Pete was young and strong. But he would grow old, like his mother. Well, so would she; she would make herself grow old fast, so as to keep pace with Pete; and when he died she must die, too, that minute! She could not stay in the forest for a single minute without him!

Having arranged this, she gave herself to imagining their life: the mother gone, and they two growing old together; growing gray, like Pete's mother. She thought of Pete's mass of black hair and looked at her own brown head, and laughed. By and by they would limp a little; Pete's mother did, when she was tired; and she stooped her shoulders; so they would do; then, by and by, they would—and here the girl stopped abruptly in her thought, a shiver ran through her frame, and she said aloud: "Not Pete first; I won't, I *won't!* But then—he would be all alone!" She sat very still; suddenly she cried out, sobbing: "Oh yes, I will! I will for him; I *couldn't* have him left all alone!"

So, for Pete's sake, she made her supreme sacrifice.

But this was to be only when they had lived long together and were very gray and stooped a great deal, and were very tired. Yet here was she, young, lithe of limb, the rich glow of health and strength throbbing in every vein, and Pete was dead! It seemed even yet, though the first wild bitterness was passed, too awful a thing to be believed. Pete in his strength, with only here and there a gray hair among the shining black ones, lying still and cold just as her mother had done. Oh! Hidden away in a hole in the ground, as they had done with her mother! She had dug the hole herself, with Pete's own spade. She had made it soft with beautiful green boughs and placed a halo of gold and scarlet leaves all about the sides, such as she knew he would like; then they two had carried him, dressed in the best he had, and laid him in it; with her own hands she had covered him from sight. And she was young and strong, and might have to live on and on until she was an old woman, without him! Was it any wonder that she flung up her hands in that despairing cry: "Oh, I don't know! I *don't know!*"

An entire day and part of another had passed since these awful things had happened, and the girl's sense of desolation seemed to be deepening with every minute. She had been sitting for hours under the solemn shadows of the great sequoias, as far away from the cabin as she had dared to go, lost in her bitter gulf of pain and dread.

When she heard Pete's mother's voice calling, a wave of fierce rebellion took hold of her soul afresh. The woman was old and gray and bent, yet there she was alive and with strength enough to ring out her voice like that, and Pete, the young and strong, was dead. He would stay dead forever. If it were not for that awful forever, if he were coming back sometime, she could bear it and wait; she could wait for years. Such a little while ago things were just as they had been as far back as she could remember, and now—

In certain moods she found herself wondering if it were not years ago, when she was young, that he went out one morning, gun in hand, and said as he passed her:

"Get your mouth ready for fresh meat, Weewona, there's the track of a bear too near the cabin for comfort; I shall bring him back with me for supper."

She had sprung up from the potatoes she was sorting and dashed after him with an eager "Oh, let me go with you! I never saw a big bear or a lion or anything worth seeing!" But he had sent her back with the assurance that a gun and a wild beast were enough to look after, without the addition of a girl. Dead bears and lions were more comfortable to look at than live ones; he would bring her one. He had been long gone, and the mother had begun to peer out through the deepening twilight; but she, Weewona, had felt no fear. Pete, she believed, was equal to many wild beasts.

He came back at last; crawled back by slow and painful effort, almost to his cabin door. He had shot his beast, but there had been a fierce fight; the creature had sprung upon him unexpectedly from the rear and wounded his shoulder, and then, somehow, he had contrived, he could not think by what stupid movement, to shoot himself, as well as the animal, and he was sore wounded, and had lost much blood.

They made wonderful efforts, the woman and the girl, working over him with energy and skill, following his directions until he was too weak to give them; working on with the energy of desperation, until the woman dropped the bottle she was using and said: "No, Pete, I'm going down the trail to find a doctor."

"Oh," Weewona said, "let me go. I can run so fast! I will find one and bring him quick!"

But Pete, though very weak, could still speak authoritatively.

"No! It's of no use. I tell you, Mother, it would do no good. I know this kind of wound; I shall be dead long before a doctor can reach me; and he couldn't do any good if he was here. No, child, don't go away; stay close by me until it is over."

The poor mother broke the self-control of years and burst into a bitter cry of defiance and determination. She would go for a doctor! She would go this minute! He *should* come in time! Pete should *not* die! In the midst of this he said, speaking faintly: "Hush, Mother, hush! I am dying." And it was true.

From force of habit, Weewona had answered the call that came to her with the penetrative forest cry: "Whee, whee, whee-*ah!*" and then immediately fierce rebellion took hold of her. She would not go back. She could not go inside that cabin with Pete's mother and leave Pete out in the night and the darkness alone; *she could not;* she could never stay in that cabin anymore; she must do *something*.

Suddenly there came to her a daring thought: What if she should follow the trail? Over there, away over there where she had never been, because she had promised Pete that she would not, was the path that she knew led down to it. Pete wouldn't care anymore, he *couldn't!* Her heart made a great and bitter wail over the thought. She might go away and never come back. Only she would not do it, of course not. She would never go away and leave Pete's mother. Pete had worked for her and taken care of her all his life; so would she. She would do everything that Pete had done, every single thing; not for her sake, but for his. It was all that was left her to do for him; even though he could not care anymore, it was sure to be what he would like if he were there. But it could do no harm now to go down the trail; Pete's mother always came back without being harmed in any way.

The temptation grew as she thought about it. It had always heretofore been dismissed from her mind as a matter of course, because Pete did not want it, and she understood that in some mysterious way her going might work harm for him. But that awful mystery, death, had put a sudden end to all that had been. Pete could not speak, could not think, could not care ever anymore. She would go. She might be late in getting back; never mind, there was a great moon, and she was not afraid of anything. The dreadfulest thing that could happen to her had come; she need not mind the rest.

Ten minutes more, and she was going by leaps and bounds down the forbidden trail. Down and down and down. The narrow, crooked path, sometimes so narrow that the surefooted girl, used to trails, had some ado in her swift flight to keep her balance. Below, away below her, water was hurrying by, and a gleaming fish occasionally darted across its shining surface. Once or twice a harmless snake moved away at her approach. She was not afraid of snakes, or ravines, or steep places, this child of the forest; but if she should meet people? Ah! that was another matter. She was, she confessed it to her inmost self, afraid of people; and yet, very curious about them. People, she knew, had been dangerous to Pete. If she could see some of them, without having them see her, that would be what she would like best. Still, what did it matter what happened to her?

She came, presently, upon a new world. The character of the trail changed; it grew wider, and smoother, and cleaner; every little way there were seats woven curiously of tree branches and trunks where one could rest. Then, suddenly, there burst upon her astonished vision a row of tents hidden among the trees, yet plainly visible from the trail.

Pete had a tent and slept in it, and he had told her about other tents, much larger, in which people lived altogether, and here they were! And people! They were not in sight, but she could hear them talking and laughing; they did not care, even though Pete was dead!

The girl's first impulse was to turn and flee back to her refuge; her second, to stand quite still, and listen for words, and find out for herself what people talked about. But, listen as she might, no word could be distinguished; just a general chatter of voices that sounded gay and happy, and deepened the girl's sense of desolation. Yet her curiosity had been stimulated to the extent that she resolved to go on, and, if possible, get near enough to hear their talk. She might never have another chance. Pete's mother might see to it that she never came again; and Pete's mother might live on and on, until she herself died: young people did die, it seemed. This might be her one opportunity. She sped on swiftly until halted by a sight that amazed her: a tent so large that it seemed to her it would cover all the clearing in which she had spent her life. She had not known that tents could be so large. And on the sunset side the curtains were rolled high, giving her, presently, a view of people, a multitude of people! She had not realized that the world contained so many! They were sitting in rows; not talking, just waiting. What could they be waiting for? What was going to happen? Once, when she and Pete were out in the woods, and thought they heard the sound of a distant bell, Pete had tried to explain to her about Sunday and church. When she had asked what it was for, he had looked very sober and been still for a long time, and then had said, with a heavy sigh: "You ought not to be growing up a heathen and a savage. I wasn't so much of a one, once; but I don't know how to explain things to you." Then she had said quickly: "Never mind; I don't want things explained; and I want to grow up right here with you." And she had never asked him again about church, because it had made him look very sober. Could this be a church? And if it was, what were the people going to do?

Hark! What was that?

It was the notes of a piano, though at that time the girl did not know it. A man stood out from the others on a raised floor and began to sing. Weewona had heard singing. Once, a long time ago, she had come upon Pete one day in the deep woods before he knew that she was there, and he was singing! She had not known that it was singing, until she had questioned. He had sung for her; and afterward, once in a long while, she had been able to coax a song from him; always when they were far away from the cabin and the main trail. But she had never heard the words that the man in the tent was singing. They floated out to her as distinctly as though he stood beside her speaking, and a glow from the setting sun glorified his face.

> "I am traveling toward life's sunset gate,
> I'm a pilgrim going home;
> For the glow of eventide I wait,

I'm a pilgrim going home.
Evening bells I seem to hear—
As the sunset gate draws near."

Now, while he was singing those two last lines, softly, tenderly, and Weewona was watching intently every movement of his face, a wonderful thing happened.

3

---◆⊠◆⊨◆---

"I Will, for Him"

SUDDENLY from out of the sunset hush that seemed to rest on everything, bells began to ring. Slow and soft at first, and of indescribable sweetness, and then to swell and rise and fill the air, and then to die away in exquisite harmony of tone, until, if the girl had known anything about heaven, she would have been sure that sounds from that glorified city had burst through space and floated down to earth. As it was, she was strangely moved. She had never heard bells ring, neither had she ever heard a hundred trained voices hum in imitation of them. She had no conception of what the strangely sweet flowing sounds were that filled the air and pulsed through all her being. The singer, pausing for a second, seeming to listen, repeated the strain:

> *"Evening bells I seem to hear,*
> *As the sunset gate draws near."*

Weewona held her breath to listen; and if she had not forgotten all about the people she would have been afraid that they could hear the beating of her heart, so loud was it in her ears. "Evening bells!" Oh, she heard them! And they were unlike any sounds of which she had even dreamed! Where were they? What were they? Where was the sunset gate? Could she find it? Oh, how? Hark! The voice was singing again; these were the words it said:

> *"I shall rise again at morning dawn,*
> *I shall put on glory, then."*

What was glory? It was surely something beautiful, if it belonged with the bells. How was he going to get it? Could there be some gotten for Pete? Oh, Pete was dead! Hark! What was that he said? Oh, what *was* it? She leaned forward breathlessly, and every word came to her clearly cut:

> *"With the shadowy veil of death withdrawn,*
> *I shall put on glory then."*

Ah! Here was one who knew about death, and knew something about it of which she had never heard. Glory! This wonderful something that was all about her had to do, it seemed, with death! Then she ought to know it; Pete ought to know it! Was it too late for Pete? If she could *only* ask him about it! Wait! There were the bells again!

> *"Evening bells I seem to hear,*
> *As the sunset gate draws near."*

Slow, and slow, and slower yet, and softer; again the singer almost stopped to listen, and again the sound rose and swelled and then moved farther and farther away, growing faint and fainter until it seemed to the absorbed listener outside the tent that the sunset gates must have opened and shut in the sounds; shut in first the sweet faint words:

"*As the sunset gate draws near,*"

and then, just a little later, shut all the gates upon the glory and the music and left the people in the dark outside.

She drew a long sobbing breath and became aware for the first time that great tears were dropping on her bare brown hands, which were clasped in a gesture of despair. The sunset gate that surely must have opened a little and let her hear, was closed again; the glory had vanished, the sun was gone, the bells had stopped and Pete was dead! If only she could find the gate! It might—oh, it might, for all she knew, be the one that opened when Death came. But what was glory? And who were the ones who put it on?

If she could only get to that voice! He could tell her what it all meant. She brushed away the tears and watched him. He sat down close to the big box out of which those new sounds had come. She did not know that it was a piano. He sat there only a few moments. Then he reached for a hat that lay on a corner of the box and, passing behind all the people that were up on the raised part with him, lifted a curtain of the tent and stepped down out of sight! Quick as thought, Weewona was off, around the great tent over to the side where he disappeared. At least she thought she was, but the twilight had deepened fast, and among the trees it was now quite dark. No person could be seen. In her haste the girl stumbled against a tent stake, lost her footing for a moment, and her sense of locality. She went quite around the tent not once, nor twice, but many times, peering into the darkness and watching eagerly for a human form. The man had disappeared.

Ten minutes before she had told herself that she could not go back to the cabin, yet it was the music that sent her there. She did not know why; she had never heard the word *conscience*; she knew nothing about duty; no one had ever said to her "You ought," yet a feeling that certainly had an "ought" in it sent her speeding back up the trail. Pete's mother was all alone, and she had called her.

"So," said Pete's mother, "you came at last! It is two hours since you answered me. Where have you been?"

"I've been—away," said Weewona, "but I've come back."

"Yes, at last. Well, never mind, it's about over, anyway."

The girl did not know what was about over, so she waited in silence. A large wooden box that closed with a padlock, and that had always stood under Pete's mother's bed, was in the middle of the floor, wide open. Weewona looked at it curiously; she had never before seen it open.

"I'm going away," said the woman. "There's no reason now why I should stay here any longer. When I come away from home, if anybody had told me it would be twelve years before I come back, and that I'd be living all alone in the woods all that time, I should have thought they was crazy."

"You had Pete," the girl said, and her tone said: "How could anybody who had Pete call herself alone!"

"Yes, I had Pete. It was for him I come, and for

him I stayed. Nobody else would have got me to. I've got others, and I've got grandchildren, and I left 'em all."

"Why did Pete come away up here?"

The question that had been on Weewona's lips for years, and been stayed because of her love for Pete, was out at last. Pete couldn't care; he was dead.

"Ain't he never told you anything? He talked a lot with you, more than he ever did with me."

The note of dull resentment in her tone did not escape the quick-witted girl. If the word had been familiar to her she would have long since known that Pete's mother was jealous of her.

"He didn't talk about himself," she said. "Only once he told me that he had a terrible trouble and did not want to talk about it or think about it, so I never asked him any questions. I tried to help him forget his trouble."

"He didn't forget, he couldn't, and it spoiled his life, and mine, too; all for a girl not so very much older than you, and he nothing but a boy. The things that boys will do in spite of their mothers! He was different from the first hour he set eyes on her; after that, he did just as she said, no matter what I thought. I couldn't do anything with him."

In all their years together, Pete's mother had never talked so much at any one time to Weewona. It was evident that she, too, felt that the reason for silence was over.

"What became of her?" the girl said, breathless with desire to know this woman who had influenced Pete.

"It's twelve years ago this very day that she died."

Weewona could hardly suppress a groan. Here was that awful tyrant Death again! And no word or hint of a sunset gate, or of glory.

"Did Pete care?" She spoke almost in a whisper. This was the only question she wanted to ask now.

"Care! He was beside himself. He was crazy! If he hadn't a-been it wouldn't ever have happened. Pete was fierce enough when he was mad, but he'd never have done a thing like that, if he hadn't gone crazy."

"What did he do?"

"He killed a man."

"Killed a man!" Weewona's whisper expressed the terror she felt. She had heard from Pete himself certain terrible stories of what had happened to men who had killed someone. She looked about her, frightened. For a single moment she forgot, and thought of this talk as hurting Pete.

"Yes," his mother said, calmly; "killed him dead. He didn't mean to. There wasn't any real murder in it, and I always told him so. He was just gone crazy with trouble. He went out to do an errand and he come across the fellow, and he said something mean to him about her. I don't s'pose he'd heard that she was dead; he just said it to stir Pete up. And there she was, lying dead in their room; and Pete up with his gun without a word and fired. He's an awful shot, Pete is, and he killed him." There was grim admiration in the mother's tone, even then, for the "awful shot."

Weewona sat in dumb terror and pain, but the mother, who had broken the silence of years, talked on.

"The man got what he deserved, anyhow. He was too mean to live. He hung about that girl every chance he could get, and followed her up, and made her talk to him when she didn't want to; so she said, and I guess it was so. There wasn't anything bad about her, only she was young and silly, and the fellow flattered her, and made believe he was going to marry her, though he knew all the time that she was going to marry Pete; and after they was married, he just kept on trying to get her to go walking with him, and coming to see her on the sly when Pete was at work. It was enough to set a fellow like Pete wild, and it did."

"Was she married to him!" Weewona spoke in a startled whisper. She knew about people being married; Pete had told her. Once he described a wedding party, how the bride was dressed and what they had for the wedding feast, not only, but the very words that the man had said when they stood up before him and were married. Could it have been his own wedding he was describing?

"Why, of course," said Pete's mother. "What did you think? Didn't I tell you she was lying dead in his house? They had been married 'most three years, and they had a little girl who was just beginning to toddle around when she died. I thought at first that was what made Pete take so to you, on account of his little girl that died, but it wasn't."

"What was it?" Weewona raised her head from the rude table where she had dropped it and fixed her great sad eyes on Pete's mother as though she would see her very thoughts.

"It's cause you made him think of his wife," the woman said, stolidly. "You did, even when you was a little bit of a thing. I saw it plain enough, but I was in hopes he wouldn't. He did, though, and that was why he named you Weewona, after her; a real Indian name, too, if ever there was one."

"Did he name me that, for her?"

"Of course. There wasn't any harm in her, either, only being as vain as a peacock, and letting that man—Lance Averill, his name was—talk to her because he told her she was handsome. She didn't care for anybody, only Pete, though, ever. But they had words, him and her, that very morning. Pete got mad and complained of her letting Lance come to the house at all; and he said he'd shoot him the first chance he got, but he didn't mean that. And then he went off fishing, and while he was gone she had her fall."

"Did she fall?"

"Why, yes. Didn't he tell you nothing about her? She climbed an old ladder to hunt a stolen nest of eggs, and tumbled clear to the bottom and hit her head on a stone. When Pete came home she didn't know him; she never spoke; and she died the next day."

"Oh, poor Pete!" The words were wrung like a cry of anguish from Weewona's lips. The mother sat with folded hands staring grimly at the blinking candle. She had known this ugly story and lived apart because of it for so many years that it had ceased to move her, but it seemed to be a relief for her to talk.

"That very night," she went on, after a few minutes of silence, "he went out to get something he wanted to have put on her coffin, and on the way home he met Lance Averill. The man was drunk or he wouldn't have said what he did, it ain't likely; but it was too much for Pete, he sat up with his gun and fired."

"What did they do to him?" The girl's voice was tense with pain and dismay, but there was grim triumph in the other voice.

"They didn't do anything. I didn't give them a chance. I got him away that very night. I didn't wait for no funeral; it wouldn't have done. You see, Lance Averill had money, and he had lots of friends. Folks thought he was a fine fellow because he would treat everybody to drinks, and was always ready for a game; and Pete didn't drink and he didn't gamble, and he kind of held himself away from folks, some of 'em thought he felt above 'em, poor as he was. Then his wife come there a stranger, and they didn't know nothing about her and didn't take to her any too well; and by and by they begun to say things about her, and that made Pete furious. He used his tongue right and left and made some threats that I knew folks wouldn't forget; the only thing left to do was to get out as quick as we could. I'll never forget that night! I had an awful time getting Pete to go. At first he wouldn't stir a step away from that coffin, but at last I got him to feeling that maybe they would insult it, if he was there, and that took him. He knew his sister would see to it that there was a decent funeral, even though her husband did just about hate Pete."

"And you came right up here on this mountain?"

"Well, I reckon we didn't! We was more than a year getting here, and had no end of trouble and escapes. It was an awful year! Three times we thought we had got far enough away from the old place, and begun to kind of settle down, and somebody would come along that we had known all our lives! Once we got a garden started, and the very day the beans peeked out, two men came along looking at land to take up, and one of 'em lived next door to Lance Averill! That was an awful narrow escape we had. Then Pete said if we was going to hide at all, we'd got to get away from human kind altogether; and he cared so little about it that I was as afraid as death all the time that he would give himself up. I was glad enough to shout when we got away up here where there wasn't any trails, nor anything else. We made a path through the woods and shot the wild critters that tried to hinder us, and just fought our way along. It's a settled place now to what it was when we first saw it."

"Poor Pete!" said Weewona.

"You've got feelings for nobody but Pete," she said, with a kind of dull resentment; "but it was harder for me than for him. He hadn't left a soul behind that he cared much for. He was dreadful thick with his sister before she got married, but when Jim and he quarreled she naturally took her husband's part. And the children—"

She made a sudden stop, her mouth working pitifully with an emotion that it had been her lifelong habit to suppress; when she spoke again her voice was broken, as the girl had never before heard it.

"Pete didn't care for the children, because they were Jim's, and he lost his own baby through Jim's fault; but the children were not to blame, and I care for 'em, and now they are grown up."

There were tears in the poor old eyes.

4

"THE CABIN WILL BE ALL ALONE"

THEY talked for hours. Weewona asked questions that had been on her heart for years, and that the closed stern lips of Pete's mother had prevented her from asking. Now that the need for silence was over, the woman evidently wanted to talk. It seemed almost as though she were making up for years of self-repression.

"And so," she said at last, "I've made up my mind to get back to the old place as soon as I can. Some of 'em must be living, and, anyhow, even if there ain't no one left that knows me, Pete's father's grave is there, and I'm going to get me laid down alongside of him, if it takes every cent I can earn the rest of my life. I give Pete all there was of me while he was alive; but now he's dead and I shall be, before long, and my place is alongside of his father."

Weewona looked at the old woman with a face of awe. She was really planning for that strange creature, Death! Planning where she would lie after he had killed her! This was wonderful! Hard as living was without Pete, Weewona did not want Death to come for her—not unless she could find the sunset gate and put on glory. The thought came to her that she might ask Pete's mother about it all. She opened her lips to do so, then closed them. She could not have told why, but she felt certain that this woman knew nothing whatever about the sunset gate.

Instead of that question, she asked a very different one, after a silence that lasted for some minutes.

"When are we to start?"

Something as nearly like embarrassment as the old woman had ever shown appeared in her face and manner. It was followed by an air of sullen determination, and her voice was hard.

"I'm going to start as soon as there is light enough for me to find the way, and I'm going alone."

Weewona gazed at her in bewilderment. It came to her mind that it was foolish in this old woman to keep up a pretense of secrecy, with the reason for it lying out under the ground, dead. Why should they not go boldly down the trail together? No one could hurt Pete now.

But she had not learned to argue with anyone but Pete, and he was not here to take her side; his mother must have her way. So, after a moment, she spoke as one who did not care how it was arranged.

"When am I to start? And how will I find you?"

There was silence for such a space that she twisted herself to get a sight of her companion's face by the light of the candle, whose charred wick had grown long enough to all but choke the tiny blaze. But the woman kept her face in shadow.

"I ain't going to be found," she said at last. "Don't I tell you I'm going alone? I'm going back where I came from, but you didn't come from there."

Weewona stared; amazement held her speechless. She tried to think just what this could mean, and seemed unable to grasp the thought. At last she said, not in terror or indignation, but with a kind of impersonal curiosity as an outsider might have done:

"What am I to do?"

The old woman made an impatient sound; then arose hastily and began to move about the bags and bundles without any apparent reason for doing so, as she said:

"How do I know? Do whatever you like, or can. You are a great big girl and ought to know how to take care of yourself. I was supporting myself a good while before I was your age; and my Laura Emmeline earned her living from the time she was thirteen. I ain't got any home—I give all that up for Pete—nor any place for you. They wouldn't have you there for an hour—even if they had a place for you, because you look so much like that girl, Pete's wife. Jim wouldn't stand that, and he's masterful and rules everybody; only Pete, he couldn't rule him. And, anyhow, they're poor, all of 'em, always were, and I guess always will be; I dunno as there will be one of 'em that's willing to make a place for me, their old grandmother, but I can work yet, and earn me a place to die in; that's all there is left, anyhow. And so can you. I'll risk but you can get along all right. There's no reason why you should take that long tramp back there. It's thousands of miles, and I've got to earn my living as I go. Pete and me rode on the cars off and on for days before we got here; but I shan't ride much. I shall tramp, and stop and do a day's work, and then tramp on. But there's folks enough all about here that will give you work to do, and you know how to work and earn your living. I made sure of that. Right down at the foot of the trail there's folks nowadays; there didn't use to be. It was getting to be a dangerous place for

Pete. I told him so the last time I went down, and since I found how near they are, and what a lot of them there was, I've been scared at every sound. Seems as if there wasn't a safe place on this earth! Maybe it's just as well that—" She drew a long, quivering sigh and did not finish her sentence. She was still moving aimlessly among her bundles.

Weewona had ceased to listen to her. A great bewilderment was upon her that absorbed all her attention. Without understanding what she had done, the girl had but that day deliberately sacrificed herself to the service and care of Pete's mother; had done it as a matter of course. Pete had cared for his mother all his life, so would she, not because she wanted to be with her—she didn't—but because it was Pete's mother; and, behold, the sacrifice had been in vain! Pete's mother did not want her, would not have her, was going away off down the trail leaving her behind—alone!

No, not quite that. The woman was talking again, and she caught the sentence:

"You won't have any trouble. There's plenty of folks will be glad to get a girl who knows how to work and is smart and willing, and you are all that. You can go down the trail with me in the morning and find out where folks live. It won't take you long to make a bundle of your things, and I can point out places to you where they've asked me more than once if I knew of any girl, and you can do the rest. There's no need of my staying to see if you find a place, because I know you will. I ain't leaving you without making plans the best I can for you. I've got four dollars that I've been saving up for years out of little bits that I could spare, and I'm going to give two of them to you. They'll keep you till you get started."

So the woman was sacrificing, too! Neither of them knew the word, but it is possible that both felt its meaning. Four dollars meant a small fortune to Pete's mother. She was sharing it with the girl. But to Weewona, who had never spent a penny in her life, it seemed of not the smallest consequence.

"And here," said Pete's mother, pausing at last in her aimless movements and squatting before the padlocked box, "is something that belongs to you."

She dived toward the bottom of the now nearly empty box and drew forth a queerly shaped little red object, which she stood on the rude table close to where Weewona was sitting.

"Your mother had that box and a handkerchief tucked into her dress in front, and that was everything she had, except the clothes on her back. It won't open, the box won't. It's a toy bank, the kind they give to children to drop their pennies into. It's got a hole in the top for the pennies to go down. There's a few of 'em rattling around in there now. You have to smash the box, though, to get them. If I was you I'd smash it now and get them out to go with your two dollars. Pennies ain't much, but every one counts. Pete wouldn't have it opened. He said you'd likely want to smash it yourself sometime, and the pennies would keep. So I packed this and the handkerchief in the bottom of the box to keep till you got old enough to know where they came from, and then I forgot all about 'em. Tonight, when I was packing up, I come across them, and here they are."

Weewona reached for the box with fingers that trembled. At last she had something of her very own. More than that, she had something that her mother's hands had handled.

Wait! What memories were these that the sight of

the queer-shaped box was stirring? There was a room, light and bright, and a pretty lady dressed in white sitting in a cushioned chair, watching a little girl as with eager baby fingers she dropped something shining into a queer little red box, and a man close beside her guided the small fingers. At first it was a dim, shadowy something almost too vague to be called a memory; then, slowly, it wheeled into vision. The man was pleasant faced, and had smiling eyes, and the woman, too, was smiling. Could the child have been herself, and the man and woman her father and mother?

Pete's mother broke the spell that memory was weaving about the silent, lonely girl.

"Well," she said, bending over to thrust a last thing into one of her bundles, "now you know all that I do about you, and it's mighty little. If you had folks hunting for you they never got out here, and I kept my ears open, too. Every time I went down the trail for months after you come, I listened to see if I could hear about anybody asking for a woman and a little girl, but I never did. I reckon your ma ran away. She had some trouble, likely, and just skipped. I always thought so. Now, you'd best fly around as fast as you can. It will be morning before you know it, and I'm bound to start early. It's more than two hours since I called you. If you had come right away you might have had everything done, and had a chance to sleep awhile. But it won't take you long just to make a bundle of your clothes. I put Pete's cup and a few of his things such as I could carry, in my bundle, and there's his knife you can have if you want. The rest of the things I've got to leave. There ain't many of them, and the land knows they ain't worth much, but I'd take 'em if I could, because they was his."

The sentence closed with a weary sigh. This woman's long exile was over, but she was finding some things even in this desolate cabin that were hard to leave. The girl looked at her as one dazed. Excitements were following one another in such rapid succession as to bewilder her.

"The cabin will be all alone," she said.

"Yes, it will," said the woman, her usually inexpressive face working strangely. "I can't lug that along. I wish I could! Pete worked hard to make it comfortable. Maybe it's better than any home I shall ever have again; I shouldn't wonder a bit if it was."

"And Pete's grave will be here all alone." It was all that Weewona could force her lips to say. Pete's mother winced under it as though a blow had struck her, but she spoke fiercely.

"What's the use of talking about that? I've *got* to leave it. I can't help myself. Don't you s'pose I would if I could? There's graves everywhere. I told you I was going to one of 'em. If Pete could lie there, too, it would be what I'd like best of anything. The only comfort I've got is to remember that the folks that lie in their graves don't care about anything anymore.

"You get your things together, and get a chance to sleep some. You'll have the day before you, though, to look about; but it will be a hard day for me, and I've got to get some sleep."

"I won't make any noise," Weewona said, and she sat quite still on the rude box seat where she had dropped, until the woman's loud breathing told that sleep had claimed her senses. Then the girl arose softly, went toward the cabin door, set it wide open and sat down on the log step in the solemn moonlight. With elbows on her knees and her chin resting in her hands, she sat and stared into space and never stirred through the long night.

With the first glimmer of a new day Pete's mother was astir. At sight of Weewona and the untouched packing, wrath arose within her.

"You ain't done a thing!" she said. "And the sun is coming up; I told you I wanted to get off real early. I won't wait for you, that's all."

Weewona started like one suddenly roused from sleep, and, springing up, began to move quickly about the cabin.

"I'll make you a warm drink," she said, "and get you a bite to eat. It won't take but a few minutes, then you can start. The sun isn't up yet."

"Yes, you look like starting! It's a good hour's work to pack a bundle; much you know about it!"

"I don't want it packed—not yet. I'm not going with you."

Pete's mother dropped the sack she was tying and stared. "Not going!" she said.

"Not now. I've got things to do before I leave the cabin for good. I didn't know we were going at all, so I didn't get ready. But you needn't wait. I know the way down the trail, and I know where houses are, and tents, and everything."

The woman gazed at her. "Well, if that don't beat anything!" she said at last. "I can't take you along. I told you how it was, but I thought, of course, you'd come down the trail and let me show you where to go. You can't stay here alone! What do you know about things?"

"I know a great deal. Pete told me lots; and besides—I can't go till I get something done here— something that I couldn't do till daylight."

"Ain't you afraid to stay here alone?"

"Why, no," said Weewona, wondering. "What is there to be afraid of?"

The woman regarded her with a puzzled air. "I don't know as there's anything," she said at last; "but I know there ain't many that would try it. But you are a queer girl; the queerest one that ever lived, I guess. I told Pete so from the first. What are you going to do?"

"Things," said Weewona, gravely. Then, after a moment's hesitation: "If you should ever come back after Pete, wouldn't you want to know just where he was? How could you tell, if folks came up here and cut trees and made everything different? That's what Pete said they would do."

"Well, how can I help it?"

"I'm going to mark the place. I can put up a board, like they do on the trail, and cut letters on it: Here Lies Peter Walsh. That is the way they mark them; Pete told me about it. I'm going to nail it to that big tree just at the foot of the grave. Pete said they wouldn't likely ever cut down that tree because it was so big. And I'll cut the letters in deep, so they won't wear off. Then, someday I'll come and take him away."

The woman looked at her strangely and spoke with sudden fierceness: "You let him alone! He belongs to me. I'm his mother."

"I know it." Weewona's voice was quiet, almost gentle. "I'll bring him to you if I can. Then you can lie there together like you said—you and Pete, and the father. Pete would like that, I guess."

"You are a strange girl," said Pete's mother again, after a silence, "the very strangest girl I ever saw."

But her voice, too, had softened, and her wrinkled old chin was quivering.

5

SHE HAD BIDDEN THE CABIN
GOOD-BYE

WEEWONA set the door of the cabin wide open and dropped herself a weary little heap on the log doorstep. She had lived through a busy, exciting day, and, now that the sun was near its setting, her work was done; she was ready to go.

She could not have told why she had spent the day just as she had. The first part of her program had been plain enough; she had meant to do that, even before she had known that she was to go away and leave it. She had expected to do it with the mother looking on; she had been glad to do it when quite alone.

No sooner was Pete's mother, with her many bundles securely tied about her and her stout stick in hand, fairly out of sight down the trail than the girl had set about her task. With painstaking care she had sawed and measured and cut and carved, and made mistakes, and gone patiently over it all again, until at last, though far from satisfying her, she felt that it was as well as she could do, and nailed it to the tree, framing the board in the most beautiful leaves she could find. Cut deep into the wood so that sun and rain could not efface them, were the words:

Here Lies Peter Walsh.
The Sunset Gate.

Weewona knew nothing about inscriptions or ep-itaphs of any sort, save that Pete had once described to her his visit to an old burial ground. The simple pitiful uncomprehended addition, "The Sunset Gate," grew out of the longing of her sore heart to have Pete share in some way in that beautiful new thought connected with the monster, Death.

This work done, the girl could not have given any reason why she proceeded to scrub every inch of cabin that she could reach. Not the floor alone but the side walls, rough and bristling with splinters though they were. The three empty shelves that had done duty as a china closet were scrubbed until they shone. Then the rough table was set out and spread, not with the clean cloth, for Pete's mother had taken that, but with an unusually smooth piece of wrapping paper that on one side was almost white. It had come up the trail, wrapped around a heavy purchase, months before, and the girl had seized upon it as a treasure, keeping it for she knew not what. Now she knew. It was almost as large as the rude table. She spread it carefully, and brought the loveliest ferns of the forest as a bordering, with a centerpiece of dark green leaves and scarlet berries.

There were three bruised and battered tin plates that Pete's mother had abandoned, and the struggle that the deserted and desolate girl passed through in connection with those rusty plates would have made a study for an artist skilled in picturing human feeling.

Twice she resolutely set one of them back on the shelf with a thud, and came forward with the others. She was spreading the home table for the last time, and she longed, oh *how* she longed, to set the plates for Pete and herself; just they two! Why should she not? Pete's mother had gone; she had chosen to go away and leave them, why must the home table be set for her?

The girl did not know why it must; for that matter she did not know why she wanted to set the table at all, with Pete under the ground. She stood before the leaf-strewn board, a plate in each hand, and stood, and *stood,* until suddenly, with a low cry, not unlike that of a wounded animal, she dashed back to the shelf, brought the other plate and set the three in their accustomed places. Pete's mother must not be shut out from that last home scene. The two tin saucepans, very old, very much bruised, one of them mended with bits of rags drawn through its holes, had been scoured with ashes until they could have served as mirrors, and were set close inside the fireplace to suggest their keeping warm some savory dishes. Even the tin can which did duty as a water pitcher, made clean and shining, was filled with fresh water from the spring and set on the table. The old tin teapot, without a cover, Pete's mother had tried in vain to crowd into her last bundle, so it too graced the feast, standing in its accustomed place beside the mother's plate; and the seats, the old woman's three-legged stool, Pete's soap box, and her nail keg, were drawn up to their places; everything was ready.

Weewona's bundle was packed. It held in trust her little three-cornered box packed inside a small rusty tin dipper out of which Pete used to drink at the spring; in her bosom was thrust the precious jackknife that had belonged to Pete, and the handkerchief that had been her mother's.

And now every last thing was done and she sat on the old log in the sunlight, giving an all-comprehensive farewell look at her surroundings; on the grave under the great tree, on the board nailed above it, with the rude letters cut deep and glorified just then by the departing sun. As she looked, her lips parted in the semblance of a smile. *"The Sunset Gate"* was all aglow with a golden light. About her untutored mind and wistful heart there hovered the thought that perhaps that light was something like the glory they put on.

The glory faded swiftly; the sun dropped lower. The girl turned and looked once more at the festive table; looked long and earnestly as if she would photograph the scene upon her heart. Then, gently, she closed the door, moving softly, as though she might disturb those left inside, took up her bundle and went away, down the trail.

She had a definite point in mind, and had in reality been steadily set toward it all day. She was going to the great tent where she had heard the song; she was going to hunt for the man who had sung those words, and ask him how to find the sunset gate and put on glory. To secure a place in which to sleep and work and earn her living was a secondary matter; the thing of first importance was the sunset gate; and as it was very near to sunset when the man sang about it, she had a vague fancy that that might be the hour when she could best find him; so she had waited for it.

She quickened her steps at the thought, and, heavily burdened though she was, almost ran down the trail; down, and down, so fast and far that she began to think she ought to come upon the tents hidden among the trees. Sudden and swift as were the changes that had come to her life, she did not realize that they might come in the same way to others. It did not so much as occur to her that these same tents might even by this time be folded away in their canvas bags to wait for another summer.

A turn in the path and she stopped short. Her forest-trained eyes recognized landmarks of tree and vine and boulder that might readily have escaped many, and she knew that she was nearing the bridge just the other side of which was the great tent; yet she had seen no tents among the trees! Never mind, there was the great spreading tent. But it was closed and silent; every curtain was dropped and not a sign of life anywhere. She went around to the entrance; no human being was to be seen.

She went over to the side where she had peeped, only the night before. She peeped again, through a tiny hole in the canvas. She saw only desolation. The seats had been stacked in great heaps, as though they were never to be used anymore. The box out of which had come the sweet sounds chiming in with the bells was gone. So were all the people, the man who had sung with the rest. A great sob came up in the desolate girl's throat and seemed to choke her; she had lost the trail! How could she hope to ever find the sunset gate and the glory?

The sun was quite gone and it was growing dark under the trees. Weewona did not care.

It did not so much as occur to her to be afraid; she had spent her life in the forest and nothing had harmed her. But where should she go? Pete's mother had told her of houses, and people living in them who would have work that she could do; she had only half heeded the words, her mind had been so busy with the sunset gate and her resolve to first find it.

So far as she had thought about the future at all, it had floated through her mind that she might perhaps go home with the man who sang, and work for him and ask him many questions, until she understood all that he had to tell about the song and glory. Now, she had no plans.

She moved mechanically, at last, down the broad, well-kept road, meeting no one, hearing no sounds save the soft whispering of leaves and, now and then, the shrill note of a belated bird, mingling with those undertone murmurings the woods keep up for ears educated, but which are unrecognizable by outsiders.

She could not be said to be planning, although vague thoughts were floating through her brain. It came to her to wonder if she should walk on all night, or lie down under some great tree and rest. Or should she go back to the cabin? That was the only trail she knew; but she turned resolutely from that thought. She had bidden the cabin good-bye; a long good-bye. Not until she could take Pete away with her did she want to see it again. It almost surprised herself to find how she shrank from breaking in on that home scene she had arranged. No indeed, she would not go back.

She marched steadily on, too wrapped in her own somberness even to wonder about the wideness and smoothness of the road, so unlike the usual trail.

Suddenly a man appeared from under a group of trees, as if he had sprung up out of the ground, so silent and swift had been his approach. Weewona had stopped to gaze up at the wonderful moon that sailed just then out of shadow. She gave a little startled exclamation at sight of the man and was darting past him when he seized her roughly and spoke in surly tones.

"Who are you, and what are you doing here?"

"Nothing," said Weewona, timidly.

"Then what are you prowling around here for? Not for any good, I'll be bound. What are you looking for?"

"For the man who sings."

"Oh, you are! Well, the man who sings is gone, and all the rest of 'em. You won't find anybody up here. Where did you come from?"

"From up the mountain."

Weewona did not know the name of the sound that the man made, but she knew it was disagreeable. It was a sneer.

"That's a likely story! Live up there with the wildcats, don't you? You look like it! Now let me tell you something that you think I don't know. You've been prowling around the big tent, trying to see what you can find; and I'll give you warning that you better not be caught around there again. There's things in there that are not to be meddled with, or looked at, till they are moved away, and I'm here to take care of them. You just let me catch you again snooping around within forty rods of that tent and you'll see what will happen. To jail you'll go, without any more words. Do you understand that?"

He shook her arm as he spoke, but the girl was already trembling like a leaf, and her teeth chattered so she could not form words. This was the awful world of which Pete had been so afraid, and from which all her life he had shielded her! This terrible man who had her by the arm was as unlike Pete as it was possible for a man to be, and no one could be farther removed than he from the man who sang. Was the horrible world into which she had come filled with men like these, or like the other? How should she ever find the others!

Part of the man's ugly words she had understood. Pete had told her about jails; she had gleaned from his mother that if they could have found Pete that night, they would have locked him up in a jail until they were ready to kill him. But why should this man want to lock her up? She had done no harm to anyone. She struggled to free herself from his hateful grasp and compelled herself to murmur: "Oh, let me go! I'll go away, ever so far away; I'll never look into the tent again."

"You'd best not!" he said grimly; but he released his hold and the girl fled past him like a frightened deer, striking in among the trees, making her own trail, and flying she knew not whither. She ran down into ravines and climbed them again with no method in her flight, beyond the desire to get as far as possible from that terrible man.

Presently, she came out upon a broad, cleared space, unlike any trail that she had ever seen. Here were cottages quite unlike the cabin, and they were lighted brilliantly. She believed that a roomful of such lights as they had used in the cabin would have made nothing like this. There was also a great central building, fairly ablaze with light. Weewona, gazing up at it as one fascinated, wondered in her hungry mind if this was what the singing man had meant by "glory." But no, for that was "something they put on."

But there were people here, many of them. Their shadows flitted about from window to window, and presently some of them appeared on the porch. They were not ugly, like the frightful man; they were chatting and laughing. Still, they were people, and she had been trained all her life to be afraid of people. Besides, that panic of terror which the gruff-voiced man had awakened was still working in her; there seemed nothing for her to do but to get away as far and as fast as possible.

Suddenly, one of the cottage doors opened and two men came out. The opening door revealed other people, and the sound of what was really merriment, but that came to her frightened ears as danger. She must get away at once.

She fled down the ravine just behind a cottage, crossed the babbling brook at a single bound, then made across the fields for the open road. She could run faster there, and no one was in sight, and at all hazards she must get so far away from those people that they could not overtake her.

One of the two men who had come out from the cottage turned and looked after her as she bounded down the ravine. "Who is that?" he asked.

"I don't know, I am sure."

"She is swift-footed anyway; and sure of herself. Look at her leap that line fence!"

"She is probably one of the numerous visitors this encampment has from the country. The people who live back from the railroad and who had hardly seen a dozen new faces in as many years, until these grounds were opened, are consumed with curiosity about it all, they say, and yet are as wild as hawks."

The elder man looked after Weewona as long as her flying feet would give him a chance, then turned and sauntered toward the hotel after his companion, suppressing, as he did so, a wistful little sigh, and beginning to whistle an old strain, familiar to his youth. Something about the fugitive, her form outlined in the brilliant moonlight, or her swift leaps over obstacles, something, he could not tell what, had awakened a train of memories that he had long been doing his utmost to forget; and the half-whistled line broke into another sigh.

He did not dream that there were reasons that would have made him willing to give all the money he had in the world for the sake of a half hour's talk with that flying figure on the country road.

6

"Who Are You, Anyhow?"

EXCITEMENT, born of her fright, urged on the girl's swift feet for an hour or more; then they began to lag, and Weewona was conscious of a great weariness. She was used to long tramps through the forest, but she was also used to a fair supply of food at regular intervals, and to being in bed and asleep almost as soon as it was dark. Her vigil of the night before had told heavily on her, and her hard day's work, broken only by hurried snatches at the cornmeal cakes left from her breakfast, added to the intense mental strain upon her, were all taking their revenge. She began to feel that she could go no farther; moreover, she was very hungry, and the last crust of cornmeal cake was gone.

Occasionally in her flight she had passed a house; they were becoming more frequent now. People lived much closer together in this strange new world than she had supposed.

Should she stop at one of the houses and ask for a bit of bread and a chance to sleep, promising to pay for it with work in the morning? Of course, she must begin to work for people right away, and get over being so much afraid of them. She resolved to stop at the very next house if she could walk long enough to reach it. Just a little way ahead was a light; there must be a house in behind the trees, and she must try to get to it.

There was a house, but there was also a dog. Weewona had not supposed that she would be afraid of dogs; she had heard too much about them from Pete, who so often wished he had one that it had been one of the hopes of her secret soul to someday get one for him.

This dog growled ominously, and as she, not understanding dog language, persisted in moving toward the closed door he snatched at her skirt, uttering the while such fierce threats that she cried out in terror.

This brought a woman to the door, who spoke in no pleasant tones.

"Tige! What's the matter? Who have you got ahold of now? A stranger, I'll be bound. Who are you, and what do you want? Let go of her, Tige. You needn't be scairt; he won't hurt you as long as I stand here; not unless you touch something that he is looking after. Let go, I say! He thinks you're prowling around where you hadn't ought to be, and he thinks about right, I guess. Who are you, anyhow?"

Who was Weewona? What was she to say for herself? It came to her as a new bewilderment; she had not planned how to reply to people's questions. She hesitated, and considered; not, however, understanding how much this added to the suspicions that not only Tige but his mistress evidently had concerning her. Tige had released her dress regretfully, under pressure, but he was still uttering those low, ominous growls.

"Well," said the woman, sharply, "can't you speak, if you've got anything to say for yourself? I can't stand here all night waiting. What do you want?"

"I was looking for a place to sleep," said Weewona, and she trembled so that it was hard to speak. "In the morning I could work to pay for it; I am very tired and hungry."

"Oh, you are! Well, what are you doing here, in the first place? Why ain't you at home, where you ought to be?"

"I haven't got any home."

The trembling of Weewona's voice as she said these desolate words would have disarmed a less suspicious person, but this woman knew more of the hard world and its ways than usually belongs to sheltered lives, and the look she gave to the trembling girl was not reassuring.

"You ain't got no home! That sounds suspicious. When girls of your age don't have homes it is generally because they don't deserve 'em. Where have you been living?"

"Up on the mountain."

"What mountain? I didn't know there was any folks living on the mountains near us. Who did you live with?"

"I lived with Pete."

"Who's Pete?"

Was there a note of contempt in her voice? Weewona, without understanding the word, resented the sound; she drew herself up with sudden dignity and spoke firmly. "He is Peter Walsh." Before her eyes seemed to glow the letters she had cut on the board:

Here Lies Peter Walsh.
The Sunset Gate.

Her dignity was lost on the woman.

"Never heard of him," she said, promptly. "Is he your brother?"

"Oh, no!"

"Well, what then? You ain't married, be you?"

"Oh, no!" more earnestly than before. "I just lived there with Pete and his mother, always."

"Oh, there was a mother, was there? Why didn't you say so in the first place? Why didn't you stay there?"

She could not see the sudden paling of Weewona's face, nor hear the thudding of her heart as she said, tremulously: "Pete is dead, and his mother went away this morning."

"And left you all alone!" the woman was plainly incredulous. "Well," she said, after a doubtful pause, "I dunno what you'll do, I'm sure. I ain't got any place for you to sleep; I'm all full. I board the boys from the mill, and they are a tough lot; though, for that matter, I guess you are no better than you should be; your story doesn't sound very probable. You'd best go on to the next house; there's only women folks there, and one old man; maybe they'll take you in for the night. Did you say you was hungry? Well, wait a minute and I'll give you some pieces. Tige, you watch you." With this, she disappeared leaving the girl in charge of a surly dog, who watched with such success that she did not dare drop down on the doorstep to rest.

Presently a paper bag was thrust into her hand after the manner in which a certain class of people feed tramps, and the desolate girl turned slowly away with the final comment of the bestower sounding in her ears.

"Don't even know enough to say 'thank you.' Here Tige, you let her alone; she's got enough to think about, I guess, without you pestering her."

The girl tried to quicken her steps. For the moment

she had forgotten Tige; she must get as far from him as possible before that door was closed.

She was out on the road at last, and the moon was near its setting. Could she go on in the dark? Could she go on at all until she had some sleep? What was to become of her? What was the matter with her that people thought her bad? She knew all about bad people; Pete had told her; but she had done nothing wrong; she wouldn't do wrong for the world, because if Pete were alive it would trouble him.

The next house, the glimmer of whose light she had seen when she reached the road, seemed to move farther and farther away as she stumbled on. Then, suddenly, the light went out.

She thought of the deserted cabin on the mountain with love and longing. The night was chill, but it would have been warm up there; she could have built a fire on the hearth, and there was a big ragged quilt that Pete's mother had been obliged to abandon; if she were only there she could wrap herself in it and go to sleep.

By the roadside was a wide-spreading tree; she managed to crawl toward it and sit down under its shadow. Then she untied her bundle and brought out from it a long, thick coat that Pete had insisted but the year before should be got for her, and wrapped herself in it; then, munching the bread from her paper bag, she fell asleep.

It was not until the east was rosy with a coming day that she awoke and sat up in bewilderment. Where was she, and what had happened? Slowly there wheeled into mental vision the events of the last few days, and her first strong feeling was one of relief that that dreadful night was gone.

She felt stiff and sore, but nevertheless refreshed by

her long, sound sleep. When she had made what toilet she could, and eaten the remainder of her bread, she was ready to tramp on. She meant to lose no time in finding a place to work; she must not risk another night on the road; Pete, who had always been careful of her, would not like that. She must not run away from people anymore.

As if to test her decision, there rattled along at that moment a noisy milk wagon, drawn by a fat gray horse. An old man was holding the reins and letting the gray horse do as he would. The man looked curiously at the girl by the roadside, who did not know that she was dressed unlike other people. She had packed away her long coat, and her queer dress, made according to Pete's mother's fancy in the fashion, as she remembered it, of a dozen years before, was sufficiently unlike the present to arrest the attention of even an old man. He let Old Gray move as slowly as he would, and stared.

"Well, I swan!" he ejaculated at last. "You didn't just get along from the ark, did you?"

This historic reference was lost on the girl. She had never heard of the ark. But something in her face moved the old man to another form of address.

"Going to town?" he asked, civilly. "If you are, you can ride as well as not; Old Gray ain't got a big load, and he don't mind if he has."

Dismay was written plainly on Weewona's face. Could she possibly do such a fearful thing! But there was her resolve not to be afraid of people anymore. Ought that to also include horses? She would have to learn to ride, sometime; Pete had said that everybody did, and her feet felt very stiff, and the man might know of a place for her to work. The conclusion was that she came timidly forward.

"Put your foot on the wheel; no, not there; so; that's the best way to get into these kind of wagons. Come far?"

"Y-yes," said Weewona, breathlessly, for they were in motion now, and she had never felt anything like it. Pete had told her much about horses and wagons, but it is one thing to be told about a horse, and quite another not only to see one for the first time, alive and moving, but actually to be seated on a board behind him!

"Don't it make you afraid?" she gasped, holding on firmly with both hands.

The old man looked at her curiously; then threw back his head and laughed, an entirely fearless, reassuring laugh.

"Afraid of Old Gray!" he chuckled. "Well, now, if that ain't a joke! I shall have to tell Mother, sure. Why, Old Gray is the gentlest, reliablest horse that ever put foot on the ground! He wouldn't hurt a fly, even after it had bit him, if he could help it. I guess you ain't used to horses, are you?"

She answered with a single word, but her voice made the old man look closely at her again, and speak soothingly: "You needn't be a mite scared; there ain't anything going to happen to you as long as Old Gray and Stephen Best have you in charge."

There was something so reassuring in his tone that after a minute she ventured to ask if he knew of a place where a girl could get work.

He replied heartily. "Why, yes, I do. It was just about this time yesterday, or maybe a little later, that Mrs. Carver hailed me as I was driving out. She wants a girl, young and spry, to help her in the kitchen. But they do say it is a pretty hard place, and I'm bound to tell you so. You see, she does her own work, not because she ain't able to pay well for having it done, but because she is so kind of persnickety about it that there can't anybody suit her. About once in three weeks, regular, she gets through with her help and is looking around for another. Maybe you wouldn't like such a place? There's lots of work, too."

"I don't care," said Weewona, gravely.

"Ain't afraid of work, eh? Well, that's the way to be; if you've got work to do, I say take a holt and do it; and if it don't stay done, as lots of work, especially women's, don't seem to, why pitch at it and do it again. That's the way Old Gray and I do every blessed morning of our lives. We get the milk all delivered in good shape, every quart and pint where it belongs, and the cans all washed up and set in the sun, and I'm blessed if the next morning we don't have to go and do it all over again! Same road, same folks, and everything. Gets kind of monotonous after a few years, and you find yourself kind of wishing there was a new tree or a new turn, or something; but there! Do your duty and it comes out right. I whistle a good deal over it, and I find it helps. I guess maybe you don't know how to whistle?"

"No."

She was given another critical look; then Stephen Best said, soberly: "It's a mean kind of a world, after all, for lots of folks, ain't it? I guess you know something about that kind. It's a terrible good thing that there's another world to make up for some of the things in this one, ain't it?"

The flash in the girl's eyes startled him; so did her single monosyllable:

"Where?"

"Why, over on t'other side, you know."

"Where is it? Is that at the sunset gate?"

He was puzzled, as well as startled. He shook his gray head, and spoke thoughtfully. "I dunno about any sunset gate, over there." But her eyes were so wistful that he found himself regretting his ignorance for her sake.

"It is where they 'put on glory,'" she explained, "and the evening bells ring."

And now her companion was more than startled. He began to have the creepy feeling which comes to some people in the presence of a diseased brain.

"I guess I wouldn't talk about it," he said, soothingly. "It kind of worries you, don't it? There's the village, and the biggest house up yonder is where the Carvers live. I reckon you'd like to live in a house as big as that? I'm going right there with milk, and I shouldn't wonder if she'd want you, first thing. Git up, Old Gray; I reckon you and me'll be late if we don't hurry."

7

"A WONDERFUL WORLD"

I GUESS she's a little off," said the milkman, watching Mrs. Carver anxiously to see if she understood, as he gave a significant tap to his forehead, "but she's a real nice girl. I took to her amazing, and I shouldn't wonder if she would turn out first-rate help."

Mrs. Carver evidently did not share his enthusiasm. She looked doubtfully at the girl waiting over by the milk wagon and gave a discouraged sigh.

"She looks like a fright to me, Mr. Best; but, then, we are in such straits for help just now that I presume I should try one fresh from the lunatic asylum, if there was any hope of her washing dishes. Did you say you knew nothing about the girl?"

"Not a blooming thing, ma'am; I just picked her up along the road because I see she needed a lift. I don't even know where she came from. She didn't appear to want to talk; but I took a notion to her, somehow; only, as I said, I guess she's a little off in some things. They're that way sometimes, you know, ma'am; kind of queer about one thing, even when they're level-headed enough in every other way."

"What one thing do you think she is queer about, Mr. Best?"

"Well, as near as I could make out, I should say it was religion."

Mrs. Carver looked relieved.

"Oh, well," she said, "she may be as queer as she likes if she will only confine it to that subject; I'll try her for a few days, anyway; she can't be worse than the last one we had. What is her name?"

"Blest if I know! I was that put about over some things she said that I didn't ask her any questions."

In five minutes more Weewona was under the fire of Mrs. Carver's questions, Old Gray and his master having gone their way.

"Have you lived out before?" This was the way the catechism opened, and the girl, making what she could of it, tried to explain.

"I lived out mostly days, as soon as the work was done; but nights I slept in the cabin."

A poorly suppressed giggle came from the inner room, and from Mrs. Carver: "The idea! I mean, of course, have you ever worked away from the cabin, for other people?"

This could be answered by a monosyllable: "No."

"Humph! Who lived with you in this cabin?"

"Pete and his mother."

Mrs. Carver gave another discouraged sigh. "Much you will know about work!" she muttered. But as this did not seem to require an answer, Weewona was silent.

"Instead of being what Mr. Best calls 'off' I guess she is half-witted," was Mrs. Carver's verdict to her daughter a half hour later.

"She is the queerest creature to talk that I ever saw; acts as though she was just learning how; and she doesn't know the meaning of the very commonest things. I don't know how I ever came to say that I would try her."

But the daughter spoke briskly. "Never mind, Mother; if she knows the name of a dishpan, or can be persuaded to use one, do let us keep her. We simply cannot get along without someone, while Kendall is here, at least."

Yet even with such dire needs, the poor stranger all but came to grief on account of her name.

"My patience!" said Mrs. Carver. "Who do you suppose is going to pronounce such an outlandish name as that a hundred times a day? 'Weewona!' What was your mother about when she gave it to you? Sounds for all the world like an Indian name; goodness! You are not Indian, are you?"

"I don't know," said Weewona, calmly.

"You don't know? That's the most extraordinary answer yet! Why don't you wake up and talk common sense? Surely, you know whether your father or your mother were Indians, don't you?"

She would have been more amazed still had she known that this girl of sixteen had not the remotest idea what she meant. It chanced that she had never heard of Indians. They might be anything, human or inhuman, for all that she could conjecture.

"My mother died," she said, desolately. Something in the tone touched a note of sympathy, and the questioner's voice grew gentler.

"When you were a little thing, do you mean? And you don't know anything about your own folks? Well, that's hard, though sometimes it turns out to be a comfort, after all. If you are a good girl yourself, your folks won't matter so much."

Mrs. Carver's mental conclusion was that the girl

had been picked up somewhere, probably by worthless people, and had "come up anyhow," instead of being brought up. She didn't believe she knew how to do a single thing in the way that decent people did, but then she could be taught, provided she had sense enough to learn; and she certainly was quite clean looking, in spite of her outlandish dress. She even had her hair in order, and that was a great deal in her favor.

Two hours later, Miss Clara went to her mother with a discovery.

"She has set the table in the queerest fashion you ever saw! You know you told her what dishes to use and that there were four of us, and where our places were? Well, she has set the table for five people, and the napkins she has piled in a dish as though they were to be served, and there's a tablespoon at each place. But the oddest thing is the decorations. When I went to see if she understood your directions, the only question she asked was if those flowers over there were for the table. She pointed to that vase on the sideboard, and I thought I'd see what she would do with them, so I said yes, if they were wanted, and if you'll believe it, she has decorated that entire table! There's a border of leaves all around the cloth, and a tiny bouquet at each plate, and a bouquet in the center, charmingly arranged. She knows how to arrange flowers, anyway, if she is half-witted."

"A very valuable accomplishment in hired help!" said the mother, contemptuously. And then: "So she has set five places? I didn't think she was of that kind. The idea of a fright like her putting on such airs! The less they know the more they presume. However, she will find that it won't do her any good. I'm not going to have my kitchen girl sit at table with us. I draw the line there in spite of your father's peculiar ideas."

"Oh, Mother! Don't let's quarrel with her about that. Have her sit in the parlor and eat off the best china and sleep in the guest room if she will only wash the dishes."

"Yes, and the way she will wash them makes me sick to think of. Oh, dear me, the insolent, slovenly, unendurable pack! I wish I need never set eyes on one of their tribe again."

Having swept into this general vortex the entire class of human beings known as "help," Mrs. Carver went to struggle with hers as to her aspirations toward equality.

She began with dignity—not to say sternness: "Don't you know I told you how many there were in my family, and where they sat at table? You can count, can't you? Who is this fifth place for?"

"Me," said Weewona, with a quiet air of innocence that the mistress believed to be insolence.

"Well, you can take the plate away and arrange the places as I told you. When I choose to have my kitchen help sit at table with me I will let you know."

This was not received in the usual way, according to Mrs. Carver's knowledge of the species. Weewona neither pouted nor slammed; she had not thought of being insolent, but she was amazed. She stood quite still and stared, until, being further ordered as to the offending plate, she found timid voice.

"Am I not to eat?" It was not surprising that her voice trembled, for she was conscious at that moment of a hunger almost too fierce to be controlled much longer.

"Oh, I have no doubt but that you will eat all that you can lay your hands on," her mistress said with a sarcasm that was utterly lost upon its victim; she knew nothing about sarcasm. "But you will clear off a corner of the kitchen table and eat your meals there. At the same time you must watch out for the call bell and be ready to wait on this table when needed."

An instant incomprehensible change passed over the girl's face, and she moved with alacrity, although the only word she said in reply was "Oh!" Instead of being offended she seemed elated. Mrs. Carver went away puzzled.

She had no mental picture such as was vivid to Weewona of that rude table up in the mountain cabin spread for three. Had it been described to her she would still have been puzzled. She could not have understood how sorely it had troubled this strange girl's heart to think of sitting at a table with others, and Pete not there; nor how hard it had been to put aside with stern will her shrinking, and tell herself that here was one of the many things that must be borne in this strange new world where Pete was not. To sit alone, mistress of the situation, free to fancy Pete sitting across from her talking with her, as he had done on those rare days when they were alone together, this was happiness. During the progress of dinner, Miss Clara, having made an errand to the kitchen, came back exploding with laughter.

"You just ought to go out there, every one of you; it is as good as going to the play! Mother, she has cleaned everything off from that big kitchen table— every single thing!"

"Goodness me!" interrupted Mrs. Carver. "What does she want with so much room? I saw she was planning to put on style. She asked me for a white cloth for the table, and I gave her one of the big kitchen towels."

"Well, you should see it! She has spread it in the middle of the table, and all around it she has made a border of those red and yellow leaves that blew off yesterday."

Miss Clara stopped to laugh, and the young man, whose seat was opposite hers, joined heartily.

"And what is funniest of all," continued the historian, "she is pretending that she has company. There is a plate set opposite hers with a piece of bread on it, and the knife and fork laid in order. Just think of that great big girl playing company!"

"She must be a rich specimen," chuckled the young man. "I guess I shall have to cultivate her acquaintance and find out who dines with her. Perhaps she needs a friendly warning about keeping company."

Mr. Carver cleared his throat preparatory to speaking. He was a man who did not talk a great deal.

"Well, now that may look funny to you," he said, slowly, "but it seems to me kind of pitiful. The idea of a young thing like that, away from home for the first time, probably——"

"She hasn't any home," interposed Mrs. Carver. "She has been living in a cabin up on the mountains with an old woman and her son ever since her mother died. Then the boy died and his mother went off and left her to look out for herself. I managed to worm that much out of the girl, though she doesn't seem to even know how to talk."

"Dear, dear! That makes it all the more pitiful. Poor, lonesome, young thing! If I were you, Sarah, I'd——"

But Mrs. Carver's hands were thrust out as if to ward off something.

"Now *don't,* Father, I beg of you, begin to harp about her eating with us. I knew that was on your mind all the time."

"No," he said, "I don't mean for all the time, but I

thought that now while she is so kind of new and lonesome if she could sit with us sometimes, maybe it would make it easier; there's lots of room. Kendall wouldn't mind sitting a little closer to me."

"Not a bit, Uncle," said the youth, heartily. "The closer I can get to you the better I like it."

His daughter regarded her father with an amused smile.

"We'll certainly have to watch out for Father," she said, gaily. "First thing you know he'll have that girl in the parlor playing on the piano."

Mr. Carver turned on her a pair of faded blue eyes and considered her thoughtfully.

"S'pose it were you, Clara?" was all he said.

She dropped him a mock curtsy. "It is me," she said, and giggled; then she dashed over to him and kissed him on his nose.

To Weewona, the first day in her new home passed more quickly than she could have imagined possible; the very strangeness of it all helping to make the hours go swiftly. There were many wonderful things that had to be examined and experimented with. For instance, water, that instead of being brought from the spring, poured itself from a hole in the wall by the mere turning of a little handle; exactly as it poured down the mountain, yet here was no mountain. Then, more bewildering still, light apparently came from the same mysterious wall, and by means equally insignificant; one had but to push in a button to flood the kitchen with light. It was a wonderful world.

Even the process of dish washing, with which she had believed herself familiar, had new phases here. Two pans were used in the service. Such riches! Her one dish in the cabin had been an old wooden affair without a handle, that Pete's mother called a bucket.

As for dishrags, hers had been well named; they were rags, indeed, and very small ones, and had to be cherished, because even rags were scarce. Her drying towel was made of several small meal bags sewed together; and they had to be scrubbed and bleached before the ugly red letters on them could be got rid of. The beautiful long crash towels that did duty here were a delight to her.

But despite the poverty of her resources, Pete's mother had known how to make dishes clean, and Weewona knew. Mrs. Carver, having given explicit and detailed explanations, stood and watched the new maid with an expression made up of satisfaction and surprise. Her next report to Clara was as follows:

"She is the most ignorant and awkward creature about some things that I ever had in my house; but she certainly knows how to work. She even washed out the dishcloth without my saying a word, and made it look clean, too."

8

"What's the Reason, Pete?"

IT was Sunday afternoon, Weewona's first Sunday away from the cabin, and the fifth day of her stay at Mrs. Carver's. The August sun was dropping low in the west when she came out to the side porch and seated herself on the upper step. Her duties for the day were done; the last dish from an unusually elaborate dinner, which was Mrs. Carver's way of observing the Sabbath, had been carefully dried and put in its place, and the kitchen was set in that immaculate order which the girl's beauty-loving eyes demanded. Now she was taking her almost first leisure to look about on the outside world.

This day, like the ones preceding it, had been crowded with strangeness. Everything in this new world was so utterly unlike the world in which she had heretofore lived that had she come from another sphere it could not have impressed her more.

She felt herself unable to explain the impression it all made on her. She tried to think it out. Suppose she were at home again in the little cabin on the mountain, and Pete was there, just as usual, but she had been away, down in the world, and he was asking her how she liked it all, what would she say?

Of course, she could tell him that some things were very nice, as well as very strange. The water in the wall, and the light beside it in the wall, too, and the one not putting the other out, as, if you knew anything about light and water, you would think would happen. And the big kitchen, with two windows, where she ate all by herself, and Mr. Best coming every morning with a can of milk, and she allowed to pat Old Gray's nose, and once to give him a lump of sugar, and Mr. Best saying: "Well, I never! Here's our girl, ain't it, Old Gray? And she's coming sometime to see Mother and the rest of us, and stay to supper; and we'll bring her back, you and me, won't we, old fellow?" Oh, she liked all that. "And the other things?" Pete would be sure to ask her that. Well, the other things couldn't be told; they were just wonderings.

"Yes, but what did you wonder about?" Pete wouldn't let her go in that way. Well, there was her room; it was nice—oh, it was a *great deal* nicer than the cabin. There was a bed, a little narrow bed, but plenty wide enough for her, and a little pillow and bed-clothes. And there was a window with glass in it, and a bright tin basin for her to wash in, and there was even a glass for her to look into! Then there was a place in the corner to hang clothes, with five hooks all her own, and a curtain before it. Could anything be nicer?

"No," Pete would say, "but where does the 'wonder' come in?"

Weewona hesitated, then imagined herself making her attempt at explanation.

"Well, the room is over the kitchen, and when the big stove is going the heat is, oh, awful! But, then, they couldn't help that; it was the way a great many of the houses were built, with tops to them, and it didn't make so much difference, anyway. You didn't stay in rooms much, daytimes, only kitchens, and nights it got cool. But then—"

Well, she hadn't "wondered" hardly at all until she went to sweep Miss Clara's room. "Oh, Pete, it is be-au-ti-ful! Three windows, great big ones, and glass in every one, and long white curtains, and the sweetest bed all dressed in white, and pictures on the walls and nice big pieces of carpet on the floor, and the floor all smooth and shining; and a big, smooth, shiny thing with boxes in that had handles and pulled out, that you called a bureau, and you kept your clothes in it all folded up. And on the top was a lovely cloth with little holes in it made on purpose, and laid all over it were pretty, bright, shining things to use. There was a little round glass with a handle, and a pitcher on purpose for flowers, and, oh, lots of things. Then, over it all was a great big glass that stayed there always—it was fastened in—and you could see yourself in it way down to your feet! What do you think of a room like that?"

Silence for a few minutes, then she said, in answer to Pete:

"Yes, of course, I thought of that. She is their girl and they would want to give her the very best things, just as you always give me; and if another girl should come along she wouldn't get them. But you see, Pete, there's two more rooms, and they are all fixed up beautifuler than hers, and one of 'em ain't used at all; just swept and dusted and shut up alone. What's the reason, Pete?"

But Pete did not answer. The girl had no words that she could put into his mouth.

Presently she ventured a suggestion. "It couldn't hardly be, could it, because they don't like me, and don't want me to have one of the nice places; because, what made them get the other room all ready before I came, when they didn't know they wouldn't like me?"

Still Pete made no answer, and Weewona gave it up. This will serve as illustration of many puzzles that beset the forest-trained girl.

There was a sound of whistling behind her, and Kendall Fletcher strolled out, with his hands in his pockets, and seated himself not far from her. He was welcomed with a friendly smile. During the four days of their acquaintance this young man had contrived to say several kind words to the stranded girl, and she was prepared to let anything he might offer have its due weight of influence.

"Resting?" he asked, pleasantly. "Kitchens must be hot places on such days as these. Beastly hot weather!"

Not knowing what sort of reply would be proper to make to this, Weewona made none.

The young man looked at her curiously. There was a whimsical smile on his handsome face. All that he had seen and heard of this addition to the family had stimulated his curiosity to know more about her, but it seemed impossible to get her to talk, and this young man was accustomed to girls who were more than willing to talk with him. He had thought this was an opportune time to draw her out. His uncle and aunt were busy with their Sunday afternoon naps, and he had declined to accompany his cousin Clara to choir rehearsal on the plea that it was too beastly hot to go anywhere. But if the girl was going to sit there like a stone and gaze into space, of what use was it to try to amuse himself with her? Couldn't she talk, or wouldn't she? He resolved to find out.

"Do you like to work in such weather as this?"

"I don't know."

"Don't know! Haven't you tried it? What did you think about it today, for instance?"

"I didn't think about it."

"Why not?" He was laughing inwardly at himself, but the girl should say something.

"No use," said Weewona, gravely.

"Why wasn't it?"

"Work had to be done, so I just did it."

"Oh, you're a philosopher, are you? Thought about something else all the time, I suppose?"

Weewona nodded.

"Something pleasant? That isn't a bad idea. Now, it is your duty to tell that pleasant thing to me, because it's too hot for me to get up a single idea, see? And we have got to help one another in this world, you know."

"Why?"

It was not the sort of reply he was expecting, and he laughed as he said:

"Why, because we've got to, of course; that's the rule, you know."

"I didn't know it. Who said so?"

This was worse still. Kendall chuckled again, though somewhat embarrassed. He was not sure that he knew how to carry on a conversation with such a very direct person.

"Anybody would think that you had never heard of the Golden Rule," he said, lightly.

"I didn't ever. Who made it, and what's it for?"

"Oh, come now!" Was this young person very cunning, and was she in this grave way poking fun at him all the while? Or was she, as Clara believed, half-witted? He made a sudden change of subject.

"Is this place like the one where you lived?"

"No."

"How is it different?"

"Every way."

"Oh, come now! Don't you want to talk to a fellow? I thought you would be lonesome, and I came out here on purpose to visit with you. You are from the mountains, aren't you? Who did you live with up there?"

"Pete and his mother."

"Nobody else?"

"No."

"Not even a dog, or a cat, or anything?"

"No."

The young man whistled. "That must have been lonesome," he said. "Who were they? Was the old woman your grandmother?"

"Oh no."

"Then how came you to live with them?"

"My mother died."

Clearly he was not getting on. He had known all this before. How should he get the girl to talking?

"And Pete died, too?" he volunteered. "And the old woman went away and left you to look out for yourself? I heard so much from my aunt. But what I want to know is about your own folks. Where is your father?"

"I don't know."

"Is he dead?"

"I don't know."

While he gazed at her, bewildered and half vexed, she was considering that last reply and finally decided to make this slow-spoken addition:

"I s'pose he is."

Fletcher caught it up quickly.

"What makes you suppose so?"

"'Cause, everybody does."

Again it was not the reply he had expected.

"Oh, well, not all at once, you know. If you are not sure of it, he may be alive. Do you remember him?"

Weewona appeared to consider this question.

"Not unless he helped me with the box," she said slowly.

"What box?"

"I've got a box of pennies; you drop them in. I stood on a chair and put them in. A man held me and kissed me. It might have been my father."

"So it might. Is that all you remember about him?"

"Once he carried me over mud and water. I was scared, but he held me tight; he said he wouldn't let me fall, and he didn't."

"Is that all? Think! Can't you remember another thing? How old were you when your mother died?"

"Pete guessed me six," she said, simply.

"Why, a child of six ought to be able to remember things! What kind of a place did you live in?"

"It was a pretty house," Weewona said, dreamily. "The room where the box was had shiny things in it, and the yard was full of flowers."

"And you played there with your father?"

Weewona shook her head.

"He went away," she said, "and Mother cried. She cried a great deal, and then we went away, and got lost."

This seemed like getting on. But try as he might, the young man could get no further word.

"And that is all you remember about them?" he said at last. "Well, that's hard lines. What is your name?"

"Weewona."

"Yes, of course; I knew that, but I mean your other name, the last one."

"I don't know."

The questioner whistled. "Not even a name!" he said, gravely. "What are you going to do?"

"Nothing."

"But everybody has to have a name! You'll be bothered to death without one. Why don't you use Pete's name? What was it, or didn't he have any, either?"

The board nailed to the great tree that shadowed a grave wheeled into Weewona's mental vision, and she replied with dignity:

"He is Mr. Peter Walsh."

But Kendall did not see the board and the grave. The girl's dignity amused him.

"Well," he said briskly, "what is to hinder you from being '*Miss* Weewona Walsh'? That's a good-sounding name, euphonious, too."

She did not understand him; but she still spoke with dignity.

"It ain't mine."

"But it will be if you take it."

Then a flash of the sturdy honesty instilled from Pete and his mother shone in the girl's eyes.

"I don't take things that ain't mine," she said.

Kendall laughed carelessly.

"It's a mountain Puritan, is it? 'Strain at a gnat and'—the rest of it, I suppose. But, come now, you've got to have a name to work with. You will need it to write in your books. Hello!" Another thought struck him. "Do you know how to read and write? Well, that's good as far as it goes. And don't you see that you will need a name to write in your books and things to keep them safe? And when you go to school— you've never been to school, have you? Lucky girl you are! School is a bore sometimes; but, then, education is a good thing to have, and you'll have to get a little, somehow. But the important thing just now is a name. If you don't have one you'll always be talked about as 'that girl up at Carver's,' or some title like that." He stopped to wonder over the wistful look that had come into her eyes. What had brought it? She ventured a question.

"Do you go to school?"

"I'm sorry to say I do. I'm not extravagantly fond of study. Between you and me, I'd fifty percent rather be at work, but my folks don't see it in that light."

"Have you got books?"

"Shoals of 'em; more than I'll ever get time to read."

Weewona so far forgot herself as to indulge in a sigh.

"Pete wanted me to have books, and study," she said, wistfully.

"He did, eh? Good for Pete." Kendall was studying her curiously. What was the sigh for? He ventured a reason. "And you didn't have any books?"

She shook her head. "Not one; they came away in the night."

Then Kendall whistled softly. What might all this mean!

"Well," he said at last, after waiting in vain for more light, "now you've got where books are, you can set to work and study them. Books are like a name— handy to have around, and a certain amount of studying is rather necessary. My cousin Clara has loads of her old schoolbooks packed away. She will let you take them if you want to."

He continued to enlarge upon this, because he liked the look that had come from the girl's eyes. He told himself that she was a queer party; but as for being half-witted, he wished he was sure of as many wits as she had.

As he watched her, he grew benevolent. Having come out here in search of amusement was no reason why he shouldn't do some good.

"You must go to Sunday school," he said. "That is where girls of your age go and learn all sorts of things."

"Out of books?"

"Yes, of course; out of one book."

"Is it arithmetic? Pete wanted me to learn arithmetic, and I mean to the first chance. Where is the Sunday school?"

She was kindling into eagerness. Kendall tried not to laugh.

"I don't think they study much arithmetic in Sunday school," he said. "They study the Bible. Don't you honestly know what the Bible is? Bless me! Aunt Sarah will have to get after you. They have a lesson out of it every Sunday, and they sing a good deal, and have prayers, of course."

Kendall Fletcher had graduated from the Sunday school years before, but for a younger generation he appreciated its value. He felt virtuous in thus extolling its merits for the benefit of this young heathen. She interrupted him with an amazing question.

9

✦

"GEE WHIZ! SHE'S 'OFF' NOW, ANYHOW!"

DO you know about the sunset gate?" The eagerness of the girl's voice and manner was intense. Kendall checked a disposition to answer banteringly and spoke in cheerful tone. Wherever the mysterious gate might be, it undoubtedly meant a great deal to her.

"I don't know; perhaps so. I know a good many gates, although most of them have less fancy names. Is it a place where there is a particularly fine view of the sunset?"

She shook her head.

"What then? Is it up on the mountain?"

"Oh, no. I don't know where it is; the bells ring, and they put on glory."

She was looking wistfully at the startled young man. He was kind, he knew about books and schools and many things, wasn't there a possibility? But no, the hope faded from her face; he did not understand.

What the startled young man thought was, *Gee whiz! she's "off" now, anyhow.* But it was funny; he would like to get details.

"Did you hear the bells?"

She nodded. "Once, just for a minute. Not the real bells, only just some to let you see how they would sound. They come when you put on glory, and that's when you die. But Pete didn't. I'm afraid he didn't know about it, and I don't know." It had become an utterly hopeless face again.

The young man in search of fun could not laugh. He essayed to comfort.

"I wouldn't worry, if I were you. Someday you'll find out all about it, maybe. You see you don't need the bells and things now, because you are not going to die."

"How do you know? They all do, don't they?"

He laughed a little, shamefacedly. These curious direct questions made a fellow feel almost creepy.

"Why, yes, of course; after a while, but it is when you are old and all wizened up and tired of life. What I meant was that you needn't think about it now."

"Pete wasn't old, and his wife wasn't, and their little baby wasn't."

"And they all died, eh? Well, that's so; they do sometimes, but it is generally old folks, you know."

He told himself that he had got to get away from this; he was beyond his bearings.

"What kind of a bank is it that you keep your pennies in? I wonder if it is like mine. I used to have one when I was a little chap. I got it full. Is yours full?"

A shake of her head was the only answer.

"How many have you? Come, let's count 'em. Perhaps you are rich."

"You have to smash the box to get 'em out."

"Smash the box! Why, that is a strange way for a bank to be made! Are you sure?"

"Pete's mother said so. He wouldn't ever open it because he said I'd want to do it myself, sometime. But I don't. I want to keep it."

"Let me see it, won't you? Perhaps I can find a way to open it without smashing."

Weewona hesitated. Though having little to conceal she was by nature secretive; but this man had been very kind to her; why shouldn't she show him her box? "I don't want it opened," she said, "but I'll show it to you."

At sight of it he whistled a surprised note or two. This was not an ordinary bank, but a velvet-covered, gold-bound affair. He thought it must have been made to order by one who had money to throw away. But for the slide in the top it might be a handsome jewel case. Too pretty a place for pennies, but they were there, all right. He shook the box gently and they gave back a pleasant sound.

"I don't believe you have to smash this to get it open," he said. "Nobody would be such a fool as to—Hello! No, you don't. Here's a spring away down at the bottom, hidden under the velvet. Want me to open it for you? Then you can see just how many pennies you have."

"I don't care," said the girl, listlessly.

She was under the spell of a bitter disappointment. Perhaps she would never find anyone who knew about that sunset gate.

All the while in her poor, sad heart she was cherishing a faint hope that in some mysterious way, known only to those for whom Death came, the garment called glory came also, and Pete had a chance for it. The question was, did he understand and seize the chance? If he did—oh, if he *did!* There was that other line that sang its refrain continually in her heart. It was about rising and putting on glory, and Death going away and letting you alone! Could that be so? Could Pete possibly be alive somewhere this minute!

She was tingling to her fingers' tips with the wonder of her own thoughts. How could she care about boxes and pennies?

"Ah ha!" It was Kendall's voice of triumph that aroused her.

"Here you are, open without any smashing. See, it opens all right. The spring had rusted. Now you can count your pen— Hello!" A sharp resonant whistle broke off in the middle of the strain. The young man's surprise was too great for whistling.

"These are no pennies," he said. "What made you think they were?" He pushed the box toward Weewona, his quick eyes having caught the gleam of gold. The top one was certainly a ten-dollar gold piece.

"What are they?" Weewona's voice was dull.

"What are they?" He mimicked her listless tone almost in indignation. "Why, they are *gold* pennies, my lady; every one of them. A very different thing from copper."

She showed not the slightest interest. Gold said nothing to her. She took up the pieces one by one, counting slowly. There were seven of them. She laid them back in their velvet bed.

"Will they shut up again?" was all she asked.

"Of course they will, but what are you made of to be no more excited than that? Did you honestly think all this while they were pennies?"

"Pete's mother said so. She said that was what Pete thought they were, and he wouldn't have it opened."

"Well, I guess he would have had it opened quick enough if he had known what was in it! Don't you understand that they are dollars? Ten-dollar gold pieces, every one of them. Seventy dollars is quite a bit of money for a girl like you. It is a shame to have kept it there all these years! It ought to have been in the bank earning more."

There was no lighting up of the eyes that had grown heavy and sad. Dollars told nothing to this girl who had never spent one in her life.

"They are pretty," she said quietly, "but you may as well shut it up again. I can keep them best so. I'll keep them always, I guess; them and my handkerchief. They're all I've got."

Kendall's mental comment as he studied the listless face that Clara was right and the girl was half-witted. How could a girl with any sense at all talk so like a fool about money? He could no more understand how one shut away all her life from this money-getting, money-loving world could grow up in utter ignorance of money's power than she could understand what it meant to him. But half-witted though she was—or because she was—she ought to be cared for and protected from herself. He began an earnest protest.

"But, Weewona, you ought not to do that. Listen to me and try to understand what I say. This money is worth a good deal to you. You are a poor girl, you know, with your own living to earn, and these gold pieces will help you quite a bit, if they are managed right. Tomorrow you ought to take them to the savings bank and put them at interest. They will give you a bank book; then when you want a little of it, you can draw it out, and the rest will be at interest, earning money for you all the while. Do you understand?"

No, she didn't. It was as though he spoke to her in Greek. What was a bank? And who would give her a book? And why need she *draw* that little box? She could easily carry it. And how could the little bits of yellow things without hands or feet earn money? They were only things, and she—what was she? It came to her curiously just then to wonder if they could die. Could just *things* die? If not, why not?

None of these questions did she ask. She could not have formed them. Besides, what was the use of asking questions? People could not answer even the very important ones. So she only sat quite still and looked at the young man who had arrested his eager flow of words in the midst of a sentence, and was gazing moodily at the flashing things in the open box and meeting the temptation of his life.

"Look here," he said suddenly. "If you don't want to put these in a bank, suppose you lend some of them to me? Say you lend me five? One, two, three, four, five. That would be fifty dollars." He counted them out and pushed them aside. "The other two you could keep in the box to rattle, and I'd keep the others for you and pay you interest for the use of them; six percent. Do you know what interest is? Well, it's what people who borrow money pay for the use of it. If you lent me these five pieces, fifty dollars, and I paid you six percent interest, six cents a year for every dollar, that would make three dollars more than the fifty that I would owe you at the end of the year. See? Well, you will when you get to studying arithmetic. And you'll find it's a real easy way of making money. I wish I had some to lend! Just sit still and fold my hands and let it earn for me. Then there's compound interest besides. You'll learn all about that, and it counts up wonderfully. Come, now, is it a bargain? I wouldn't think of doing it, only it happens that just now I'm awfully in need of fifty dollars. Fact is, I haven't done much this day but think how I was going to get it. I never once thought of you, though. I just came out here to help you pass the time, and here you turn out to be my helper! You'll let me have it, I know, because, as I explained to you, it will be earning money all the time, and that will be a great deal better than to keep it shut up in a box."

He was talking very fast, and Weewona, hearing little that he said, was gazing at him with troubled eyes. He wanted to borrow five of her yellow pieces, so much she understood. She did not want to lend them for the sole reason that they were all she had that represented home. She would not have put it in that way, but that was really what her heart meant. Still, he had been kind to her—very kind. He had not laughed at her in the way that Miss Clara did, nor had he spoken sharply as Miss Clara's mother did. Not that Weewona minded that in the least. Pete's mother very often spoke sharply. So far as this girl could know, all women did. Pete had not, and this man did not, and she felt kindly toward him. Why not let him have the gold pieces? She would still have two to keep.

"You would bring them back?" she said, at last.

"As sure as sunrise," the young fellow said, promptly; "or sunset. You are more interested in sunsets than you are in sunrises, aren't you?" And he laughed. "Then I'm to take them, am I? It's a bargain?"

"I s'pose so, if you want them. You said they would help you?"

"More than you can understand." He was grave enough now.

"Well, then, take 'em." She pushed five of the gold pieces toward him and closed her box with a snap over the others. He clutched at them eagerly and hurried them into his pocketbook.

"Now you must have a note," he said, in a business-like tone. "That is what people give when they borrow money. You can put it away in that treasure box, and whenever you look at the box it will make you think of me, you see."

He tore a leaf from his pocket diary and wrote rapidly. Weewona looked on gravely, yet interested. Pete had written slowly and laboriously, but this pen went with a dash.

"There!" he said, stopping midway. "Here we are again at that question of a name. How am I going to give a note of hand without a *name* to give it to? 'One year from date I promise to pay to Weewona'—and there I stop. Weewona who?"

"It doesn't matter."

"Yes, but it does. It isn't legal without it. I might mean Weewona Smith, or Jones, or Brown, and nobody could tell which I meant. You see, there can be hundreds of Weewonas."

"There aren't," said the girl, positively. "Pete said there was only one woman in the world by that name, and I was the only girl."

Kendall Fletcher stopped to laugh.

"Oh, he did! Well, he was a great fellow, but all the same I wish you would choose a name. You might take mine. 'Weewona Fletcher.' How would you like that?"

"It isn't mine," she said, with a kind of dignity that made his face flush.

"No, but when you don't know your own, why can't you choose one for convenience? I'm honest, you'll need to. Let's pick out a name, since you don't like mine. We'll make one up that we have never heard of before. Would you like that?"

"I won't have a name," she said, looking steadily at him, "until I find one that I've some right to. My mother had a name. I'll try to find out what it is."

He whistled. "How the dickens will you set about it?"

But he had to be content with that. Weewona had turned her back on him and was secreting the velvet box.

"Hold on," he said. "Let me give you the note." He finished rapidly and signed his name amid flourishes. "Kendall Morse Fletcher."

"There!" he said. "That's as good as I can make it. You will know that 'Weewona' means you, and so will I. And for all practical purposes I guess that will do. I'm awfully obliged to you. Look here, we won't say anything about this little business between us, shall we?"

"I don't know what you mean."

"Why, I mean we won't talk about it to my aunt, you know, or Miss Clara, or anybody. It is just between ourselves. Isn't that the best way?"

"I don't talk," said Weewona, and she turned away from him.

There was nothing for him but to whistle again, a low, perplexed whistle, as he sauntered toward the gate, having had a glimpse of his cousin Clara in the near distance. He had a feeling that he had been dismissed, and that, too, with a sort of cold dignity.

"She isn't half-witted whatever she is," he told himself, abandoning that theory forever. "And she isn't luny, either, except in a certain direction. She's just 'off' about that sunset gate business; a religious muddle of some kind. Somebody ought to help her. I wonder if Aunt Sarah could? What's these folks' religion worth if they can't help a little girl like that?"

And Mr. Kendall Fletcher, who had no religion, strode down the road to meet his cousin, half indignant with all the people he knew who professed to have, because, somehow, they did not seem to him fitted to help.

10

WHY HE PLAYED THE FOOL

IT was all very well for Kendall Fletcher to whistle and pretend that he was in a genial mood as he joined his cousin Clara. He took her singing books and inquired interestedly as to the choir practice, and laughed in uproarious fashion when she mimicked the fellow who tried to sing tenor; but all the time he knew that he despised himself. He fully concurred in the verdict that he gave to "the fellow in the glass," when he brushed his hair the next morning.

"You can smile and whistle and make believe as much as you want to, but all the same you are the meanest chap between here and the coast of Maine. You have been taking advantage of a girl's ignorance, that's what you have done."

He still whistled from force of habit as he rushed about his room, glad that if he carried out his plans there was need for haste.

At the breakfast table he astonished the family.

"Seems to me this is a very sudden move," his aunt Sarah said, while his uncle exclaimed in genuine concern, "It was only yesterday morning that you said you hardly expected to get off this week; you surely didn't have any letters yesterday to hurry you?"

"That's all true, Aunt Sarah. It's my conscience that's hurrying me.

"You didn't suppose I had any, eh?" This in response to Clara's significant laugh. "Well, I have, a little; I keep it packed away in hot weather, but it is cooler this morning, you see.

"No, sir; no bad news." This to his uncle. "But it is getting late in the season, you know, and Mother is growing anxious to see me; and, since I've got to go sometime, I made up my mind in the night I might as well start.

"No, Aunt Sarah, thank you, I shall not wait for the express; the other train is a bore, I know, but it will land me in town two hours earlier than the afternoon express, and, once having decided to go, I go in a hurry. I'm that kind of chap."

All the while there was a mental explanation, which, if his aunt could have heard would have rendered her speechless with amazement and anxiety. It ran in this wise: "You cowardly scamp! You don't want to stay one hour longer than you can help in the same house with that girl you have cheated; that is what's hurrying you, and you know it." Nor did it relieve the tension in the least to have another inner self splutter indignantly:

"It's no such thing; I didn't cheat her. It was a fair and square business transaction."

At that moment came Weewona with a plate of flannel cakes; the sight of her gave Kendall the opportunity he wished. He began as soon as the door closed after her:

"Aunt Sarah, you won't need to go to missionary meetings for a while; you have a little heathen right at your door. Do you know, that girl never heard until yesterday of such a book as the Bible? And she wants to know if they study arithmetic in Sunday school; if they do, she wants to go!"

He stopped to join in Clara's laughter, while his aunt said, anxiously:

"I hope, Kendall, you haven't been talking irreverent nonsense to that poor girl!"

"There is no telling what he has talked to her," chimed in Clara. "He wouldn't go and help me with the choir, because it was too hot to do anything but take a nap; and, as soon as I turned the corner, I saw him seated on the steps with her; it's my belief that he spent the whole afternoon out there teaching her wickedness."

"That is because you judge others by yourself," retorted Kendall. Then, gravely, "I spent some time in trying to help her; she needs help about as much as any heathen who could be found. But it was out of my line; I hope you can do it, Aunt Sarah."

Clara, however, was not to be subdued. Before her mother could make any reply, her laughing voice pushed in.

"As true as I live, Mother, it is a good thing that Ken is going home; that little heathen with her big eyes has struck him, all at once. If he were to stay here, there would be long talks on doorsteps, such as were held yesterday, and all sorts of goings-on. In fact, I am not sure but they have established confidential relations already. Have you promised to write to her, Ken?"

It was the merest nonsense; she expected a merry retort, and stopped, amazed at the effect of her words. The color overspread her cousin's face, even to his forehead, and he darted an angry glance at her from his handsome eyes.

"Why, Ken!" she said. "What in the world? Can't you take a joke? You couldn't *think* that I was in earnest!"

He tried to laugh it off and appear as unconcerned as he had been expected to be, but he was too angry with himself to be successful. Why need he have been such a fool as to blush like a girl? But that reference to confidential relations had been too close a home thrust. He could not get back to his natural manner, and was glad of the need for haste.

When at last, after hurried good-byes, he found himself seated in an eastward-bound train, with his soft hat pulled well over his eyes under pretense of taking a nap, he gave himself up to as uncomfortable a train of thought as, in his heretofore free and easy life, he had ever indulged. What an extraordinary scrape this was in which he found himself! Could it be that he was Kendall Morse Fletcher, only son of Morse K. Fletcher, the lawyer who was noted throughout the state for his unswerving loyalty to truth and righteousness?

He was not in the least like his father in face or manner; he had heard from his babyhood that he was "all Carver," having inherited apparently all the graces and foibles of the Carver family; but he had told himself that there was one thing in which he resembled and meant to resemble his father: he hated meanness. Men had told him that his dead father would not have been guilty of a mean act, or a questionable one, even though he could have made a fortune thereby. His son had early registered a resolve to have the same said of himself.

Yet there he sat with his hat drawn down over his eyes, feeling so mean, whenever he thought of that nameless girl whose gold pieces were in his pocket, that it seemed to him he could never look anyone in the face again.

"It is all owing to that confounded Averill," he muttered. "If I had never laid eyes on him, I shouldn't be in any such scrape." This, by the way, whether it was a Fletcher or a Carver trait, was strongly marked in Kendall Fletcher, the disposition to blame other than himself for all his misdoings as well as misfortunes. He was an only son, and his father had been five years dead. His mother had been the petted darling of a large family, the youngest child—Fletcher's uncle, James Carver, being the oldest. She had early gone from her childhood home to be the darling of Morse K. Fletcher, the rising young lawyer. People who knew them both fairly well said that the only foolish thing Fletcher ever did was to marry that little yellow-haired beauty, Effie Carver. She was pretty, and she was sweet, and the busy lawyer had adored her. Now that he was gone, his still young and handsome widow adored his memory, and thought that she lived only for the sake of his son; but, as she had spent a very large part of her life in thinking of and enjoying herself, that duty still claimed much of her time. They had been left far from wealthy. Mr. Fletcher had been too young and too just a man to have made a fortune. Indeed, their affairs required the most careful handling to furnish an income sufficient for mother and son.

Kendall was being held rigidly to his father's plans for him, that of a college and, he had hoped, a legal education. But Kendall, although a passable scholar, managing to keep himself in fairly decent standing with his class, was no student from the love of it, as his father had been; and, chafing under the restraints of limited means, would have been more than glad to turn his back on college and "get to work to make his fortune." But his mother, like all winsome, willful people, could be set in her way on occasion, and had set herself firmly against such innovations.

"The idea of a Fletcher not having a college education!" was her main argument. "And a son of Morse K. Fletcher at that!" This climax was supposed to be unanswerable.

For the rest, the boy managed life very much as he chose, so that he was always ready to attend his mother on her modest little excursions into the world—and to be at home promptly to act as host when she gave her quiet little dinners, with two, or at most four, favored guests. A model of propriety and economy was Mrs. Fletcher, although her sister-in-law, Kendall's Aunt Sarah, would have exclaimed in horror over the cost of one of those quiet little dinners. But then, Mrs. Fletcher was not at any time in favor with her sister-in-law. Mrs. Carver had been known to confide in Clara to the extent of owning that she never could understand how "your father" could speak of Effie as his favorite sister, when she was "the only silly one of the family!"

Mrs. Carver's chief objection to her nephew, of whom, on the whole, she was fond, was that he looked too much like his mother.

The studies, or festivities, or something else of the past winter had been too much for Kendall Fletcher; and his mother, who had been invited to spend two months at the shore with a dear friend of her girlhood, had been more than willing to have him accept his uncle's hearty invitation to come to the country for the summer. Kendall, who was fond of his uncle and amused by his aunt Sarah, had been glad to go. There had been another reason why he told himself that he should be glad to get out of sight and sound of "that beastly city," for a while at least, "and out of sight of that confounded Averill," he would add savagely under his breath. Now, Averill was his classmate and supposedly intimate friend. Perhaps it will never be known why college boys so frequently choose for their intimate associates those who have the worst possible influence over them. However, Kendall could not really be said to have chosen this one; rather he had been chosen by him in a marked and flattering way, for Averill was popular. It could not have been because Kendall Fletcher, always well dressed and with an air of prosperity about him, had the name of having plenty of money; but certainly Averill liked to be intimate with those who had full pockets.

From the first his influence over Kendall had been distinctly bad. Not that he was vicious, or reckless; on the contrary, he was cool and calculating in his disposition, managing to keep himself well out of scrapes, even when he was known to a few as the ringleader. People who knew very little about him liked him exceedingly. Among these was Mrs. Fletcher.

"That young Averill is the nicest boy you bring home with you; bring him often; I think his society is good for you."

Kendall laughed, his free and easy laugh, but to a close listener the tone was significant in which he asked:

"In what way, Mother?"

"He is so unlike you, dear. He is cool and quiet; the sort of boy who would do nothing rash; while you are a creature of impulse, you know. I don't see why you couldn't have been more like your father in that respect."

Kendall laughed again. "No, Mother," he said. "You are right; Averill will never do anything rash; he will only stand by and watch the other fellows do it."

One way in which Averill had helped the youth whom he had taken up was in teaching him the mysteries of cards. Kendall distinctly remembered when the subject of card playing had been brought up at home.

"The fellows want me to come down this evening and get introduced to a game of cards. They seem to think it is a huge joke that I have never played. I suppose that is all right, is it? You have no commands for me this evening?"

"No," his mother said, musingly. "I think not; the Webster girls are coming in to spend the evening, but they mustn't expect to find you here to help entertain them every time they come."

"I think that's all right—" She had interrupted herself apparently to think something over, and began again after a little. "Your father didn't play cards, but I suppose it was chiefly because he hadn't time. I never heard him say much about them; only about gambling. Of course, he didn't approve of that. Your Aunt Sarah, it is true, thinks that cards pave the way to ruin; but, then, she thinks all forms of recreation sinful. I don't believe they used to play cards so much in old times as they do now. One cannot go anywhere of an evening without coming in contact with them. I was even persuaded to take a hand myself the other day at the Olivers!"

She laughed half apologetically, then hastened to add: "Really, I found it very pleasant. I thought then that it would be nice if you and I could have a game occasionally. I like home amusements for boys. Does you friend Averill play?"

"Oh, yes, Mother, he plays; in fact, he is the one who is especially anxious to instruct your hopeful son."

Whereupon she had given unqualified approval to his plans for the evening.

He had been an adept pupil, developing an enthusiasm for the game which his teacher did not seem to share, and delighting his mother, one evening, in winning from Averill himself. Thenceforward, cards became a prominent feature of Mrs. Fletcher's little social "at homes," which grew increasingly popular and frequent.

"Of course," said Kendall's mother, "you will never play for money; no gentleman does that."

And Kendall, highly amused over her knowledge of gentlemen, laughed and whistled. This was the only admonition he received with regard to card playing.

He had occasion to remember the first game he ever played for money. A stranger, a guest of Averill's, was the moving spirit of the game. Evidently he was an adept with cards, and he confessed that they seemed rather slow without a stake of some sort; it made no difference to him whether it was pins, or buttons; just something to create a little fun. Kendall could not have told, afterward, the steps by which he was beguiled that night. He knew that his head ached, and that was one reason why he had played the fool.

That headache needs explaining. No young athlete was ever freer from it, as a rule, than he. It was Averill again who was at fault. He was with him at his brother-in-law's house, calling on his young sister, Miss Maude Averill, who had come from the Averill home, wherever that was, to spend the remainder of the season with her married sister. She was a brilliant little witch, with great black eyes that had a hundred changeful expressions. But the fact that Fletcher had occasion to remember was that she had brought to her sister a case of homemade wine, and the callers were invited to test it.

"My mother," said Averill, proudly, "can make better wine than anybody in our county, and that is saying a great deal."

Now, Kendall believed himself posted as to all kinds of liquors; his father had had views with regard to them. Kendall himself had signed the total abstinence pledge in a big, round hand in his early boyhood, and had been a proud and prominent member of a Loyal Legion, until it died a natural death before he was twelve, because no leader could be found to carry on the meetings. But that word *homemade* was the trap in which he had been caught. Of course, homemade wines were as innocent as lemonade. Yet certainly no wine that he had ever tasted had been like that! He had exclaimed over it at first, and been rallied by his friend, and almost openly laughed at by the bright-eyed Maude, for not being equal to the stimulus of even homemade wine! So, though he felt the liquid in a new, strange manner, to his very fingertips, he had drained his glass and allowed the attentive Maude to give him a second one. Then they had gone, by appointment, Averill and he and Averill's friend, to the room of one of the "fellows" who boarded at a family hotel downtown, the object of the visit being to enjoy a quiet game together.

11

THE UNUSUAL HAPPENED

IT was on that evening that Averill's friend chose to press his wish to have a little interest added to the game by using a small stake, and pressed it so vigorously that Kendall, with his headache and a general feeling of bewilderment that he did not understand, did not see his way clear to refusing without positive rudeness. It certainly made the game more exciting.

It was Averill's friend who, a little later, pocketed Kendall's five-dollar gold piece with a smiling apology:

"Here's a wish for your better luck next time."

They had not meant to play late; indeed, Kendall remembered afterward that he had promised to be at home in time to attend a friend of his mother to her rooms; but all thought of this seemed to have passed from his mind, and he expressed his willingness to try his luck once more, only he had no money with him. It was then that Averill at his elbow asked a suggestive question:

"By the way, Fletcher, did you do that little errand for me this afternoon?"

"Yes, and no," said Fletcher, thrusting his hand into his breast pocket and bringing out a roll. "Mr. Gray had gone before I got around; he took the three o'clock train instead of the night express, as you supposed. So I brought it back."

Now "it" was a roll of money that had come into Fletcher's keeping in this wise.

"Oh, hold on," Averill had said as he was turning away that afternoon. "Did you say you were going to the express office? Then you can't do a little errand for me, can't you? Or, rather, for my respected brother-in-law; he started this morning on his long route, and among other things that he didn't get around to is this fifty dollars to be handed to Gray, at the *Times* office, you know. Dick was particular about it being done today, because Gray is going East by tonight's express, I believe; and if my exam keeps me all the afternoon I shall have close work getting around there. Could you do it as well as not?"

"Be delighted," said Kendall. And this was the roll which he pushed toward Averill, who did not offer to take it, but bent over his friend and spoke low.

"Why not borrow it, Ken, and have your fun out? It is rather awkward that we are such an impecunious set, when this is Willard's last night with us. You could use this as well as not, because Gray will have to wait now until he gets back, or, at least, until my brother-in-law can attend to it. You are sure to win next time. Willard said last night that you were a better player than he."

If it had not been for those two glasses of home-made wine and that "confounded headache," Kendall was sure he would not have been such a fool as to listen to this. Why, he had never borrowed a penny in his life! It was another of the things about which his father had had views. But the others were waiting for their game.

"Help us out, that's a good fellow," the host said, smiling.

"And clean them out this time, Ken," urged Averill, who thought himself used up with his "exam" and was not playing.

Kendall lost, of course, and, angry over such unparalleled luck, tried again, and again lost. Then there was an accident; to this day he didn't know how it happened. His headache he knew was by that time almost unbearable, and he managed somehow to hit against one of the heavy chairs and knock the corner of it through the big plate-glass window; and when the proprietor of the hotel came up to see what the trouble was, he quietly but firmly insisted on immediate payment for the glass. So when Kendall awoke in his room next morning, with his head still aching and a general sense of misery about him, it was presently to the realization that he had not only spent all his ready money, but had borrowed fifty dollars and spent that. Is it any wonder that his head continued to ache?

The trouble grew upon him. At first he hoped that he could secure an advance from his mother on his next quarter's allowance and meet it somehow, although the entire allowance had already been mentally appropriated and was being waited for. But, behold, the first remark his mother made at that breakfast table was:

"Ken, dear, do you suppose you can lend me ten dollars for a week or two? If you cannot I don't know what I am to do. I am positively in disgrace over an unpaid bill; and Mr. Gladden has already advanced for me on the next quarter, so I can't ask him again. I don't know how it is, but our expenses have been fearful this quarter. We really must retrench, somehow, though I am sure I don't know how."

Of what use to ask his mother to lend him fifty dollars! There was no help for it; he should have to swallow his pride and ask Averill to wait for a few weeks. To be sure he did not see how he was to raise it then, but, of course, it would have to be raised somehow.

The asking had been infinitely more disagreeable than he had supposed. Indeed, it had developed an entirely new situation. Averill had shrugged his shoulders in a disagreeable way he had, on occasion, and replied:

"My dear fellow, you don't owe *me* anything. You must talk to my beloved brother-in-law about that."

"But I thought," said Kendall, dumbfounded, "I meant, of course, to borrow it of you."

"Sorry for you, dear boy, if you had been obliged to; I hadn't a quarter of the amount you spent on hand."

"But you urged it upon me. You said I could have it as well as not!"

"So you could, for all me. It wasn't mine. I was merely reminding you that you had it in your possession and that my brother-in-law was not at home to receive it. I have absolutely nothing to do with the matter except to explain, if he inquires about Mr. Gray's bill, who took the money in charge to pay it. However, we need not discuss that. You will make everything straight, of course, before my brother-in-law gets back."

All this happened just at the close of the college year, and will help to account for the fact that Kendall Fletcher was glad to get away—"to think things over."

That he could whistle through those summer days, and hold endless good-natured sparrings with his cousin Clara, and seem to them all to be having a jolly good time, goes to show either the volatile nature of Kendall Fletcher, or the dual nature of man.

There was a Kendall Fletcher, who was miserable enough, and who spent hours, during which he was supposed to be sleeping, wondering how he could possibly raise an extra fifty dollars, and if he could not, what would become of him. If it were only Averill, he could manage to pay the fellow five dollars at a time, with interest, and make him wait; Averill had money enough. But urge as he would—and he had written a volume to him—he could not get Averill to assume an ounce of responsibility about that money. The last letter had been decisive. Kendall had lain flat on his back in his room and read it over again for the fourth time just before he came down to the side steps that Sabbath to entertain Weewona. This was the way it read:

> *My beloved Fletcher:* Has the summer heat been too much for you, old chap? It isn't softening of the brain, is it? Who would suppose you to be the son of a famous lawyer! I am sorry that that strange delusion about you owing me money still continues. Why, man alive! I had no more to do with that money than had the historic babes in the woods. It had been handed to me to pay a bill for another man, and I passed the errand on to you with your full and free consent. What could be a plainer or more simple piece of business than that? Just because, to help you out of an embarrassment, I good-naturedly suggested that you borrow that money until the next day if you wanted to, you persist in talking as though you borrowed it of me! If you weren't in such a mess I should joke with you over the

folly of that idea. You know as well as I do that I never have money to lend.

But the time has come when, as a friend, I advise you to cease harping on a fancy and get down to business. My respected brother-in-law, who generally looks after his money matters pretty carefully, has notified us that he will be at home early next week, and I hear that Gray will be back by the last of the week. Of course, very soon after these two arrivals, explanations will be in order. I'm always ready to serve my friends if I can, and if it will be of the slightest satisfaction to you to send the money to me, of course I can explain to my brother-in-law that Gray was not at home, and therefore the money was held, without having your name appear at all. But I suggest this simply to save you an embarrassment and not because I have any responsibility in the matter. I suppose it is hardly necessary to add that in event of the fifty dollars not being forthcoming by Wednesday of next week at the latest, I shall be compelled to explain the situation, not only to my brother, but to Gray. From something in my brother-in-law's last letter I should infer that Gray had been writing to him about the matter, and he is not a man who enjoys that sort of thing. It is to be hoped that this latest volume from me will make everything clear to you, and give us a chance to drop the subject. I have written about it already *ad nauseam*.

I suppose it is hardly necessary to add that you are the meanest skunk in the country! was Fletcher's mental comment as he once more read that sympathetic letter. *If this business doesn't give me a chance to drop you so low that I shall never have to look at you again, my name is not Kendall Morse Fletcher, that's all.*

But the means by which it had been made possible for Averill to be dropped brought a flush of shame to the young man's face.

He went directly from the station to Averill's room, not waiting even to see his mother, and a brief and stormy interview followed, though the storm, it must be confessed, was chiefly on Fletcher's side.

The money once safe in Averill's possession—and its delay had caused him no little anxiety—he was more than willing to forget his annoyance and keep friendship with his popular and easily influenced classmate.

His voice was cordiality itself as he said, with easy grace: "My dear fellow, let us congratulate each other. What an everlasting nuisance that paltry fifty dollars has made of itself! Of course, I supposed at the time that the loan was only for that evening, but I know how such things go. Money slips through a fellow's fingers somehow, and it is hard to catch it again. My respected brother-in-law, with all due regard to his virtues, is not the sweetest-tempered person in the world when it comes to borrowing money, and I'll own that I was a bit worried about you, old fellow. I'm glad it's all right."

This gave Fletcher exactly the opportunity that his angry soul desired.

"Thank you for nothing," he said, haughtily. "I am evidently expected to be overwhelmed with gratitude for your assistance and solicitude, but I am not able to see it in that light. What I want to say, once for all, is that I never dreamed of borrowing money of your brother-in-law, and you knew it. What I understood and what you meant me to understand was that you were offering me the loan of the money of which you had charge, as if it were your own. What I expected you to do when I explained matters, and asked a favor, was to hand over fifty dollars from your own funds to your brother-in-law, which you and I both know you could have done without inconvenience had you chosen, and wait until I was ready to pay you. I did not, and do not, consider this a wonderful favor for one to ask of a fellow whom he supposes is his friend. That you did not choose to do it, and practically accused me of borrowing without leave, proved to me the sort of man you are, and I have no desire to be considered any longer a friend of yours."

He poured this out as fast as his angry tongue could serve him, ignoring all attempts to interrupt him, and when he reached a period, turned and rushed away.

It is, perhaps, unusual for an act of which a person is ashamed to have a distinctly uplifting influence; the downward trend is only too apparent in most such cases; but for Kendall Fletcher the unusual happened.

As often as he thought of that strange girl in his uncle's home whose lightly prized gold pieces had helped him out of his first serious embarrassment, he felt a thrill of something very like self-contempt. He understood perfectly that it was the girl's utter ignorance of the use and value of money which had made his act possible, and that he would be ashamed to have even the most careless of his acquaintances know of it. He chafed under it and was sure that he must do something, and that speedily, to recover self-respect. If he could not earn fifty dollars he must save it, and to save money he must reorder his life.

In some respects this was easy. The very thought of cards had become offensive to him. They brought back too vividly the evening of his disgrace. True, he told himself that had it not been for that homemade wine he would not have become a tool for Averill's friend. "No more homemade wine for me," he said, and drew himself up to his full height, feeling that by so much he resembled his father.

"I'll be like him in that respect, at least," he said. By the same token he was moved to let Miss Maude Averill alone, although she was back again with her sister for the winter, and was making every effort to be friendly with him. On one occasion, meeting him at some public function, she took the pains to explain that he was not expected to ignore her sister and herself because he and Hal had quarreled.

"Hal won't tell me about it," she said with a pout, "and he insists that it is all your fault, but I told him I was sure he had been mean; he is capable of it. Still, you mustn't include us in his punishment. Come and see us."

"You bet I won't!" This more forceful than elegant response was fortunately entirely to himself, but it emphasizes the situation. It was good for him in more ways than one that the break with Averill inclined him also to break with Miss Maude.

12

"I Need Coaching, You See"

STRANDED from his former intimates, where Averill had been rather the leading spirit, and disinclined just then to look up new friends, Kendall, who must do something with a good deal of energy, decided to study.

Up to this point his studying had been planned with a view to keeping himself unconditioned, while his energies had been spent in having a good time.

Plunging into study with all his mental powers, he made the discovery that there was keen enjoyment in work of that kind.

Very soon his professors discovered and commented on the change in him.

"Fletcher has waked up, hasn't he?" they said. "Shouldn't wonder if he would do something now."

One of them spoke approvingly to him of his work, and the young man was surprised to find what keen pleasure there was in this new experience. The nearest approach to commendation that he had heretofore received had been:

"Fletcher, you could handle that topic well if you would only take hold of it."

Of course his classmates noted and wondered over the change.

"Getting to be a regular grind!" one of them said, looking after him as he strode away, shouldering a strap-load of books. He had just declined an invitation to a "lark" on the plea that he hadn't time.

"He doesn't have time for anything, these days, but just digging in; I wonder what's struck him."

"It's that row with Averill," explained another, and the first speaker chuckled.

"Gracious! We fellows better get up a row with someone, then, if it will make us take hold as he has; that chap will carry off the honors yet."

As for Fletcher's mother, she was looking on bewildered.

"Why haven't you time, Ken?" she questioned. "What makes you so much busier this winter than usual? Mercy me! You haven't been *conditioned,* have you? I should die of mortification if you were. Your father never thought much of boys who got conditioned; though to be sure very nice fellows seem to, nowadays."

With the vaguest ideas as to what the objectionable condition really meant, Mrs. Fletcher was, nevertheless, relieved to find that Kendall had escaped it, and she watched with a curious protesting pride over the new developments.

"He is going to be like his father, after all," she said, in explaining her absence from some society function with the statement that Kendall had not had time to escort her. "His father never had time for recreation, either; I always had to coax until I was tired whenever I got him into society. Kendall has always been *so* different! But as he grows older I can see that he grows more and more like his father. It is in the blood, I suppose."

The tone was a curious mixture of martyrdom at the hands of an unnatural son, and abounding pride in his strong character. She had been satisfied with him before; she had been proud of his beauty and his grace of manner, and his perfect ease in society; but she told herself that, after all, it was what was to be expected that she should have a chance to be proud of the scholarship of Morse K. Fletcher's son.

In many ways the winter upon which he had entered with so much embarrassment was proving a valuable one to Kendall Fletcher. Gradually he formed new friendships among the more studious of the college men, and found his recreation in lines that had not interested him before.

Yet he was not at any time satisfied with himself. Try as he would, money saving to a youth brought up as he had been, with expensive habits and tastes, was a hard matter; and his mother's habits made it harder still. She was continually appealing to him for the loan of a quarter, or fifty cents, or a dollar, and, whatever she did with others, it was her boast that she kept no "hard and fast accounts" with her boy.

"When either of us has any money," she said gaily to her intimate friends, "the other is welcome to it, and when neither has any we just have to go without until next quarter day."

With such financial arrangements the fifty-dollar fund grew very slowly indeed, and was often drawn from to meet necessities. And Kendall Fletcher knew all the while that whatever might be thought of him by others, he should never respect himself until he had paid back the loan. Sometimes his lip curled in derisive scorn over his use of that word *loan*. The "steal" would be a more appropriate name, he told himself fiercely.

In a sense, it was almost surprising what an effect that transaction came to have on Kendall Fletcher. He had wasted much time and many opportunities without a qualm of conscience; people all around him were doing the same; some fellows were born digs and some weren't, and that was all there was about it. He had felt not an hour's disturbance over cards; everybody played cards; but he didn't believe in playing for money.

"I had rather be the loser than the winner," he had said once to Averill as they stood watching a game until one of the boys went away with empty pockets. He had been impressed by the saddened face of the loser, and it seemed like robbery. Averill had laughed and said: "You'll get over such squeamishness after you've won a few dollars." He hadn't believed him at the time; but still, of course, respectable people did such things. Such had been his former attitude. He had felt angry with himself when he lost money at cards, but at the same time there had been no real loss of self-respect. And the wine drinking, with the mental confusion that followed it, that had been annoying, certainly, but it was an accident that might have happened to anyone. Just a silly joke, he supposed, on the part of that insufferable Maude; he had believed her word, that was all, being in the habit of associating with young ladies who could be trusted. He could hear himself saying something of that kind to Averill. There were times when Kendall felt that it would be a pleasure to say to somebody what he thought of that kind of a girl. Homemade wine, indeed! Still, there was no self-abasement in all this. He had not meant to drink liquor, and he had learned a lesson, not to fall into traps set by that sort of young ladies.

But those five gold pieces were on a different plane. It was infinitely worse, he told himself, than it would have been to borrow money of Averill's brother-in-law; for it had always to be taken into account that this girl was a child, with a child's indifference to money because she shared a child's ignorance; with a child's trusting nature, also, believing that whatever one wanted, who had been kind to her, he should have.

And he, Kendall Morse Fletcher, the son of a man to whom ignorance and innocence never appealed in vain, had betrayed her trust!

It was of no use to tell himself that he meant to return every penny of the money with interest. "Oh, bosh!" he said angrily, "so does every common dabbler in other people's money. As if I didn't know that the average swindler always begins in that way!"

And he hated himself. If he had not plunged into study with all his might, so compelling his brain to work in other channels part of the time, he would have plunged into—something else that brought forgetfulness.

Such being the state of things, the young man almost of necessity thought much about the girl he had injured. What was she doing with herself? he wondered. Had she mustered courage to ask Clara about the schoolbooks? He might have done so much for her if he had not been in such a confounded panic to sneak off. It was all because Clara had been such a fool, prating about "confidential relations" between them! Well—fiercely—why should he have resented that? Wasn't it true? Hadn't he bound the girl to secrecy?

One of the things that made this naturally open-minded young person recoil from himself was the knowledge that he must keep this whole matter a profound secret. He had the aversion to unnecessary secrets that belongs to well-balanced minds. Why, he asked himself, if there was nothing to be ashamed of, hadn't he said boldly to his aunt Sarah that he had borrowed fifty dollars of Weewona and given her his note for it? He was compelled to laugh a little over the picture his fancy instantly drew of his aunt's amazed face, had there been any such announcement.

There were other thoughts connected with Weewona that troubled him. How utterly desolate the girl was! She had lost "Pete," and he seemed to be all her world. What had the strange creature meant by "the sunset gate," and "putting on glory"? Something that had to do with religion; but how pitiful it was that she did not even know enough about it to ask intelligent questions! Still, if she had, could he have answered them? There seemed to be no one to help her. He was skeptical as to his aunt Sarah; he told himself gloomily that her kind of religion wasn't calculated to help a girl like Weewona. He wondered whose kind would. And again he felt half angry with himself because he had no kind of his own to offer.

"A fellow ought to be able to answer intelligently questions about such matters!" he told himself contemptuously. "At least a fellow brought up as I have been; or, if he didn't, he ought to find out how. Only a fool is both ignorant and indifferent."

How had he been brought up? He took himself well in hand to try to discover. Had he been what is called religiously educated? He had been a fairly regular churchgoer when quite a youngster. His father had believed in churchgoing, had been more strict about it than his mother, although she was a church member and he was not. They had both grown careless, he and his mother, since the father's death. They kept their seat, of course, in the old church, and his mother, he believed, contributed regularly to the support of the church, as his father had done; but all sorts of trivialities were now allowed to detain her from its services; and for himself he had ceased to think of such a thing as regular attendance. Most of his friends studied on Sundays, and since he had taken up study with a will, it had seemed to him a good quiet day for work; his mother found it a good day for sleeping.

All this did not seem to afford the sort of religion that could help anybody. There was the Sunday school, to be sure. He had belonged to that institution from the time he could talk, until—well, until he dropped out, some years ago. He had begun with "Who was the first man?" and had gone on through various grades of lesson leaves and quarterlies. He knew the histories of all the striking Old Testament worthies, and had reveled in the spectacular portions of the New Testament; but had never in his life had brought home to him, so that he realized it, the claim that the Lord Jesus Christ had on himself. Principles of Christian living had been instilled; integrity, honor, obedience to just laws, these were part of his inheritance, as well as training; but of God as a Father, whom all human beings were in honor bound to obey, and Jesus Christ as the revelation of the Father, whose atonement alone opened the way for real sonship, he knew almost as little, so far as practical purposes were concerned, as Weewona herself. Her questions that he could not understand had been the first to set him to thinking how appalling his ignorance of such matters really was.

This was further emphasized by an incident that occurred during the spring.

A student by the name of Templeton, with whom he had become intimate since he joined the debating forces, dropped out of active work at a critical time, just when an intercollegiate debate of special importance was due, and the college was looking to him to win laurels for them. Thus unexpectedly it fell to Fletcher to take the place of importance in the contest, and much grumbling resulted. Templeton they knew, but what could this fellow do? However, they won the debate, and upon Fletcher fell the noisy acclamations of honor from his jubilant mates.

It was while he was in the full flush of a really unexpected victory that it occurred to Kendall that he ought to visit his friend Templeton and give him a detailed account of the evening.

"How is he, anyway?" he asked of Templeton's roommate. "Able to receive callers, I suppose?"

"He's pretty well banged up, that's a fact," the young man said, gloomily.

"Not getting on, eh? It's nothing but a cold, is it?"

"I don't know what it is. I know that if he belonged to me, I should—oh, yes, he is up, about his room; too restless to keep still. He'll see you all right, be glad to. He was asking for you yesterday; wants to hear about the debate, I suppose, at first hand."

But Templeton had not seemed to be deeply interested in the debate. He listened, it is true, to Fletcher's glowing account, interrupting it by frequent and sometimes violent coughing; but at first Fletcher had hardly been able to talk, so shocked was he by the change that a few days had wrought. Then he had plunged in, with the feeling that he must try to entertain this sick man and make him forget himself.

He was not prepared for a sudden change of subject at the first pause.

"Well, old man, I'm up against it."

Fletcher did not understand. His mind was still on the debate.

"Missed the time of your life, didn't you?" he said soothingly. "After you had worked so hard to get ready, too; it was tough! But I'll tell you what, Tempy, it was you who won, after all, and I told the fellows so. If you hadn't coached me up and made me think what the other side would be likely to say, we should never have made it. You must be sure to be ready for the next one, though; that's the great thing, after all."

Templeton leaned back in his easy chair, after another attack of coughing, and wiped the perspiration from his forehead, as he said:

"That's all right, Fletcher, I'm glad you won; I thought you would. But I wasn't thinking of the debate at all; I've got something else to think about. It's all up with me, you know, the college, and a profession, and all the rest; I've reached the end of my rope."

"Nonsense!" Fletcher had said, with almost a bluster of heartiness. "You've got the blues, and no wonder; it's all on account of that beastly cough; there's nothing like it to take the courage out of a fellow. Just you wait until real summer weather comes, and see how fast you will gain; by commencement week you won't know yourself. By the way, did you know we were going to elect you class poet? We are; the committee settled that last night."

"Fletcher," said the young man, sitting erect and speaking with slow, impressive emphasis, "the only way I shall ever represent my class will be in a coffin; I'm going that way, and I'm going fast. I don't want to waste any more time in being cheered up and told that it isn't so, because I know better. The question for me now is how to get ready for that. I need coaching, you see. Do you happen to know of anyone who can do that kind of thing for me?"

13

HE GROPED ALONE

FLETCHER had not known how to answer such a question. He was more embarrassed than he had ever been before in his life. He told himself that he had been taken by surprise; that he had no thought of Templeton being seriously ill. If he had known—well, what would have been the effect if he had known?

He had asked himself that question after he had closed the interview as best he could and gone. Being honest, he confessed to himself that the result would have been he would have stayed away and shirked responsibility on the plea that Templeton was too ill to receive calls.

The interview oppressed him; he could not get away from it. In vain he racked his brain for someone among his acquaintances who could help his friend. He reminded himself that the poor fellow had no mother, and, being loyal to his own, shut away as quickly as he could the thought that some mothers were no good, anyhow, in such emergencies.

But, after all, was this an emergency? Wasn't it highly probable that Templeton, unused to being housed, had a fit of the blues, just as he said, and would be all right in a few days?

Comforting his heart with this hope he refrained for nearly a week from asking after the invalid's state, and was rewarded by hearing finally that he was decidedly better.

This made the hopeful young man hilarious, and he went, in a few days, to see his friend again and rally him on the gloomy forebodings he had indulged.

"I was pretty low in mind," said Templeton, "and I don't mind owning that I'm astonished over this change for the better; I didn't expect it. Still, Fletcher, aren't we fellows acting like fools? We spend years in getting ready to live here. Time and money are poured out freely in the effort, and people looking on call us wise. All the time we know to a certainty—and it is about the only thing we are certain of—that we are due somewhere else, some-time—for anything we know the time may be next year, or next week; but we don't do the first thing toward getting ready for the move. Isn't that folly?"

"A fellow can't go around mooning over dying all the while," said Fletcher. "He wouldn't be fit for living if he did."

"Of course not. Who said anything about 'moon-ing'? You and I are not mooning over the sheepskin we expect to get next year, but we are working for it for all we are worth, and we know precious well that if we don't we won't get it. What I mean is, that a good deal of our planning has it in view, and I wonder why we are so indifferent as to the other? That is, until we get sick. Isn't there an element of cowardice in that? I say, Fletcher, what do you be-lieve about these things, anyhow? You believe in God, don't you?"

"My dear boy! Of course I do. Did you take me for a heathen?"

"No, I didn't; I knew you went to church oftener than some of us, anyhow; and I knew that your father used to go regularly. My grandfather told me about him when I was a little chap. He thought your father stood next to the minister in wisdom and goodness.

"There's my grandfather, now," he broke off to say. "If he were living he could coach a fellow about all these things, but I never paid any attention to what he said on such subjects, and he has been gone these six years. I tell you what it is, Fletcher, I believe we're fools. You ought to be able to help a fellow, with a father such as you had and a good mother. If I had a mother, now—a chap takes the world at a disadvantage whose mother dies before he can remember. Still, we don't use the advantages we have. Take yourself for an illustration. You've had lots of advantages, as I've just been pointing out, yet what do you know about it all? Suppose, instead of getting better, I had done as I expected to and gone the other way, and suppose when you came to see me this evening you had found me at my last gasp, what would you have done? Honest, now, have you got a word to say that would give a chap a lift in such an emergency? I don't believe you would even have mentioned such a thing as a prayer, would you? Come!"

Fletcher laughed. "You needn't pursue your cross-questioning any farther," he said, good-naturedly. "I yield every point. Let's be eternally glad that you are not in need of any ministrations in that line. I've brought Prexie's last notes over to read to you, so you can see what you have got to come to in a few weeks. So glad you are all right again, Tempy."

But that had been the last of his congratulations.

Several weeks of damp and generally disagreeable weather followed, during which Templeton took cold. When next heard from he was very ill; indeed, so ill that his nearest relative, an uncle, had been sent for, and the doctor gave little encouragement.

Kendall Fletcher was appalled. It came upon him with all the force of a first surprise. His optimistic nature had seized upon the belief that his friend was out of all danger, and would soon be back at his work.

Moreover, it was impossible for him to forget the searching words that had been spoken during that last interview. Templeton had been quite right; it was of no use for him to try to be helpful in such an emergency; he had nothing to say, and it was true that he did not know how to pray. There was a prayer that his father had taught him when he was a little chap, and he had used it until he was ashamed, being a big boy, to say it anymore. As the words came back to him, he wondered why. There was really nothing very childish about it:

> Now I lay me down to sleep,
> I pray thee, Lord, my soul to keep.
> If I should die before I wake,
> I pray thee, Lord, my soul to take.

Why wasn't that a good prayer for manhood as well as childhood? Why couldn't Templeton use it? If he was really going to die, and his soul was going to live, why not ask to have it go to God? Yet, on the other hand, why should he want to go to God? He had given that Being very little thought indeed during all the years of his life; why want to live with him eternally? Yet he felt that this was just what he craved for his friend. It was all mystery.

Then he thought of Weewona and the "sunset gate" and the "putting on glory." "That's when you die," the strange girl had said. "But Pete didn't know how, and I don't." Had she, perhaps, found it? If she were there, might she possibly help Templeton? What folly! But there must be somebody who could help him.

"Does he ever ask for me?" was the question that he finally obliged himself to ask of Templeton's former roommate. He had hesitated over it for days, with a dread of the possible answer. He shrank intolerably from visiting the sick man; the memory of those strange talks and of his utter inability to meet the need they voiced, rose up between them.

It seemed to him that he could hear Templeton's hoarse voice and see the glitter in his eyes as he said those words: "I need coaching, you see." He would have given all his college course in a moment for the knowledge that would have enabled him to supply that need.

"No," said Templeton's friend. "He doesn't really ask for anybody now; just lies and sleeps, when the cough will let him. You see, they keep him under the influence of opiates a good deal to deaden the suffering."

"Have they absolutely no hope of his rallying again?"

"Oh, dear, no! Why, his uncle is making all arrangements to have the body taken to the family burial place."

Fletcher looked his utter distress.

"The *body!*" he said. "What a fearful expression." The remainder of his thought, which he did not give aloud, was this: *When "it" was lying in the family burial place, where would Templeton be? Somebody ought to help*

*him, and that speedily. Ministers? What were they for if not
for such emergencies?*

He went to church the next Sunday with a view to
discovering the fitness of the minister for Templeton's
needs. It seemed a startling coincidence that the
theme of the sermon was immortality. "If a man dies,
shall he live again?" Fletcher listened as for his life.

The subject was handled logically in three sections,
suggested by three classes of people: Those who do
not think about immortality, those who fear it, and
those who desire it.

The speaker believed that the first class included
the mass of the people. He declared that the normal
attitude concerning death seemed to be one of inat-
tention, or evasion. This made Fletcher think of Templeton's earnest question: "Aren't we all acting like
fools?"

He followed the theme to its close, listening as he
had never listened to a sermon before, and was disappointed.

"He didn't seem to me to get anywhere," was his
comment to a fellow student who joined him at the
close of the service and began a discussion of the
sermon. "His plan was perfectly clear, but I think he
omitted his climax altogether."

The other man laughed, as he said: "Good thing, I
think, that he omitted something. We should have had
a cold dinner if he hadn't."

"Well, but, Lane, isn't that a just criticism? Are you
any more certain than you were that immortality is
worthwhile? And if you were, do you know any better
how to manage in view of it for hearing him?"

"Oh, as to immortality," said Lane, with a shrug of
his handsome shoulders, "I'm not troubling myself
about that—the present is more than I can manage."

"You belong, then, to the class he mentioned, who decline to think of such subjects?"

"Why not? Didn't he prove that a very respectable majority were of that mind? What interests you so especially, old fellow? I didn't know that such themes were any more in your line than mine."

"I was thinking of Templeton," said Fletcher, gravely.

"Ah, yes, poor Templeton! He is pretty nearly done with life they tell me."

"With this life, at least. I suppose you are ready to admit the possibility that there is another? I believe you were, like myself, brought up in the church?"

"Oh, yes, indeed; grew until my teens, at least, under the shadow of the sanctuary, Sunday school and all; but as to your question, I shall have to confess that I belong to the class over which the reverend-doctor waxed fierce this morning. I don't know anything about it, and so far as I was able to discover, neither does he. There is no possibility, so far as I know, of our reaching the facts, except by an experiment that neither of us is ready to make. Why, isn't it the highest wisdom to think nothing about it? Poor Templeton will soon be in a position, I suppose, to enlighten us, if he could come back to do it, but that doesn't seem to be the style."

There was clearly no use in pursuing the subject further with this flippant youth, who set aside the teachings of his early boyhood with a laugh and a shrug. Fletcher did not even remind him of the sentence in the sermon that had made a deep impression on himself. He took the sentence in shorthand as it was spoken, and glanced at it as soon as he had turned the corner from Lane's view. "To sift your feelings and make yourselves clear as to what they really are is a procedure which has a direct bearing upon the pursuit of positive knowledge; for unless you think it important to know the truth, you will never pursue it, nor encourage those who do."

It occurred to Fletcher as almost amusing that, up to this time, no question had ever risen in his mind as to the biblical and Sunday school teaching in this regard. Was the half doubt that the preacher had raised indicative of real advance on the part of a listener? Still, of course, a preacher could not put everything into a single sermon. Doubtless he had convictions about a great many things that he had not chosen to present that morning. Suppose he should get him to call on Templeton, who had attended his church as often as he had any? He ought to be able to help one who had reached such straits.

The thought grew upon him and he lost no time in putting it into execution.

Dr. Evarts was courteously interested in the young man. He did not remember him; there were multitudes of young men who were occasional attendants at his church, but that made no difference, of course; he would be glad to call.

It was several days before Fletcher had opportunity to learn the result; then he came upon Templeton's former roommate, who he knew kept in constant touch with him.

"Do you know if Templeton had a call from Dr. Evarts?" he asked.

"Yes, he did; he was in on Tuesday; made quite a call; introduced himself; told Templeton you asked him to come. He showed a great deal of sense in visiting the sick; didn't try to make the poor fellow talk, you know, but did most of the talking himself. He told some amusing incidents of his college life, and told them well. I thought he would chirk Templeton up a little."

"And didn't he?"

"No, he didn't. He gave him only the faintest semblance of a smile in return for all his efforts. I suppose the fact is, the poor fellow is really too weak to be amused. By the way, he sent you a message, though I can't make anything out of it. I think he must have been a trifle flighty. It was soon after Dr. Evarts left. He had turned with his face to the wall, and had lain quite still for some minutes. I thought he was sleeping, but he suddenly turned back and looked at me. 'Tell Fletcher,' he said, 'that wasn't of any use, he doesn't know how to coach for this.' Can you get any notion of what he meant?"

How well Kendall understood! It haunted him; he could not give up the hope of trying to help.

A newcomer in the history department at college had taken a Bible class in the Sunday school. It was said among the students that he had studied theology. In the hope that he might be one to inspire Templeton with courage, Fletcher, on the following Sunday, made his way to the newly organized Bible class.

Here again he came upon the question of life after death. The lesson had to do with the words of Jesus: "I go to prepare a place for you." Their familiar ring sent a thrill through the young man's heart. He found himself wishing that he knew just how to repeat them to Templeton, and just what words to follow them with. He began to listen intently. But the text of the lesson was not being adhered to closely. Instead, they drifted into a discussion of what heaven is like. The teacher, in response to a question, said he did not suppose there was anyone in the class who could look forward with satisfaction to the traditional heaven.

The fact was we had to get away from many of the teachings of childhood before we were ready to study this subject at all. That, he said, was one invaluable benefit that would result from the form of study known as higher criticism. It cleared away the mists, taught us how to distinguish between history and poetry, between actual events and allegorical representations; in short, between fact and fiction.

Fletcher, being appealed to for corroboration of this, asked what the facts were. Leaving out all allegory and imagery, what, for instance, should one believe who was about to change worlds? In other words, what was there for one to do who had lived a fair moral life here, but had given little or no thought to the life hereafter?

It was a point-blank question, such as Fletcher would not have been likely to ask had his mind not been filled with thoughts of Templeton.

The professor hesitated.

"Well, as to that," he said, at last, "there is room for a great deal of talk, of course, and much difference of opinion; but, after all, in the last analysis it narrows down to the knowledge of an all-loving Father, who is able and willing to do his best for his children both here and hereafter."

Fletcher listened through the hour, and came away without carrying out the half-formed resolution to speak to the teacher about his friend. He had a feeling that Templeton would think that this man also did not know how to "coach" for the event he was anticipating.

After that he gave it up. He did not call again on Templeton. He even avoided, as much as possible, asking after his welfare. He plunged into study and tried to forget that there was such a thing as sickness or death.

And Templeton, starting out in life from a Christian home, with his feet set on the right trail, nevertheless lost his way and groped alone.

14

❧

"WEEWONA WESTERVEL"

WEEWONA, just ready to descend the steps of Mrs. Carver's back porch, had been arrested by Mrs. Carver's voice.

She was older by more than a year than she had been on that morning when Mr. Best left her standing forlornly by his milk wagon while he went to intercede for her with Mrs. Carver.

She looked much more than a year older; indeed, one who had seen her at that time and not since would not have recognized her at all. Much of the change could be accounted for by the changed dress. She wore a neat suit of brown wool goods, and her becoming hat was of a lighter shade of brown, relieved by a touch of vivid red. Her dress fitted her form perfectly, and was made with that careful attention to minute details which distinguishes well-made garments from the cheaper grade of suits. Every stitch in this one had been taken by Weewona's hands. Pete's mother had done her good service in teaching her to be an expert needlewoman.

Moreover, the clothes were worn with what Clara Carver called "an air."

"I don't see where she gets it, Mother; I really don't. Just think, she has spent all her life up on a mountain with two ignorant people; never going anywhere nor seeing anybody, and look at her! She carries her head like a fine lady."

"She spent the first years of her life somewhere else," said wise Mrs. Carver, "and they are what tell. Just as likely as not her mother was one of those fashionable creatures we read about, whose vanity and fine dressing get them into trouble and they run away from home. I only hope that the girl hasn't inherited bad blood as well as a fine figure."

"Well," said Clara, "I wish I had her skill in my fingers. Look how she fixed over that old hat of mine! It never looked as pretty as it does now, even when it was brand-new. I'm going to have her make my hats after this. Let's keep her always, Mother; she can do all our sewing just as well as not."

That Weewona's figure was fine, there was no denying. Her shape had rounded out and become womanly, and she had lost that half-startled, hunted look with which she had first met civilization. There were numberless other ways in which she was changed.

Very soon after Kendall Fletcher's hint to her about the schoolbooks, she had summoned courage to ask Miss Clara to lend them. Miss Clara had been willing and contemptuous.

"Dear me, yes; you can have them, of course; I don't want them; I'm sure I don't know why I kept them. But you can't do anything with them without a teacher. And, besides, I don't see how you are going to have time for such things."

"The idea!" she said to her mother. "That is some of Kendall's work. I knew that boy had put some queer notions into her head by the way she looked at him that last morning."

But Mrs. Carver approved. The girl had a good deal of leisure time, of course; all servant girls did; she wished *she* had as much! And she might much better be fussing over schoolbooks than reading silly stories, as most girls of her class did.

"She won't do a thing with them," grumbled Clara. "Just have them tumbling about in the way."

But Clara was mistaken; Weewona did "things" with them. She began with an arithmetic, chiefly because Pete had wanted her to study it and had taught her what he could, without books and with little knowledge of his own. There was also in the girl's mind the memory of Kendall Fletcher's admonition to acquaint herself with something called "interest" that she would find in an arithmetic. She looked for it, and absorbed herself in its definitions and tables, making calculations from them based on five gold pieces. Amazed over the result she grew to have a dim idea of the power of compound interest, and the value of those borrowed gold pieces.

But the schoolbooks did far more for her than that: they took possession of her; they absorbed every leisure moment; they gave her no time for brooding, or for desolation; they kept her quick of step and eager to dispose of work, that she might have more time for them. And always in them all, grammar, spelling book, *Fourth Reader,* everything that was a book, she kept continually on the alert for the sunset gate; indeed, much of her desire to learn grew out of a fixed determination to find out about that gate.

Faint possibilities of knowledge concerning it were suggested from time to time, or, rather, hints that there were people who possessed that knowledge. For instance, there were certain lines in the book named *Fourth Reader* that she had seized upon with wondering hunger, and memorized at once:

> *Tell me not in mournful numbers*
> *Life is but an empty dream;*
> *That the soul is dead that slumbers,*
> *And things are not what they seem.*
> *Life is real, life is earnest,*
> *And the grave is not its goal;*
> *"Dust thou art, to dust returnest,"*
> *Was not spoken of the soul.*

Over these words she studied, as she worked at her dishes or her sweeping, in a way that hymns are seldom studied.

"Tell me not . . . that the soul is dead that slumbers." That was really what it said; what did it mean? What was the soul? Was it, perhaps, something that did not die, after all, but just went to sleep and after a while woke up and put on glory? The greatness of this thought all but took her breath. She felt that she *must* find out, somehow, what those words meant.

Among the books that Miss Clara had half contemptuously tossed at her from that wonderful box in the attic was a little fat brown volume, much worn and defaced and with one cover gone. Weewona, attempting to read it, had found it very bewildering; just words, words, *words!* in long columns, page after page, and they seemed not to belong together. Could anybody really like to read such a book as that?

One never-to-be-forgotten afternoon it dawned upon her what that book meant. It told the meaning of words! She was doing the dinner dishes when the great thought broke on her mind, and she was sorely tempted to slight the dishcloth and get away; but the rigid training of Pete's mother, backed by a rugged inherited conscience, prevailed, and when she finally fled to her books, the dishcloth hung in spotless condition in the sunshine to dry.

"And the grave is not its goal." The girl had said those words over, all through the dinner-serving and dish washing. *Grave* she knew only too well, but what was *goal*? Oh, the pitifulness of it, that a girl in this land of schools and freedom, well past her seventeenth year, should have to sit helpless and almost despairing before that fat brown book, without an idea of the way to find in its wilderness of words the one she sought! *Almost* despairing, but not quite, it presently occurred to her that by reading every word in the book the one she sought would be found, if, indeed, it was there at all. It was a formidable task, but she girded up her will and resolved. Did her guardian angel, of whom she knew nothing, attend her especially just then, that the book fell open of itself among the *g*s? Glancing swiftly down the page she made the discovery that every word on it began with *g*. It was so with the next page and the next! And they were followed with page after page of words beginning with *h*. After that she turned pages to right and left recklessly in a fever of discovery. Oh, joy! The words were sorted, just as she sorted her dishes and her clothes for the wash. Now she could find *goal* without a great deal of work if it should be that the word was there. And it was. "A starting post." Was she wiser now? She studied over the phrase and its possible meanings for the remainder of that day, and by morning had reached a resolve. When Old Gray and his master and the milk wagon appeared at the back door, Weewona was on the watch, ready with her question.

"Mr. Best, what is a starting post?"

"A starting post," said the old man, and he lifted his hat to run his fingers in a perplexed way through a few spears of gray hair. "Let me see if I can explain it. Why, when folks run a race, you know, they have a place, sometimes it is a post and sometimes it isn't, but they call it a starting post, and to win the race they've got to get back to it the first one; so what they all want more than anything else after they have started is to get back there. See?"

"I guess so," said Weewona, thoughtfully; and all the while she was caring for the milk she was considering it.

"And the grave is not its . . . starting post." Did it mean that that wasn't where people wanted to get? But what did it matter whether they wanted to, or not, since they all got there? She was perplexed. She had grown very shy of asking questions; it had taken some courage to bring herself to ask about the starting post. Her efforts after information had been too constantly met with an astonishment that was mingled with dismay, or with bursts of merriment at her expense. Especially had she become quite silent about the sunset gate and the putting on of glory. With a no less resolute determination to know what the song meant, she had resolved upon other ways of finding out.

Her last spoken efforts had been with Clara Carver. It was on a Sunday afternoon, and Clara, at the piano, was trying a Sunday school hymn. Weewona was not far away; the sound of the piano drew her by an irresistible force as close to it as she dared to come. The words being sung were as an unknown tongue to her, but a strain in the melody caught her with a reminder, and she ventured her question.

"Do you know the sunset gate?"

The singer shook her head. "Never heard of it. Is it a song?"

"I don't know—or, yes, they sing about it; but I mean, do you know where it is and how they get there? Do they have to be dead before they can put on glory?"

The music stopped with a discord and the musician stared, then laughed, a puzzled, half-frightened laugh.

"Goodness!" she said. "What are you talking about? Where did you get such queer notions?"

Then, later: "Mother, I'm just scared over having her in the house. I tell you she is downright luny!"

This Weewona overheard. She did not know what *luny* meant, but it was something that scared people. Even that kind, good Mr. Best had acted a little bit scared when she asked him about the gate. It was at that time that she resolved upon silence.

She had another word to look up. Profiting by her previous experience she looked eagerly among the long rows beginning with *s* and found it; only to gaze blankly at the strange word that defined it:

"Soul: The immortal spirit of man." It must mean something that belonged to people, but what? She made a dash for that word *immortal,* elated beyond measure because her scheme of taking the first letter of the word again served her well; and the definition made her pale with excitement; here it was at last: "Immortal, that which never dies." What could it all mean but that there was something in people that lived forever? Then Pete was alive; and, perhaps, oh, *perhaps,* he had "put on glory."

It is hardly possible to put into words the effect that this revelation had upon the lonely girl. The desire to know all about life that was to be known took hold of her with a consuming power. It made her study as few schoolgirls have ever done; and, in spite of all the drawbacks, lack of time, of training, absence of teachers, absolute ignorance of where to begin, she made amazing progress. She became enamored of study for study's sake; she begrudged the hours she must spend in sleep, and would doubtless have curtailed them to her injury had not Mrs. Carver's laws with regard to the putting out of lights at certain hours been rigidly enforced. She begrudged the hours spent in sewing, yet she must, for the fiat had gone forth. Miss Clara had announced that she must be put into decent order to answer the doorbell and to wait on table when they had company, and, finally, to go to Sunday school.

"Mother, why don't we get that girl fixed up for Sunday school?" She asked the question with some asperity and explained her reason. "That irresponsible Mrs. Ames, who is always ferreting out new scholars, keeps both eyes on her and pours out questions on me every time I meet her."

The sewing was fascinating. Weewona had never sewed on such garments as under Mrs. Carver's skillful purchasing were now planned for her. The material had been bought, of course, with her own money; not the two gold pieces in the three-cornered box, about which she was silent, but money that she had earned. The question of wages had been settled by Mrs. Carver before Weewona began the study of arithmetic.

"I am going to pay you ten dollars a month," she had said, benevolently. "That is large wages for a girl of only sixteen who has never worked out; but you need clothes, and so I shall pay it from the very first."

She did not say—perhaps at the time she really did not remember—that Weewona was an exceptionally strong and well-trained worker; that she knew how to cook plain food extremely well; that she kept everything she had to do with beautifully neat and clean, and that she had what her mistress called a "knack for turning off work"; in short, that she was by far the best help that the energetic and particular Mrs. Carver had ever had in her house. Yet, because she was young and had never worked out before, of course she could not expect the sixteen dollars a month that had been paid for good help. Everybody considered ten dollars very good wages for a beginner.

Weewona was satisfied; she would have been satisfied with five dollars, or even three; but this was because of her ignorance. Were Kendall Fletcher and his aunt, then, on the same plane of morals?

The Sunday school had opened for her at last. There came a day when, in the neatest of suits, she joined the multitude of girls and boys making their way to the church. At least, they seemed a multitude to her.

Her heart beat high with expectation. Was she not on her way to school, that desire of Pete's heart for her?

She was promptly placed in one of the Bible classes, being duly enrolled as a member. Always she remembered the little thrill of pride with which she met this first opportunity to pronounce her adopted name before others, and the eagerness with which she watched to see it written in beautiful characters on the roll book: "Weewona Westervel."

15

·⊹⊱✠⊰⊹·

"SHE DOESN'T BELONG HERE"

THE question of a name had given the homeless and friendless girl more trouble than she had supposed so unimportant a matter could. Immediately following Kendall Fletcher's criticism of her namelessness she began to take careful note of others, and to discover that all the people who came to the house seemed to have two names. Also, that all of those whose names were frequently on Miss Clara's lips were blessed in like manner. They were "Anna Jones" and "Fanny Chester" and "Charlie Smith" and "Joe Weston." She watched the coming of the mail, and read the addresses. Always it was "Mr. James Carver" and "Miss Clara Carver." She studied the milk bills and noted that they were sure to be signed "Stephen Best." Clearly she must have another name; how to secure it became a daily study. The discovery of her very own name was set to one side as something to be waited for, and one for immediate use was what absorbed her. The more she thought about it the more she grew to dislike the idea of being known simply as "that girl at Carver's."

These thoughts were busy within her as she stood one afternoon at the little window in her room, with the small fine handkerchief that had been her mother's in her hand. Often she took it out to hold, when the sense of homelessness and loneliness were strong upon her. It came nearer to her by far than those cold gold pieces; it was something that her mother's fingers had held. She had just received at the door and shown to the parlor a mother and daughter who had come to call. She had heard the girl say "Mother" in the tone of one to whom the name expressed utmost confidence. She could not have described the effect of this upon her; it seemed to emphasize her sense of desolation. She held the handkerchief close to her heart; it was all she had. Suddenly her eye was caught by a shadow on the whiteness, a dim outline as of something that had once been written. She had watched Miss Clara but the day before marking her handkerchiefs. Could there possibly have been once a name written on hers? She strained her eyes to study it, but the short autumn day was darkening, and her small north window did not at any time furnish a strong light. She rushed down to the south window in the kitchen and, fairly standing in it, devoured the faded shadow. Certainly there was once something written there.

There followed literally hours of study; it consumed all her leisure time for days. She stretched the handkerchief over a block and gazed and puzzled. She stretched it the other way, on the cross lines of the weave, and grew sure that there had once been a name written there. Bit by bit she picked it out, carefully forming on paper what she believed was a copy of the shadow. After a while she grew sure of it. By slow degrees a name began to live before her. A part of a

W, then an *e* and then what might be, and she believed was, an *s.* At last she had it formed, all that she could make out, at least, though a shadow at the end of the *l* made her think that there might have been another letter; but so much she believed was plain: "Wester-vel." Here was a name to which she had a right, "Wee-wona Westervel." Her joy over it was great. Nothing that had happened to her compared with it, and she told herself that she was happier than she had thought she could be without Pete.

Sunday school, however, had failed of being the brilliant success that Weewona's daydreams had suggested. The girls in the class were of another world than hers. They fluttered their ribbons and tossed their plumed hats and looked askance at the large-eyed, dark-skinned stranger, and had nothing to say to her, though they whispered about her. She heard one of them assuring the others that she was part Indian. Perhaps she was. Who knew? And if she were, what of it? They looked as though, for some reason, it would be a disgrace. Weewona was uncomfortable.

Nor was this all; the lesson was not what she had imagined it would be. They talked about matters that she did not understand and was not interested in.

The teacher had much to say about one Paul, who took a long journey; she did not know for what reason, nor why it was of interest to talk about. The girls did not seem to think it was; they whispered together about the new gloves of one and the hair ribbon of another while the teacher was speaking. Weewona thought they disturbed her.

Suddenly she turned to Weewona and asked: "Can you tell me what happened to Paul at Lystra?"

The girl felt her face growing red, but she replied promptly that she did not know. She had never seen him or heard of him before. Whereupon all the girls tittered as though she had said something funny; even the teacher seemed to be amused; Weewona had no idea why. She wondered why they constantly spoke of the man as "Paul," without any other name. She was surprised to discover that all over the school they seemed to be talking about him. She heard his name from the class back of theirs, and again across the aisle. He must have been doing something either very good or very bad; she wondered which? She listened with a view of discovering and did not succeed. Then she lost herself in a wonderment as to whether Pete had known him, or had he just taken that journey about which they were all talking? She determined to risk one question. She would shape it so that there could be nothing in it to awaken a laugh. She waited until the teacher turned toward her again, then spoke timidly: "Is Paul dead?"

She had certainly not been prepared for the outburst that this awakened. The girls all but shouted, and the teacher, while trying to repress them, evidently found it difficult not to join in the laugh.

"My *dear* girl!" she said, then stopped, her face in a broad smile. In the confusion thus awakened, the question was forgotten and Weewona went home without discovering whether or not Paul was dead. But she did not forget that she had asked. The girls took care of that. They bandied the words about in giggling whispers all the way down the aisle and even into the street. The last sound she heard, as she turned the corner and began to climb the hill, was the mirthful outburst: "Girls, is Paul dead?" and then a shout of laughter. And now Weewona's lips were sealed against all questions.

After that for several weeks she kept her seat in the

class, listening when a word caught her mind that seemed understandable, but for the most part in a kind of mental fog; unable because of the lack of a little foundation knowledge to understand what they were talking about.

The teacher was evidently in doubt what to do with her. Apparently she finally decided to smile on her and do nothing.

The girls continued to study her curiously, but not one of them ventured to speak to her in a friendly way. They were not intentionally cruel girls; they were simply absorbed in their own bright, free and easy selves, and indifferent as to those who did not fit in.

"She doesn't belong here, anyway," Weewona heard one of them say with a toss of her gay ribbons. Weewona agreed with her; but the question was, where did she belong?

By and by she dropped out of Sunday school; without any violent wrench, rather, by general consent. Miss Clara had company, and Mrs. Carver remarked that she did not see how Weewona was to be spared for Sunday school that morning with all the work there was to be done. It was Weewona herself who offered to stay and do it.

On the following Sunday Mrs. Carver was ill, and, of course, Weewona could not be spared. So one thing and another hindered, and the indefatigable Mrs. Ames did not look up the stray lamb, chiefly because the lamb's teacher said:

"Oh, dear Mrs. Ames, don't go after her yet; give me time to think what I shall do with her. She does not belong in our class at all; she ought to be in the primary room, only she is so large, of course. But, really, Mrs. Ames, she is frightfully ignorant. Don't you think she asked me if Paul was dead! Fancy it! Perhaps the poor thing is half-witted, but her eyes don't look like that."

Finally Mrs. Carver remarked that perhaps it would be as well for Weewona to give up Sunday school and go to church, evenings, instead. So the girl tried the evening service and liked it better than she had the Sunday school. She liked the singing; often the words that were sung thrilled her. Also, she liked the praying, although she did not pretend to understand it. She was more or less familiar with the name of God, having often seen it in books; besides, Pete had told her about him. She could recall the very spot in the woods and see the great sequoia under which she sat when she questioned him. Pete was chopping wood, but he arrested his axe to answer her.

"God made you, of course; he made everything and everybody. Don't you know I told you that yesterday?"

"Yes, but what did he do it for?"

"Well, now, that's something that I have never found out."

"Pete, you said some folks talked to him; how do they? Does he answer?"

"They think so, I suppose. They *talk,* anyhow. They call it praying."

"What kind of folks are they, Pete? Great big, strong, rich ones?"

"Yes," Pete had answered. "That's about it, I guess; grand people who live in fine houses and think they are better than common folks. That's all the kind I know about, anyhow."

And that was all that the poor fellow knew about prayer!

Weewona at church, still under the spell of wanting to belong only to Pete, had no idea of trying to join in the prayer, yet felt thrilled and awed when many people bowed their heads as the preacher talked to one unseen.

Of the sermons she made very little. Occasionally a sentence would set her to wondering, and if there had been anyone whom she dared to question, she would have made the attempt to understand.

But, for the most part, she let the preacher's voice lead her off into her dream world, where, in the forest with Pete, she roved wild and free, and was happy. Or, as she grew to understand books better, she retired with them into a world of her own imagining, and lived a life as unlike the real one as her fertile brain could plan.

But always she kept a kind of extra sense alert, on the watch for any possible reference to that sunset gate, or the glory, and somehow—it would have been impossible for her to explain how or why—she came to associate the two with the thought of God. Perhaps this was the real reason why the attitude of prayer hushed and thrilled her.

In these ways she lived her lonely, set-apart life; no one molested her, very few noticed her, and those few asked an indifferent question or two, and discovered that she was a girl that the Carvers had "picked up somewhere" to work for them.

The minister's wife had noticed her, smiled on her and had several times said "Good evening" in friendly tones. Also, she had told her husband that that girl from Carver's was quite nice-looking, and had beautiful eyes, and that it was a shame she wasn't in Sunday school and the young people's meetings. Something really ought to be done about it; he ought to call and have a talk with Mrs. Carver. And he, poor man, said, with an expressive shrug of his shoulders, that perhaps she remembered that Mrs. Carver was not the most angelic person in the world to talk with when it came to a question upon which they might differ. Didn't his wife remember how hard they had tried to get her to send Joe Barnes to the winter term of school?

Still, being pressed, he admitted that perhaps they ought to find out about the girl, and that he and she would go up to Carver's sometime and see what they could accomplish. But he was a very busy man, and his wife was a very busy woman, with a home and many babies to look after; and with intentions so excellent that they comforted themselves with them whenever they saw the girl, the months slipped by and they did not go.

There was also another family that had kind intentions toward Weewona. Farmer Best rarely saw her moving about her neat kitchen that he did not come home and tell his wife that he did wish they could do something for that girl; that she always looked as neat as a pin, and that even Mrs. Carver spoke well of her work; but she had a lonesome look in her eyes that made him feel all the while as though she was looking for something that she could not find.

"Let's have her down here, Mother, to stay to supper, and maybe all night, and try to hearten her up."

And "Mother" was more than willing. But it was curious how impossible it had been to find just the right afternoon for this visit. As often as it was planned there was sure to be in the way an all-important reason why Weewona could not be spared. As the months passed and she became more and more helpful and responsible, it grew increasingly hard to spare her, and at last Mr. Best became discouraged and said no more about it.

So the winter passed and the summer followed it, and for the first time in that notable housekeeper's experience, Mrs. Carver's home settled into peace. Weewona could actually be trusted; she did as she was told, and did it the third and fourth and fortieth time without being watched.

Her studious habits, so far from being a drawback, were pronounced by Mrs. Carver to be distinctly beneficial. They made her contented at home, that good lady said. She did not want to be continually running somewhere, after the manner of most girls of her class. Nor was she sighing for company; and if she did have a light in her room the minute the sun went down, instead of sitting in the twilight as most girls liked to do, she was not the one to grudge her a little electricity if it was put to good use. So Mrs. Carver felt benevolent and happy.

Into the peace of this unusually comfortable home, there burst, one day, a bombshell, set off by Weewona herself.

16

"Child, Come with Me"

AT least Mrs. Carver could hardly have been more amazed had it been a veritable bombshell. Weewona wanted to work for her room and board and go to school.

"The idea!" said Mrs. Carver, in extreme disgust. And, "The idea!" echoed Clara Carver on being told of Weewona's aspirations. Then, as if that were not strong enough, she repeated: "The perfect idea! Just as we have got settled down to something like living; much housework she could do in four hours!"

"I should like to know who has been putting such notions into her head," said Mrs. Carver. "She must have heard that the Blaisdells have a girl who does that; and charming times they have, too! Mrs. Blaisdell says there are forever some extra doings at the school that take the girl away just when she is needed most. I should rather have no help at all than that kind."

"I wonder when she thinks the sewing would come in that I told her I wanted done this fall?" said Clara. "That just comes of encouraging her notions about studying. I told you that you would spoil her;

she is getting above her work. The next thing she will be setting up for a teacher! You haven't got to do it, though; that's one comfort. I should let her know once for all that no such scheme was possible, and that the sooner she gave it up entirely, the better it would be for her. You will have to be right up and down with her, Mother, and make her understand from the very first that we will have no such nonsense."

"I did, of course," said the worried woman, "but she may not give it up easily, for all that. She looks to me as though she could have a mind of her own if she chose."

"Well, so can we. Don't you give in to her, Mother, one inch. Tell her she has more privileges now than most servant girls, every single evening to herself, and often part of the afternoon. We simply can't get along with any schoolgirl folly this winter; you know we are going to have company. For pity's sake, don't you give in!"

"What is the use of talking to me about 'giving in'?" said Mrs. Carver, who knew that this was not one of her failings. "If the girl has made up her mind to work for her board and go to school, I can't compel her to stay here and work for wages, can I?"

"Yes, Mother, you can. You must set your foot down that she has got to give up all such notions. I'll risk but that she will come to her senses as soon as she sees that she can't manage us. We have been so awfully good to her that she presumes on us. But if you are firm she will simply *have* to give up. You know perfectly well that there isn't a family within miles of the schoolhouse who would take her to work for them. Why, there are only a few, you know, who keep help at all; and they don't have that kind. People who would be willing to get along with what a girl could do before and after school couldn't afford to board her; the Blaisdells are the only ones around here who ever did such a thing. Oh, she will be glad to stay and behave herself."

Thus fortified, Mrs. Carver grew strong in her determination to remain very firm should the subject be broached again, as she suspected it would; for the girl's quiet reply to her previous firmness had been: "I'm sorry, ma'am, but I must go to school this fall."

However, days and weeks passed with no further word from Weewona, and with duties faithfully performed. Mrs. Carver told her daughter that she was happily disappointed, and that she guessed, after all, the girl knew enough to see on which side her bread was buttered. Then she added magnanimously:

"But she certainly is doing remarkably well; and I believe I will raise her wages to twelve dollars a month. I think I will tell her so, next month; that will help to keep her contented."

But she did not. Precisely one month to an hour from the day on which she had expressed her wish, or, rather, if Mrs. Carver had taken note, her determination to go to school, Weewona appeared at the sitting-room door neatly dressed for the street, a large package in her hand and a larger one waiting for her on the side porch. The morning work was carefully done; Mrs. Carver had just passed through her meat kitchen and grown stronger in her determination to further bind this excellent help to herself by that advance of wages.

"I'm going now, ma'am, if you please," said Weewona, respectfully.

"Going where?" was the astonished question. It was one of Weewona's strong recommendations that she never went anywhere.

"I'm going away, ma'am, to find a place where I can work for my board and go to school. You know I told you about it just a month ago."

Astonishment held Mrs. Carver silent for several seconds; then she exclaimed, "Well, of all things in this world! What on earth can you mean? Pray, where do you think you are going?"

"I thought," said Weewona, still with utmost respect, "that I would go to Center on the train. I have heard that it is a large place, and that they have a good school. I can leave my bundles at the station and walk through the town, stopping at the houses until I find a place."

"Well!" said Mrs. Carver again, "if this isn't the limit! Do you really pretend to say that you are planning to leave me in this way, after all I have done for you, without even giving notice?"

"Why, no, ma'am," said the astonished girl. "It is a month today since I gave notice, don't you remember? I said I must go to school, and I asked if I might stay here and work for you nights and mornings and Saturdays, and you said you couldn't possibly do it; that you needed all a girl's time. So then I began to look for chances. I've had two of them, to go with people who were boarding at the hotel; but you told me, you know, a long time ago how help should always give a month's notice, if they were going away; and so I told them I couldn't leave until my month was up, and that would be too late for them. I did the best I knew how; and if that wasn't just the way to give notice, I'm sorry; I meant it for that, anyway."

Then, for the second time, Mrs. Carver said: "Well, of all things in this world! There's gratitude for you! I've never done for a girl in my life as I have for you; bought your clothes for you and cut them out and planned them; and taught you how to do dozens of things that you had never heard of before, and this is the way you pay me! It serves me right, though, for being foolish enough to take in a tramp girl without a rag to her back."

Weewona, much troubled, had no word to say. She did not understand Mrs. Carver's evident indignation. Had she not done exactly as that lady had advised? Had she not been plainly told that Mrs. Carver would not for a moment think of such a thing as having a girl who gave her only four hours of time each day, and had she not replied that she was sorry, but that she had decided that she must go to school, and must begin with fall? She felt that she had complied with all the conditions, and had nothing with which to reproach herself. She stood for a moment in doubt as to what was expected of her, then turned and silently left the room.

It was ten minutes later that she stood on the side porch arrested by Mrs. Carver's voice. It was the kind of voice that made Weewona think of starch that was too stiff.

"When you have tested your notions to your satisfaction, and found out the folly of them, you can come back here if you want to. I am not one to turn a young girl out on the streets to beg, no matter how badly she treats me."

"I thank you very much," said Weewona, earnestly. Then she added, softly, "Good-bye," feeling almost certain she was bidding a final good-bye to the house that had first sheltered her. She was sorry not to be able to stay; but the thought of turning from her purpose did not even occur to her.

Several times during her stay at Mrs. Carver's, Weewona had had a chance to stand, all but breathless, watching an incoming or an outgoing train, but to be actually seated on one of the flying things was an entirely new sensation. Still, she was wiser in many ways than she had been on that day when she held breathlessly to the seat of Mr. Best's wagon, feeling that Old Gray was rushing her to swift destruction. By no outward sign did the neatly dressed, quiet girl in the seat nearest the door indicate that her heart was thumping like a sledgehammer, and that her limbs were trembling so that she could not have walked a step.

She had herself well in hand, however, and it was not long before the heart was doing its work in the usual manner, leaving its owner at leisure to look about her.

In the seat just in front of her was a pale-faced, hollow-eyed child, whose shrunken limb, as well as the tiny, gold-mounted, velvet-padded crutches waiting in the corner, told the pitiful story of pain and helplessness.

Children of any age were a continual wonder and fascination to Weewona. She never forgot her first sight of them as three or four trooped by Mrs. Carver's doors on the way to school, and ever since she had made the most of her few opportunities to study them. The suffering little face appealed to her at once.

The child was evidently very tired, and she was undeniably cross. She wanted water, and the water, when it came, was "horrid!" She wanted ice water, and she didn't want to drink out of that ugly, thick glass; she must have her own silver cup. On being reminded that the cup had, by mistake, been packed in the trunk, she cried weakly and said that she must have it anyway.

The mother, herself pale and worn, was kept in a

constant state of anxious solicitude, and looked as though she had almost reached the limit of her resources.

"The poor child misses her nurse," the lady explained, with a wan smile, to a sympathetic fellow passenger. "She left me only yesterday, without warning, and I found it impossible to supply her place. So unfortunate, with the fatigue of a long journey in prospect; it tires her very much to travel."

During one of the mother's journeys to the next car in search of cooler water, Weewona leaned forward and spoke to the child, who was struggling with a knot in her ribbons.

"Shall I untie that for you? Do you want to take it off? I should think you would; it is warm here, isn't it?"

"It is horrid!" said the child, fretfully. "I hate it."

"Oh, do you? That must be because you are tired. I like it very much; I never went so fast before."

"So fast!" The child forgot her discomfort for a moment in her surprise. "Why, this is a pokey old train that keeps stopping all the time. We lost the express and it was all Maria's fault too."

"That was a pity," said Weewona, sympathetically, "but this seems to me to fairly fly; you see, I was never on a train before."

And now the child stared in amazement.

"Never! Do you mean never in your life? Honest? And you a great big girl! Why haven't you? But I wish I need never be on one again; I hate them. They make my head ache. It aches now."

"Poor head! Could I rub it for you a little? And if I told you a story while I was doing it, wouldn't that help the ache a little bit?"

The first faint glimmer of a smile that Weewona had

seen appeared on the pale face, as the child admitted that she liked stories.

When the mother hurried back from the next car, feeling that she had been long gone and fearing the worst, she found a trim young stranger in her seat making gentle passes over the aching head while she talked, and the patient quiet and interested. With a sigh of relief the mother dropped into the chair behind and waited. The train thundered on. Weewona, who had only a thirty-mile journey to make, began to wonder what would happen if the train reached Center before the story was concluded; but she did not allow the thought to break the connection. She talked on without pause, her voice gradually dropping lower and still lower as she saw the child's eyelids drooping heavily. At last she signaled the mother for pillows, and between them they made the little sleeper comfortable.

"So grateful to you," murmured the mother, as she tucked the traveling rug in carefully. "She has not slept since four this morning, and she was all tired out. It is wonderful that she let you touch her; when she gets one of these nervous spells she cries if a stranger looks at her. You evidently know how to manage sick children. Are you going through?"

Just what that meant, Weewona did not know, but she ventured a reply.

"I am going to Center. I want to find a place there before night; and I am a stranger."

"What kind of a place?" questioned the lady, giving her a swift glance that took in every detail of her neat dress and general appearance. "You look to me like a schoolgirl."

A vivid flush overspread Weewona's face; how delightful to look like a schoolgirl! Thus encouraged it was easy to tell, under questioning, the story of her plans and hopes. Before she had really finished it the lady's hand was upon her arm and her voice was cordial, even eager.

"Child, come home with me; I think you must be the very girl for whom I have been looking ever so long. I live just around the corner from one of the best schools in the city, and if Electa continues to have a fancy for you, you will earn your board and room many times over by just caring for her, mornings and evenings, which are her worst times. The poor child is so nervous with continued pain that she takes a dislike to the people who have to do for her, unless they are gentle and refined and, in short, understand children, as you seem to. Are you willing to go home with me and try it for a month? It is a long way from here; we have to ride all day and all night. That is another reason why I should like to have you go; I need you on this journey. Maria left me in the lurch at the last minute; she was the cause of our losing the express, and there isn't even a comfortable chair-car on this train! Since you have no relatives to leave, I should not think you would mind the distance; it will give you a chance to see more of the country.

"Why, child, of course I would pay all traveling expenses, and if we suit each other as well as I think we shall, I should be glad to make the situation permanent. It is a great thing to find help that Electa fancies; she is, of course, my first consideration; and the mornings and evenings, when a schoolgirl would be at leisure, are just the parts of the day for which I have found it hard to plan."

Thus easily was Weewona's immediate future settled for her. When the train stopped at Center, the place that had been for four weeks the center of her hopes and ambitions, she was so busy trying to make a more comfortable disposal of Electa's lame foot that she did not even notice the call.

That evening in the Carver home the supper dishes waited late for their washing. "Don't you worry," Clara Carver had said to her mother, "she will be back all right on the seven o'clock train. People in Center don't stand around on their doorsteps waiting to give stray girls room and board. She will find out that it is a silly thing to throw up such a home as she has here. I should make her understand if I were you that it isn't everybody who would take her back after such a performance."

But Mrs. Carver had no chance to do this. The seven o'clock train arrived, and Weewona did not.

17

"She Is Really Our Second Girl"

IT was months afterward that Weewona, rushing about the dining room of the Ordway home trying to make up for lost time, received light on certain matters that had puzzled her.

It was one of her duties in this home to put the dining room in order after dinner, and make the table ready for breakfast.

This, presumably, was included in her two hours of evening service, but the child, Electa, always came first and when she chose to fill the two hours, the dining room had to suffer. On this evening the little invalid had been more restless than usual, and the two hours were gone; but Weewona, knowing what annoyance would result in the morning if this work was neglected, borrowed a half hour from her own time.

The young ladies, Miss Edith and Miss Faye, were at work in the sewing room that opened by folding doors from the dining room; they were wide open now, only the portieres being drawn. While the ladies sewed they carried on a vigorous conversation. Weewona, who could not put a much-used room in order without making a reasonable amount of noise, felt sure that they knew of her presence; presumably they did not care if she overheard their talk. Their voices were very distinct.

"It really is becoming awkward," she heard Miss Faye declare. "It looks strange to people. She is an unusually nice-looking girl, and Electa is so fond of her that everyone who talks to the child hears of her; they know she belongs here. Warren Hayne asked me last night why we 'Lookouts' weren't after that pretty girl who seemed to be hiding in our house."

Then Miss Edith, in a still louder voice: "Well, now, Faye, what is the use of talking to me about it? There is nothing to hinder her going to the meetings whenever she has time. She hears the invitation from the pulpit. As to asking her to join regularly, you know as well as I do how awkward that would be. Could we take her with us to the socials and introduce her as a friend of ours? And when the socials are here, as they are so often, how would we manage then? She is really our second girl; that's the plain truth, and everybody will know it; and it isn't the custom here to invite one's help to social gatherings, as you know very well. There are some of the young people who could not be depended upon to treat her nicely, under such circumstances."

"People make very silly distinctions, I think," Faye said, irritably. "Weewona is every bit as well appearing and knows as much as dozens of girls in our set; I don't see any reason why she shouldn't associate with them."

"Perhaps there isn't; but you can't make society over to suit your own ideas, and you know perfectly well what the result would be if we should attempt anything of the kind. I, for one, am not ready to pose as a reformer. I say, let well enough alone. Weewona can come to the meetings whenever she pleases."

"Hush!" said Faye, imperatively. "You are talking too loud, and even mentioning names! She is in there at work and she can't help but hear you. We needn't insult her to her face if we are too cowardly to keep from doing it behind her back."

She was right. Weewona could not help but hear, though an instinct of honor kept her making as much noise as she conveniently could. The effect upon her was not what it would have been on the average girl brought up in the usual way. She was quietly glad that she had heard. The conversation made plainer to her some things about which she had wondered. It was because she was a housework helper, then, that she was never asked to do what other girls were doing. She was a "second girl," and over that phrase she studied curiously. Were there "first" girls, and were they better thought of than second ones? Was there a possibility that she might, sometime, become a "first" girl? It was another puzzle which she felt that she must work out. She had noticed once or twice the pulpit invitations to those young people's meetings; they had sounded cordial. She had heard a social announced in connection with them, and had even helped Miss Faye in numbering cards for a game to be played there. She had wondered if she were included in that cordial invitation, and why the young ladies did not ask if she were going; now she knew. She had thought of going regularly to that young people's meeting; now she knew that she would not.

It was not a definite or indignant resolve to have nothing to do with it; it was simply a shrinking back. She must understand life better before she would know just how to order hers. Meantime, it was safe to wait.

She had learned some things, though hardly the reasons for them. She knew, for instance, that she must say "Miss Edith" and "Miss Faye," while other girls of her age who came informally to the house, said always "Edith" and "Faye." She had wondered why. Was this also because she was a "second" girl?

All of which, in connection with many other little things that might be told, will help to explain some of the conditions of mind that grew out of Weewona's stay in this Christian home.

It was a Christian home. Mr. Ordway, the head of the house, was a church member and regular attendant, and his wife was connected officially with all the affairs of the church—financial, social, or religious. The only son of the house was a student of theology, and the young ladies were prominent workers in all lines of church activity.

Morning prayers were a part of the established order of the house, and the only reason why Weewona was not more frequently present at that function was because Electa, awakening earlier than was expected, chose to need her just then.

After Weewona's partial enlightenment with regard to social distinctions, it interested her curiously to discover that here was a function in which distinctions were not observed; even the cook was invited to a sitting at family prayers. Weewona was not there very often; she found herself shrinking from many things that she had once thought she would be eager to learn at the first opportunity. She told herself that she was still eager, but that people did not know the things that she wanted to know.

She grew daily more skeptical as to their knowledge of that sunset gate; her attendance at church was not helping her in that regard; the old trouble was in the way, the knowledge usually obtained in a primary Sunday school room would have enabled her to understand much that was now utterly obscure. She was not at all regular in her attendance; Electa managed that; she was growing more and more willing to have Weewona take the mother's place on Sunday evenings as well as morning. "She can tell stories, new ones," the petted child explained, "and I know all of yours, Mamma." And the mother smiled and sighed, and was more than willing to accept the cordially offered help. Electa had been long ill, and the mother's inventive faculty, never large, was exhausted.

As for the child, she was a sorrowful skeptic. Sometimes she expressed herself very plainly in a childish and yet unchildlike way.

One Sunday evening, when Weewona was in charge, her unbelieving mood was pronounced.

"I don't want to say my prayers tonight," she said, fretfully. "I'm tired of them; perhaps I won't ever say them anymore. Do you believe it does any good to say over a lot of prayers all the time? Nobody seems to hear; nobody answers, anyhow. I never had an answer to a prayer in my life. Do you suppose anybody does?"

"I don't know," said truthful Weewona.

"Well, I don't believe they do. You have heard Papa pray, haven't you? Of course you have, mornings, when I let you go downstairs. Well, he asks for a lot of things that he never gets. I've heard him ever so many times, and I've kept watch, and I know he didn't get them. He used to ask for me to get well, but—" she glanced about the room, as if fearful that someone beside Weewona would hear, and lowered her voice— "he doesn't do it anymore; at least, I don't believe he does; I haven't heard him for a long time. Do you ever hear him?"

"Sometimes," admitted Weewona.

"Well, he doesn't get that, you see, and I don't know why he keeps asking for it when he knows it's no good. The doctor told him I wouldn't ever get the least little bit well; that I would just keep on growing lamer and lamer all the time. Now, what's the use of praying about that?"

"Perhaps," said Weewona, faintly, "the doctor is mistaken."

"No, he isn't. I know I'm getting lamer, and my back is growing crookeder. Every time I look at myself in the glass I can see that I'm a lot crookeder. I'll be an ugly little old woman, all humped up! I hate it!"

The worn little face looked old and fierce. In some respects this child of scarcely eight years was already old.

Weewona regarded her pitifully and knew not what to say. Being truthful by nature she could not try to prop her up with smooth words that meant nothing, for she had heard of the doctor's verdict, though how Electa knew what had been carefully kept from her, the young nurse could not imagine. She moved about the room trying to find something out of place, while she racked her brains for something of sufficiently startling interest to draw the child's thoughts from herself. She was not quick enough. Electa began again in a quieter, but deeply sad tone.

"I should think I would want to die, but I don't. I hate living, and being all humped up and bent over and stared at. I can't begin to tell you how I hate it; but I'm scared over dying. Should you think anybody could ever like to be dead?"

A sudden rush of loneliness and desperate homesickness, such as sometimes swept over Weewona at thought of the mountain cabin and Pete, caught her now, and she said, almost fiercely, "Yes, I should! I think I should like it better than anything else in the world."

"What! To be put in the ground and covered all up? Ugh! I shouldn't. I should hate it.

"I know," she added, after another pathetic pause. "People say we don't stay in the ground. They say we—the part that is really us, you know—don't go into the ground at all; but I don't see how they know. Mamma talks about heaven sometimes when she feels bad about me, but I can't *think* heaven, can you? It doesn't seem anywhere, and graves do, you know. I've seen them. I saw Uncle Dick put into the ground. Did you ever see a grave, to come close to when it was wide open?"

"Yes," said Weewona. "But, Electa, I wouldn't talk about such things anymore if I were you. If you do, you will not get to sleep."

"I don't want to go to sleep, and I want to talk. Do you suppose the souls of people get out of their graves and go to heaven? How could they? And how do we know we have got any souls?"

"I don't know," said Weewona. "Why don't you ask your mother to explain all about it?"

"I can't," said the child, sorrowfully. "Mamma cries; it makes her feel bad about me, you know. She says, 'Oh, my darling, *don't!*' and then she cries. Mamma thinks I'm going to die, pretty soon, I know she does; so I can't talk to her, nor to Papa. Besides, how would they know about it? They have never been to heaven. That's it—nobody ever has, who came back and told. Don't you wish they would? If there were just one man, or little girl, even, that God would let go to heaven and look around and talk with some angels, and then come back and tell about it, wouldn't that be too lovely! Why do you suppose he doesn't do it?"

"Electa, won't you say your prayers now and try to go to sleep? Your mamma will not like to have you lying awake so long."

"I can't help it; you can't make yourself sleepy when you are not sleepy one bit, and I told you I was tired of my prayers. I have said, 'Now I lay me down to sleep,' ever since I can remember. I wonder if I ever mean it? You know it says:

> "'*If I should die before I wake,*
> *I pray thee, Lord, my soul to take.*'

"What do I want him to take it for? Do you honestly believe that heaven is a nice, beautiful place, where everybody has a good time, and where crooked little girls get straight and well, and run about like other people?"

Oh, for knowledge enough to answer the questions of this little old child, with her pain-drawn face and crooked body! Weewona, in her ignorance, longed for wisdom to do so, even as Kendall Fletcher, in his knowledge, had longed for it.

But, though in some things she had been disappointed in life, Weewona was far from being unhappy; in truth, she was too busy to have time for unhappiness; and she was always able to remember gleefully that one great desire of her heart had been accomplished—she was a schoolgirl.

There had been trials connected with this experience, but they daily lessened. At first, the tall girl, who looked every hour of her age, seemed strangely out of place among the little girls and boys with whom her grade placed her. Had she grown up thus far in the atmosphere of schools she could hardly have borne the situation, with the ridicule that resulted.

But as it was, much of the ridicule she did not understand. To her it was simply a matter of a girl having grown tall before she had her chance at school, and she could not understand why such a thing should amuse anybody. The quiet patience with which she bore the ridicule, coupled with the excellent lessons that she always had, began, in time, to command respect. Moreover, she was always kind, always ready to help even the youngest and least important.

On the whole, in the course of a few weeks, Weewona became popular with her classmates, and loud was the lamentation among them when, after the midyear examinations, she was advanced to the next grade, where, if she was still much behind her years, the contrast was by no means so sharply marked as before.

By the time her first year at school was concluded, her teachers assured her that by making good use of the long vacation she would be able to advance again to the grade where there were some pupils as old as herself, and where the disparity that had been so glaring at first would cease to be noticeable.

Of course, during all this time she had learned many things besides lessons from books. She knew now what kinds of questions would make people stare and call her queer, or "off." By dint of skillful questioning and observation she had learned the meaning of that word. She avoided all questions that would tend toward its use, and for the things that she was still determined to know, not found in textbooks, bided her time. The sunset gate, for instance, though by no means forgotten, was kept in abeyance.

The girl fancied that she could now tell, by merely looking at people, those who would be likely to know about it, and she believed that they were few.

In the home that had so opportunely opened to receive her she was still as much of a fixture as they could arrange.

The embarrassments that the eldest daughter had foreseen growing out of Weewona's instincts of refinement and the speed with which she assimilated culture had never arisen. The girl had shown wonderful skill in the difficult art of "knowing her place," and had never in any way obtruded herself. She never even intruded upon the family circle in the home where she so skillfully fitted in, but kept herself to herself, and to Electa, with a good sense and devotion that were rare.

18

"SHE MAY HAVE INHERITED CONSCIENCE"

OF course the ever-recurring question: "Where-withal shall I be clothed?" came up for consideration, and threatened embarrassments. Care for it as daintily as she could, Weewona's brown suit began to show signs of wear. Then there were shoes and various other needs that were beginning to press their claims. No one beside herself seemed to notice these things, or think of them; but Weewona one morning surprised and dismayed Mrs. Ordway with a plan that she had carefully worked out. She could secure a room where she could board herself by sweeping the office across the hall from it once a week and dusting it every morning. Then she had found that she could secure five hours of housework each day at twenty cents an hour, which would give her six dollars a week. She had made careful calculations and believed that for two dollars a week she could buy her food, and with the other four she could, by degrees, furnish herself with necessary clothing. By all of which it will be seen that Weewona was a much better financier than she had been when she lent her gold pieces to Kendall Fletcher. Mrs. Ordway's respect for the girl deepened while she listened. There also deepened the determination to keep this capable young woman in her employ if possible.

She broke out volubly. Weewona must not think of leaving them; it would be too hard on Electa. How could she, who seemed to love the child so dearly, bear to plan such a course! There was a better way than that. If she could spare five hours each day from her studies, so much the better for Mrs. Ordway. Indeed, that good lady would like nothing better than to secure the girl's entire time. She made the suggestion with the upward inflection; if Weewona desired to accept it there was a chance. But the look in the girl's eyes seemed to answer her, for she said:

"So I supposed." Well, then, she would be glad to pay her twenty-five cents for the extra hour, and that would give her a dollar and a half a week for incidental expenses. As for clothes, dresses and things of that kind, the girls had some that they were going to dispose of; she wondered that they had not thought of giving them to her. Of course, being in society, they had to have fresh dresses quite often, and Weewona would find that those which, for one reason or another, they had laid aside would make over into better dresses than she could afford to buy; the material was always of the best; she did not believe in buying cheap things. As for boarding herself on two dollars a week, that, the good lady was sure, was out of the question; it would be slow starvation. She really must not think of it.

And Weewona, glad not to have to learn new ways, and try to please new people; glad to have the matter of clothes settled for her by those who knew all about such things; glad, above all, not to leave Electa, stayed.

And the months passed with few outward changes, save that Electa grew, as she said, "crookeder and crookeder." She also grew weaker and more exacting, though she was rarely out of temper with Weewona. The mother said, with something between a smile and a sigh, that that girl could do anything she wanted to with the child, and more and more the child was left to her care.

Weewona made acquaintances, of course, among the schoolgirls and boys. Some of them had brothers and sisters who belonged to the same social circle as the Ordway girls, but with these she got no further than a friendly recognition as they passed on the streets. Socially they did not meet at all; not because some of them would not have been willing had they thought of it, but—Weewona's out-of-school hours belonged to another world. This they tacitly accepted and gave it no more heed; at least, so far as girls were concerned. Among the boys it was somewhat different. Being boys, they naturally paid less attention to class distinctions than the girls were being trained to do.

Certain of them sought out and made friendship with the bright-eyed girl who "simply walked through her lessons," as they phrased it. One young fellow in particular was persistent in his efforts to show her kindnesses. He was older than most of the high school boys; was, indeed, a conditioned college boy who was "coaching up" on certain studies in which he had dropped below the mark. He was a handsome fellow, belonging to a good family, and was much sought after.

There came an eventful evening in which he invited Weewona to attend a concert in his company. It was her first evening out in the world in company with one of nearly her own age, and she prepared for it with the conscious flutter that must always accompany first things. In her newly made-over crimson gown that had once been Edith Ordway's, and that became her as it never had Edith, she looked sufficiently distinguished beside her handsome escort to be stared at and inquired after.

She heard much about it the next day. One of the more outspoken among the schoolgirls challenged her after this manner:

"Say, Weewee, you made an out-and-out hit last night, do you know it? You looked as handsome as a witch in that red dress, and Jack Leeson was too swell for anything! He is the most stylish boy in town. How did you happen to catch him?"

Although Weewona shrank instinctively from the innate coarseness of this kind of talk, it was not in human nature not to be interested in having had "the most stylish boy in town" for one's companion. She did not know that the stylish boy had also the name of being "fast." She only knew that he belonged to one of the "first families," and by dint of careful study and observation she had come to have a fair conception of what that phrase meant. She also knew that the young man was very nice to her. He was careful to take off his hat to her when they met, and in other little ways belonging to polite life distinguished her as an acquaintance of his. When he invited her to one of the fine concerts of the season she was glad. And when, on the following Sunday evening, he came boldly to the Ordways' to ask if he might take her to the young people's meeting, she was pleased.

But Mrs. Ordway was not; she was anxious. "I don't

like it," she said to her husband. "Not that there is anything very bad about Jack Leeson, is there? But he has the name of being rather wild, and Weewona is as ignorant as a child about all such things. He will be sure to put notions into her head. He doesn't mean anything but fun, of course, but his fun may be hard on the girl. Do you think I ought to stop it? This is the third time, now, that she has been out with him."

"I don't know how you can," Mr. Ordway said, arresting his hairbrush to consider. "We have no authority over the girl."

"Oh, Weewona won't do anything that I really advise against. She is very conscientious. I don't know how she happens to have such proper ideas of duty and conscience; she is not religiously inclined. She told me she would much rather than not stay with Electa, that she did not care to go to church; and I notice that she is very willing to be excused from prayers."

"She may have inherited conscience," Mr. Ordway said.

"Oh, I don't think that is probable. She must have had a common origin, or else not a respectable one. Respectable people do not drop their relations as completely as she has been dropped. She has no idea who any of her relatives were."

"There is nothing about that girl to suggest slum life," Mr. Ordway said, positively; and his wife, with a wise shake of her head, replied:

"No, I'm afraid it suggests something worse; that is one reason why I don't like to see her with Jack Leeson, though I must say I trust her more than I would some girls in our church."

While this conversation was in progress, Jack Leeson and his companion were taking the longest way to church, intent, the one on the girl who just now amused him, and the other on the subject under discussion. It was really their first continued talk together, and Jack Leeson had himself begun it by saying:

"I hope you are not bent on young people's meeting this evening? I have other plans. It is a glorious evening, and a walk in the park would be about seventy-five times more interesting."

"But you asked if I would go with you to the meeting!" Weewona's look and tone expressed her astonishment.

"Of course; that was for Madame Ordway's benefit. I happen to know that she has straitlaced ideas about Sunday. Besides, I meant to bring up at the church in time for the doxology, or whatever it is they close with; that's quite time enough. I'll take you over to Forest Park; there are some charming moonlight strolls over there. It is prettier than Prospect Park, to my thinking."

But he had reckoned wide of his mark. Weewona's voice was firmness personified. "Mr. Leeson, I told Mrs. Ordway that I was going to the young people's meeting, and what I say I generally do. But I need not keep you from the park. I am not in the least afraid to go to church alone."

Jack Leeson was astonished and immensely amused. He suppressed a whistle, and replied in a seriocomic strain:

"Dear me, what dignity and propriety! I am properly squelched and am sure now that you descend straight from the Puritans. No, thank you, I don't care to ramble about the park alone. To church we go, though there were ten glorious moons instead of one to woo us. It's all right; I don't mind in the least. I go to the young people's meeting occasionally all by myself just for fun. But I don't remember seeing you there."

"I am hardly ever there," said Weewona. "But do you call it fun? I shouldn't think that was just the word."

"Why not? It is great fun, I assure you, to see those youngsters hop up one after another and mouth over words that they don't understand; mimicking their elders and imagining that they are saying it themselves. They always remind me of a company of trained parrots."

This interested Weewona, as all new ideas did.

"Why do you think they don't understand what they are talking about? she asked. "I fancied that they did."

He laughed good-naturedly. "It is the most charitable thing to think," he said. "If they do understand, they are a lot of precious hypocrites. Have you ever heard that little Minnie Tabor hold forth? It's great fun. She's up on words, you know; can pour them out in class by the ton, and not know a blooming thing about the lesson, either. Well, the last night I was at this meeting I heard her get off in her prettiest voice, such a voice as a full-fledged angel might be supposed to have, a lot of stuff about having 'groped all day after something higher.' She longed she said, for a 'deep experience, a more entire consecration of her all to the Master,' and a lot more of that kind of bosh. What was that but mimicry if it wasn't humbug pure and simple? Minnie Tabor never longed for anything in her life but fun, and she is consecrated to having a good time. I spent the Saturday evening before that meeting with her, and I never heard a girl rattle on as she did in my life!"

"And you think she is just pretending? What object can she have in going to those meetings and saying such things?"

"Oh, she thinks she means it, all right. I didn't say they were hypocrites; I said they were poll parrots. It is the custom nowadays to have young people's meetings; kind of a church function; and the minister expects his young folks to attend, and keep the thing going."

"What thing?"

"Why, the whole affair; the church, you know, and all it stands for, I suppose."

"That's what I am trying to find out. What does the church stand for?"

"Oh, see here! I'm not the fellow to be examined on church history, I can tell you. When it comes to that, I know as little about it as I do about tomorrow's Latin, and that's owning to a good deal of ignorance. I dare say you could tell more about the church in five minutes than I could in a week."

"But you are mistaken. I don't understand the church at all. I know almost nothing about it, and I want to learn. Why do they want churches built up? Why do they have preachers and go once a week to hear them talk, and all the rest of it? I've been wanting to know about it this long time."

Jack Leeson regarded her curiously, a puzzled look on his face.

"Why," he began, hesitatingly, "of course you know what the churches started with. They are built on the Bible, you know, and people are bound to follow its directions, or think they are. If a fellow really did, in these days, I guess they'd send him to the lunatic asylum; but that's where they get their bylaws."

"Where did they get the Bible?"

"See here, I believe you are guying me! You want to give me a chance to show just how little I do know."

"No, I'm not thinking of you at all. I haven't lived in a city full of churches all my life, as you have. I don't know about these things, and there are reasons why I want to learn."

"Well, you have come to the wrong chap as true as you live. I never looked into these things much, although, as you say, I've had chances enough. The Bible is all right, of course. I believe in it, and the church, too, in a way, although I consider it a good deal of a bore to go to it, especially on moonlit nights."

"Why do you believe in the Bible?"

"Gracious! Because I do, of course. Most decent people believe in a good deal of it. Why, bless you! My grandfather was a clergyman, and so are two of my uncles. The Bible is inspired, you know."

"Do you mean that God wrote it?"

"Of course; or told people what to write. Let me see, what did I study once about the Bible being handed down? We had it in our class in the days when I went to Sunday school. There was a lot about Hebrew manuscripts and Greek manuscripts, and the trouble people took to get them carefully copied. I don't remember a dozen lines there were in the book, but I know it was quite convincing that the Bible had been handed down to us straight and was to be trusted. Oh, the churches are all right, and so is the young people's meeting, if the youngsters do talk about what they don't understand. That doesn't hurt them, and it amuses those who listen. Here we are at the church. Are you still resolved to sacrifice the evening, or have we had church enough? I'm sure I've talked more religion tonight than I have in a year before. Must we go in?"

For answer, Weewona herself pushed open the chapel door and entered, and the handsome youth shrugged his shoulders, made a queer half-amused, half-petulant grimace, and followed.

19

"SUCH AN IMPOSSIBLE GIRL"

AN imp of mischief went into the church with Jack Leeson that evening. No sooner were they seated than to Weewona's distress he began to whisper. They were late, thanks to having taken that longest way, and a high school boy was speaking.

"I tell you, boys," he was saying, "we aren't half in earnest about this thing. If we went at it with the energy that we give to the baseball team, folks would believe we meant it."

"Suppose he should try it!" whispered Jack Leeson. "I'd put five dollars into their treasury for the sake of hearing him give one yell here such as he produces on the ball ground. Wouldn't it make that solemn-faced minister stare!" And he laughed, not quite softly.

"Hush!" said Weewona, red-faced with embarrassment. "He is staring at you."

A young girl arose and began to speak.

"Now look out for creeps!" whispered Jack. "Minnie Tabor has her angel face on."

"The topic appeals to me tonight," said the girl, "in a different way from what it does to you, because it is intimately associated with my mother. She had what I might call a consuming ambition for her daughter."

"Um!" murmured Jack. "That's what her daughter has for herself, the ambition to be called the sweetest duck in the whole pond." The sweet voice, with more than a touch of pathos in it, continued.

"She desired for her child, without regard to outward conditions or circumstances, that she might grow each day a little more like Jesus Christ. Her constant prayer for me was that I might be conformed to his image."

"Oh, larks!" murmured Jack. "No wonder she died of disappointment."

"Please, don't!" said distressed Weewona. The sweet, tremulous voice went on.

"My mother, as you know, is gone to heaven, and there are times when I miss her so that it seems to me I cannot live any longer without her."

"Boo, hoo!" whispered Jack; and, in answer to the flash from Weewona's eyes, "Tears are in order now, don't you hear them in her voice? She expects her audience to be sympathetic; that's Minnie's great stunt."

He was not utterly heartless; he had simply yielded to the temptation to be what he called funny, at all hazards. He knew Minnie Tabor only in social life, and on the occasions when he had met her intimately she had been in high spirits; she was one of those whom youth and environment, and an abundant flow of animal spirits tempt to go further in the interests of merriment than in quiet moments they wish they had. Jack Leeson, having really very little knowledge of human nature, and giving only surface judgment to most things, had judged the girl accordingly. He did not even know that fun and frolic were entirely compatible with a sincere Christian life. He believed that the fun was genuine, therefore the other must be something put on. To be sure, he saw no great harm in that; he was even willing to own that Minnie Tabor was charming when she was "doing either the pathetic or the pious; combined they were irresistible."

"But the hardest part of it all is to know that I have sorely disappointed her." It was Minnie's voice again, and this time it broke into a sob as she sat down. Jack Leeson softly imitated the sob, to the great delight of several young people who occupied back seats.

The leader of the meeting spoke promptly: "We have all fallen far below the mark which those who love us best set for us. Let us join with our pastor in prayer for our friend here, and for each other, that we may be lifted, all of us, to a higher plane."

Whereupon Jack Leeson performed a rapid pantomime for Weewona's benefit of someone being lifted and set down with a thud on higher ground. If he hoped to provoke a smile on the stern face beside him, he was disappointed. Instead, if he had but known her better, he would have understood that her eyes expressed only indignation.

"But before we pray," said the leader, "I want to ask if there is not one here tonight who would like to make a start toward Christ? Someone, I mean, who never professed to belong to him, but who is thinking about it, and asking himself if now is not the time. Let me tell you that you will never find a better time than this, and I ask you to just rise in your seat and stand a moment, thus saying that you would like to have us pray especially for you. We will wait just a moment."

Jack Leeson nudged his companion's elbow. "Now's your chance!" he whispered. "Hop up, while they are waiting and staring. It will create a sensation and encourage the poor things; they don't expect anything of the kind. I would do it myself if I were not too well known."

And then Weewona flashed a glance at him which he understood, and for five minutes he was quiet. Had he been observing, he would have noted that there was little chance for staring; every head save the leader's and those of a very few outsiders like themselves, was already bowed. No one arose on the invitation; but presently the pastor's voice in prayer broke the stillness. It was a very tender prayer, brief, earnest, solemn, athrob with personality, yet singularly quieting in its effect. With especial fervor and tenderness were those remembered who had need of Jesus Christ as a Savior, but were not willing to ask for him. Then, while heads were still bowed, somebody began to sing softly, others joining, until there was a murmur of tender song throughout the room, every word as distinct as though one voice were reciting.

> *"Tell me, my Savior, where thou dost feed thy flock,*
> *Resting beside the rock, cool in the shade?*
> *Why should I be as one turning aside alone,*
> *Left, when thy sheep have gone, where I have*
>   *strayed?*
>
> *"Seek me, my Savior, for I have lost the way;*
> *I will thy voice obey; speak to me here.*
> *Help me to find the gate where all thy chosen wait,*
> *Ere it shall be too late; oh, call me near!"*

As the harmony flowed out, filling the soul with its sweetness and strength, Weewona was back again under the great trees, peeping into the tent, listening to that marvelous story of the sunset gate. Behold, here it was again! The gate! And a distinct call for help in finding it!

> "Help me to find the gate where all thy chosen
> wait."

Could that be other than the gate where they "put on glory"?

Were these young people, then, all praying to die? If so, did they expect to have their prayer answered? Or were they, as the little Electa thought, "just saying over words because they were nice good words, and made people feel better, somehow, while they were saying them"?

Even so, she longed to be of their number. Her very soul took hold of that pitiful question in the song:

> "Why should I be as one turning aside alone?"

Why, indeed! Oh, for someone to have understood the dense ignorance of this groping soul! She would have risen to her feet in an instant on that invitation had she understood what it was that she was thus to ask. No feeling of timidity held her back; she was simply lost on the very trail itself, with all about her earnest souls who could have pointed out the steps had they but known that she needed help. Even the mocking spirit at her side had sufficient theoretical knowledge to have set her right with regard to the foundation facts of the Christian religion had he chosen to do so. It is not certain that he would not have tried, had he understood her need. The little that he knew concerning religious truth he supposed was common to all intelligent people.

The young man's conduct did not improve, as the

hour passed. He had been a good deal annoyed at first over the discovery that he could not bend to his wishes the girl he had chosen to honor with his company. He had allowed this feeling to merge into the comic and help him in turning everything he saw and heard into ridicule. At first, he made no effort to control this tendency, and then he passed so completely under its power that it would have required more of an effort of will than he cared to make to control it.

Despite the troubled and indignant glances that Weewona gave him, he continued to whisper, to the evident annoyance of others beside herself. The pastor of the church, who knew him well, kept glancing their way with a troubled air. Finally he changed his seat to one just back of them, and when Jack's parody on the hymn that was being sung reached his ears he leaned forward and touched the young fellow's arm with a murmured, "I wouldn't, Jack, if I were you."

"Wouldn't you?" said Jack, cheerfully. "I wonder how you found that out! The trouble with the proposition is, that you are not me; I don't see how we are going to manage it."

To Jack's intense delight, Weewona, instead of joining the ranks of those who were passing from the parlor into the main audience room for the second service, directly when the meeting was closed turned with decision toward the outside door. Jack followed her promptly.

"Had enough of meetings, have you?" he said gleefully. "So have I. Now we'll have time for a stroll in the park; and the moon has waited for us. Isn't she doing her level best just now?"

But Weewona spoke with a sharpness that was new to him.

"Mr. Leeson, if you want to know why I didn't stay to church, it was because I was ashamed to be seen any longer in your company. I don't know much about churches, nor religion, but I know enough to see that respectable people treat the church respectfully while they are in it, and consider it a disgrace to behave so as to be spoken to. I am going straight home; but you needn't take the trouble to go with me. I'm not in the least afraid."

"Upon my word!" said Jack, who was obliged to quicken his pace in order to keep up with her. "You are an independent person, I must say, and plain spoken! A trifle too much so, between friends, it seems to me. Of course, I didn't mean any harm, and didn't disturb anybody, unless it was the parson; he's a spoony sort of fellow, and a little stirring up now and then will do him good. Come, Weewona, don't be cross and spoil our fine evening. You don't get an evening to yourself often enough to waste it. Turn around with me and we'll have the time of our lives."

He caught at her arm, but she drew herself away and spoke firmly.

"No, I am not going to the park. I am going home at once, and I am indignant. I consider that I have been insulted. I have been made conspicuous in a public place and looked upon as a person who did not know how to behave decently—all because I was in bad company."

"Upon my word!" he said again, and this time he was angry. "'Bad company,' indeed! You seem to forget to whom you are talking. That's pretty well for one who has taken you up as I have, in spite of your being the Ordways' hired help. There isn't another fellow in our set that would have done it, and this is the thanks I get!"

And now Weewona was furious. But she showed it only by a still colder and more self-controlled tone, as she said:

"Mr. Leeson, I will thank you very much if you will turn around and go the other way, or stand still, if you prefer. I mean to go on, and I wish to go alone. I will save you further trouble now or at any other time on my account. Having been so good as to take me up, be so very good as to drop me and let me alone."

Jack Leeson was so astonished that he almost halted, and stared in bewilderment. Could he believe his ears? He was used to girls in high circles who were elated over his attentions. Why, wasn't he Justyn J. Leeson's only son? Yet here was a girl who worked out for her living, actually so angry that she seemed to be dismissing him! And all for what? Because he had whispered a little in a "kid" prayer meeting! She was still walking very fast and in the direction of home. Evidently there was to be no stroll in the park for that time at least. He had wasted an entire evening on a pigheaded girl who did not know any better than to quarrel with him! His temper got the better of him entirely.

"Well!" he said. "This goes ahead of any treatment I ever expected to receive! You can stay at home after this until you are gray before I shall give you another chance out. I shall drop you too low down ever to find you again."

It was a babyish speech, as well as a mean one, and five minutes afterward Jack Leeson would have given much for a chance to take it back. But he lost his chance. Weewona, still walking rapidly, suddenly addressed one of two elderly women whom they had overtaken.

"Mrs. Warner?" Both women stopped and turned,

and the girl's words came fast. "May I walk the rest of the way home in your company?"

"Surely," began the elder of the two. "Who is it? Why, it's little Electa's 'Weewee,' isn't it? Certainly, child, you are very welcome."

"Then, Mr. Leeson, I need not trouble you to go any farther; Mrs. Warner lives across the street from us."

And so, for the first time in his life, Jack Leeson was summarily dismissed.

Mrs. Ordway, who resolved on that Sunday evening that the very next time Weewona asked permission to go out with Jack Leeson to speak plainly to her, had no opportunity. Days and weeks passed without any requests being made, and with no appearance on Jack's part.

Mrs. Ordway did not know that the young fellow, having given his anger time to cool, magnanimously resolved to forgive; and after waiting long enough to teach the "little spitfire" a lesson, give her another chance. He had heard it hinted that she had Indian blood in her veins and he believed it.

Yet, even so, she interested and amused him; she was different from any other girl he had ever known; her very quarrel with him was unlike anybody else.

One afternoon, after several weeks of waiting, he stood on the steps leading from the superintendent's office and waited for Weewona to appear from the classroom where he knew she was.

Then he joined her quite as though they had parted the day before on excellent terms.

"I've got tickets for the Academy Farce, tonight," he said in his most nonchalant tone. "I had a hard time getting them, too; put it off too long. I had no idea there would be such a rush. I should like to take you with me. Shall I call for you as early as half past seven? We shall have to start early on account of the crowd; they aren't going to hold the seats after eight."

"Thank you," said Weewona, "but I am not going to the farce; and you seem to have forgotten that I have been dropped." Whereupon she signaled a passing car and left him standing on the sidewalk, not so angry as he was puzzled over such an impossible girl.

After that, he let her severely alone. "She will find," he said, "that she has gone too far." He fancied her sitting disconsolately over her lost hopes. Not even then did he understand that this was not pique upon Weewona's part, but a deliberate resolve that she could not afford to risk her good name with such as he. He had been kind to her, and there was a sense in which she missed him; but, after all, if he had cared for her as a friend, would he have persisted in his conduct at that meeting after he saw that it annoyed her, and especially after being spoken to by the minister? She decided that she could not afford to trust such kindness.

"He has simply dropped her," Mrs. Ordway told her husband, in a tone of relief, after some weeks had passed.

20

◆═◈═◆

"Is It Mere Story?"

DON'T you think, Dudley, there is another one!"

"Another what?" Mr. Ordway asked, glancing up from the paper he was reading.

"Oh, another boy, or man it is, this time. Dear me! I had no idea that Wona would ever trouble me in such ways."

"Is it Weewona again? I thought she settled down after Jack Leeson dropped her."

"So she did; but that was—why, that must have been more than a year ago; time flies so fast! She hasn't given me an hour of trouble since, until lately. It began while you were East."

"What began? What has happened?"

"Why, she has walked home from the library three times with Mr. Selling; or, at least, he has walked with her, and he has asked her to go with him to the Wendell lecture tonight."

"Selling!" The newspaper dropped to the floor, and Mr. Ordway, having indulged in that single word, whistled softly.

"Yes," said Mrs. Ordway, answering what she believed was his thought.

"Mr. Selling. She looks high, doesn't she? What do you suppose he means by noticing her?"

"Oh, he means kindness, I guess; philanthropy, or some notion of the sort. He is that kind of a man, I fancy; at least, he isn't Jack Leeson's kind. But a man like Selling can turn the head of a girl quicker than a dozen Jack Leesons could."

"Yes, indeed! Especially a girl like Wona, and mean nothing but kindness all the time. I wish he would keep his philanthropy for boys. But there isn't a single plausible reason for keeping Weewona at home to-night."

"Oh, let her go, of course," said Mr. Ordway, resuming his paper. "She must take her chances like other girls in this world. She will get to the Wendell lecture, at least, and the tickets cost a dollar apiece."

So Weewona went to the Wendell lecture.

Mrs. Ordway was right; it was more than a year since the girl had taken that indignant walk home from church with Jack Leeson.

Calculating from the date that Pete had arranged as covering her probable years, she had now passed her eighteenth anniversary. Date of birth had, of course, been impossible to determine, but here Pete had come again to the rescue, and fixed upon the day of her arrival at his cabin as the one that they would consider her birthday. Always, thereafter, he had remembered the eighteenth day of June by some special treat or token. When he was gone, the day dropped out of notice, until Electa discovered it, and the eighteenth anniversary was marked by a gift from her of as beautiful a Bible as her father could find on sale.

This was not Weewona's first acquaintance with the Bible. Electa had chosen her gift with discrimination. Her own interest in the Book dated back to a certain

Sunday afternoon a few months before the birthday, in which, after turning in all the positions that her limited strength would permit, she declared herself tired of everything.

No, she did not want to be read to; she was especially tired of everything that there was to read. Fairy tales were silly; she was tired of people and things that could not be.

All her storybooks of real people were stupid. The people were always going skating or tramping or picnicking; out of doors and on their feet the whole time. She almost hated them. Then she had a sudden fancy. Weewona was to get the library stepladder and climb to the very top shelf of her closet, the wide shelf away up above all the others. There were some books packed away there that she used to have when she was a little bit of a girl. There was one in particular, a piece of poetry about a little sick girl lying in bed. Perhaps she would like to hear it read again. She couldn't remember just how it ended.

Weewona searched patiently, but the poem so described was not to be found. However, she found something; a box, large and heavy, and so pretty in itself that there must be something pretty inside.

Electa exclaimed over it with delight, "It's my new Bible that Uncle Gus sent me ever so long ago! Papa said it was too nice a Bible for me to have around until I got bigger, so Mamma had it packed away on that high shelf, and I forgot all about it. Open it, quick! I forget how it is bound, but I know it is lovely."

It certainly was, and the frail little girl showed more interest in it than she had exhibited for some weeks.

"It has pictures in it," she said. "Lots of them. Look, there is one on almost every page, and there are some great big pictures taking up the whole page, that are lovely. I don't care for the reading; I mean, it reads like any other Bible, but I shall like to look at some of the pictures."

The book rest was set on the bed and the little girl turned the leaves of the handsome volume, studying picture after picture with unusual interest.

"Oh, Weewee!" she said. "Here is one of a little sick girl; no, I think she is dead. I don't remember any story about her; is there one?"

"I don't know," said Weewona. The child lay back on her pillow, her little flash of strength exhausted.

"Look, please," she said, "and read it to me. If she died I ought to know about it, because——" A long drawn-out, unchildlike sigh completed the sentence, and Weewona turned away quickly to hide tears. But she found the story and read it. To both it was a first time for that old, simple, wonderful story.

"There came a man named Jairus . . . and he fell down at Jesus' feet, and besought him that he would come into his house, for he had one only daughter, about twelve years of age, and she lay dying. . . . While he yet spake, there cometh one . . . saying to him, Thy daughter is dead, trouble not the Master."

"Horrid old thing!" interrupted Electa. "Why didn't he wait until the man got home? Go on."

"But when Jesus heard it, he answered him, saying, Fear not, believe only and she shall be made whole."

"Oh, my!" said Electa. "Hear that! Read on fast!"

"And when he came into the house . . . all wept and bewailed her, but he said, Weep not, she is not dead, but sleepeth. And they laughed him to scorn, knowing that she was dead. And he . . . took her by the hand, and called, saying, Maid, arise. And her spirit came again, and she arose up straightway."

"Oh *my!*" said Electa again. "Do you suppose she was really dead?"

"It says so."

"Yes, I know, but—well, it's Bible, and of course, we ought to believe it. What did he mean, though, by saying, 'She is not dead, but sleepeth'?"

Weewona hesitated. Exposition of the Bible was new work to her. At last, bringing her common sense to bear on the question, she said: "He might have meant that death was no more to him than sleep; that he could waken from the one as easily as from the other."

"Yes, so he might. I suppose that is what he did mean. Oh, dear! Do you suppose if he were here he would do such things now? Of course, he could, or he wouldn't be God. Why, he could without being here, for that matter, couldn't he? I wonder why he doesn't, anymore? Perhaps he does, only we don't hear about them. But, then, Papa has asked him lots of times. Weewee, why don't you say something? Do you think he might possibly cure me if I should coax and coax a great long while?"

"I don't know," said the distressed Weewona. What was she to say to this longing little soul? If she only knew how to answer!

"But you don't believe he will, do you?" said the shrewd little questioner. "And I don't, either."

Again came that long, drawn-out, unchildlike sigh.

But the Bible with pictures was not suffered to return to the top shelf and oblivion. It became a continued source of interest to both Electa and her nurse. Bible stories that Electa had known from almost babyhood and that Weewona had never before heard were read and reread and talked over, and Weewona realized with each passing day that her interest in the life of the one called Jesus was deepening. Every day the longing grew to know more about it all; to understand it; to be able to answer Electa's questions with an assurance that would satisfy her. Above all things else to be able to help her get ready—if there was such a thing as getting ready—for that awful hour that was coming to her with steady feet.

If Mrs. Ordway had known that this girl's interest in Mr. Selling's attentions had to do with an intense desire to help her little charge, she would have been astonished.

Weewona knew that Mr. Selling taught a class in Bible literature at the college. Ought not a man who taught Bible literature understand Bible teaching?

All the time that she was walking home from the library by Mr. Selling's side, giving such intelligent attention to what he was talking about that her questions pleased him, there was an undercurrent of thought passing in Weewona's mind. Suppose she could get to feeling well enough acquainted with this man to ask him questions about Electa's Bible, just what would she ask first? How give expression to that which she wished most to know?

Her knowledge of the Bible was, she feared, too limited for intelligent questions. She had begun to read it through; begun, as she supposed every reasonable person should, at the beginning. She had very little time for personal reading, and had only now reached Deuteronomy. It could not be said that she enjoyed the reading. She understood very little of it, and much of the time it was absolutely unintelligible to her; yet she came, occasionally, to what seemed like detached bits that thrilled her, and made her long to understand more. This, aside from the stories that she read for Electa's benefit, constituted her present acquaintance with the book. She had begun to feel that she could not make intelligent progress in reading it through without knowing a few things about it.

It was this state of things that caused Weewona to look forward with marked satisfaction to the taking of that long walk to Bannard Hall, where the Wendell lecture was to be given. There would surely be a chance to ask questions if she could but plan them, so as to learn the things she most needed to know.

On Mr. Selling's part there was also much interest awaiting. He fancied this girl, because she was keen of brain and had made remarkable use of limited opportunities.

He had asked a few questions about her and perfectly understood her position in the Ordway household. So far from having the shallow mind that would have advised him to socially ignore a young woman in such a position, this gentleman allowed himself an amused smile over the sensation he would undoubtedly create in certain circles when he appeared at Bannard Hall in such company. But he had another and distinctly selfish reason for giving this girl the honor of his society. Mr. Selling was writing a book; he had already tried a few of its most telling passages upon her, without letting her suspect their authorship. Her keen delight in their style and her appreciative questions had been as elixir to the hungry author. Therefore, he was looking forward to those long walks to and from the hall, but it was not from the Bible that he meant to quote.

Weewona gave him no time to get started on his own line of conversation; for once, she took the initiative.

"I want to ask you," she said, "about your class in Bible literature. I should like so very much to belong to it, but I suppose it is open only for advanced students?"

"Oh, no," he said, kindly. "It is not held exclusively for advanced students. A special permit to join it can be secured on entering college, and you will be ready for that very soon, will you not?"

"Oh, no, indeed; I have another year in high school, and, besides, I have no hope of college."

"Is that so? I am sorry. You have talent that ought to be cultivated. I have noticed especially your appreciation of good literature, which reminds me of a passage, not exactly from the Bible, that I would like to discuss with you."

But she was not ready to hear it. "I wanted to ask," she went on, hurriedly, ignoring the passage to be quoted, "if you could put me in the way of what I need just now? Some book, perhaps, or several books that I could study, not from a literary point of view. I presume it is quite elementary knowledge of which I stand in need. I never had any Bible training, Mr. Selling. I am so ignorant of the book that I do not know how to set about studying it."

She had not meant to explain so fully, but his silence seemed to invite her to do so. His reply, however, was disappointing. It was simply to the effect that the Bible was rather a puzzling book to study as a whole; he was not surprised at its having a formidable look.

Still, once started, she was not easily turned from her object.

"I have been reading the first part of it," she persisted. "I am just now in Deuteronomy, but beyond being charmed by certain isolated verses, I have made nothing out of it, and I have been very eager for a chance to ask someone who knew, what it all means."

He laughed lightly. "The Bible? That is a very large

question; too large, I am afraid, for one evening. It means many things."

"Yes, of course; but what I mean is, what is it all for? Why do people study it so generally now? Is it different from every other book, Mr. Selling?"

"Different how?"

"Well, for one thing, in authority. Did God say it?"

Mr. Selling laughed again. "You are going too fast," he said, lightly. "You will have me beyond my depth in five minutes. I am not a preacher, you know."

"But you are a teacher of the Bible?"

"Heaven forbid! Only of its literature; that is very fine, and I enjoy the class exceedingly. But we do not meddle with its distinctive teachings, save as they affect literature."

"Then you cannot help me? I cannot tell you how disappointed I am. There are reasons why I am extremely anxious to find out about some things as soon as possible."

There was no mistaking the disappointment in her tone. Mr. Selling looked down upon her from his greater height with a compassionate smile.

"What is it that you want to know?" he asked. "Try me on something concrete. I might be able to help you, after all. Have you come across an insurmountable obstacle to your faith?"

"I have no faith," she said, gravely. "And there is nothing concrete to ask about, until I know how to ask. What puzzles me is, how to take it. Those first books, for instance. Is it history, or is it mere story?"

21

OH, TO KNOW!

THAT depends," he said, and he could not seem to speak other than lightly. "Some of it is history, without doubt; but it is history much mixed with fable, allegory, imagery, what you will."

"Then how is one to tell which is truth?"

"Oh, there are ways of picking out the essential truths; at least I presume so. To be strictly truthful, I have never given that phase of the subject very much attention."

Again Weewona felt the pressure of a bitter disappointment; she had been so sure that a teacher of the Bible would understand the Bible. She made a desperate plunge into the center of her subject.

"Mr. Selling, is there a life to be lived after people are through with this one?"

He was not even yet ready to be serious. "That is certainly concrete enough!" he said, "and vigorous for such a warm evening as this. Still, I'll make a venture. I am disposed to think on the whole that there is, although I am far from being as certain of it as the theologians would have me. As I told you, I am a student of the literature of the Bible only, and not of its dogmas."

Uneducated girl though she was, Weewona could not help a lurking contempt for what seemed to her the weakness of such a statement; a little of the feeling showed in her reply.

"I should think that one who had opportunity for study, and enough knowledge to understand it, would hardly be satisfied without knowing all that could be known on such a subject."

"Oh, I don't know. I'm inclined to think with the immortal Horace that those who discharge all their duties to the living haven't much time for peering into the life beyond."

Weewona returned to her old childish wail. "People are dying all the time, young people as well as old—" and she thought of the little Electa—"they need help; I should think if one could learn how to help them he would want to."

Mr. Selling seemed to have no answer ready. The truth was that he was at that moment thinking of the passage from his manuscript which he was especially anxious to talk over, and wondering by what means he could best get this girl away from the uninteresting topic that seemed to be absorbing her. She was not ready yet to give him his chance. After a moment's waiting, she made another effort.

"Mr. Selling, is what is called the New Testament on a surer foundation than the Old? All that about Jesus, for instance, is that history?"

"Well, probably; a good deal of it, at least; though there are errors in the New Testament also. Still, as you say, the central figure is the great thing."

"And everything said of him is true?"

"Oh, I didn't say that; but his teachings have, in the

main, been handed down correctly, and his character has borne the test of the severest criticism. By the way, that reminds me of a criticism that I want to quote for your consideration, something quite in point."

He was almost off to his manuscript, but the persistent girl intercepted him.

"One moment, please; won't you tell me what the errors are? It is really a very important question to me. Had he, and has he still, power over—death, for instance?"

Her voice shook a little; the issues hanging upon this answer were to her so vital; there was the story of the little maid fresh in her mind; and there was the little maid, Electa, fading before her eyes.

"Well, as to that," said Mr. Selling, reluctantly forced from his quotation, "people differ, you know. Personally, I admit that I consider all miracles as standing on very shaky ground. There is enough in the Bible that is grand and enduring without pinning our minds to childish tales about the spectacular and the marvelous. Such tales are for children and have their uses, no doubt; but you do not need to tarry over them, Miss Westervel; your mind is fitted for something better."

She was not elated; on the contrary, she was dismayed. Could this really be true! If it were, then poor Electa, with her growing absorption in the story of the dead child, and her growing faith in the Voice that had said, "Maid, arise!" was feeding on husks. Her soul revolted from such a decision.

"But surely," she said, "surely, Mr. Selling, there must be more to such accounts than this! The New Testament is full of them, and they are read from the pulpit continually. Would ministers read them to their people if they were mere creations of fancy, and even preach about them? Why, the churches are built on the New Testament, are they not? And if only pieces of it are trustworthy, why do they keep the false mixed in with the true? What are the churches for but to lead the people?"

"Softly, softly!" said Mr. Selling. "I am being submerged by an avalanche of questions. Let me see, where shall I begin? The church, you know, is only one element at work in the process of civilization; a powerful element, of course, but having its limitations. At present it is an important part of our social organization. Habit, and that curious mistress known as public opinion, are sustaining it just now along certain old lines that modern scholarship does not stand for, and that will pass away as we develop. Individual churches here and there are already taking the lead, gliding into social organizations, spiritual in tone, and with a moral object in view, and an undeniably great work to accomplish. Whatever may in the future become of the claim of Christianity to be a revelation, it can be claimed as a historic fact with a mission to accomplish. Now, I wonder if I may not give you my quotation? It is really something about which I wish to consult you. It has an imagery in it which is perfectly clear to me, because I know what I mean in using it, but whether or not it will strike a clear-brained listener who does not know beforehand what is being aimed at, is the question."

Afterward, Weewona realized that she listened halfheartedly, and gave little evidence of being clear-brained. Had she spoken the whole truth, she would have said that she did not care what his quotation meant, that compared with the great themes on which she had been seeking light it was of no consequence in the world; though, of course, she tried to rally her thoughts and give courteous heed. Her disappointment was greater than she had thought it could be. Unconsciously she had been building much hope on this opportunity; it had seemed to her the best that was likely to come to her, and to fail so utterly was bitter.

What was now to be done? Was there really no one who could give her light in time to help Electa?

It was of no use to think of the child's father and mother, tender and loving as they were, and both of them members of the church. For reasons that Weewona did not understand, Electa kept her questions on all themes pertaining to religion for her ear alone. The child was not communicative as to her reasons for this beyond the fact that Mamma always cried when asked any such questions, and Papa did not understand how little girls felt.

"They both talk to me about when I will be well and strong like other girls," she said one day, "and I know they don't believe a bit of it, but they think it comforts me."

For several weeks after her memorable attempt at learning from Mr. Selling, the inevitable effect of the interview was strong upon Weewona. She still read from the "picture Bible" to Electa whatever portions the child fancied, but she talked as little about them as Electa would allow, avoiding any direct statements, and she hid her own Bible away in a drawer. Of what use to read it, since she did not know and had no means of finding out what portions of it were authentic?

But this condition of things did not last. The necessary reaction on a mind constituted like hers came to help her.

There was a renewal of that feeling of almost

contempt for a man who was engaged in teaching from a book that, by his own admission, had very much to do with civilization, having in it a central figure whose character had "withstood the severest criticism," and on whose principles not only the church, but social life in general was founded, yet did not care enough about it to study closely into its teachings or to help others to do so! What weight should be attached to the opinions of such a man?

After a while, she unlocked her Bible from its hiding place and gave it again the place of honor on her study table. It is true that she had not much time for study; vacation work that had accumulated during term time was pressing, and Electa's increasing weakness called for added attention; but such moments as she could snatch for her very own were again spent on the book in a puzzled search for light.

On Mr. Selling's part, there had also been an awakening. He went home from the Wendell lecture feeling very much dissatisfied with the evening, at least the part which had to do with the companion he had chosen. His quotations had not produced upon her the effect that he had expected. In truth they had seemed to produce no effect whatever. The girl had asked no questions, and part of the time had hardly seemed to hear what he was saying. The possibly obscure passage about which he had expected an avalanche of eager questions had apparently been so obscure as to fail of notice altogether.

He had evidently been deceived in the girl, had mistaken a spurt of interest for real intelligence and appreciation. He had been an idiot, of course. Why should he have expected a girl like that, hampered by heredity and environment, to be appreciative of higher literature? Of course, all he had been trying to do was to give her an uplift, but she really was not worthy of it. So Mr. Selling dropped her. All that Weewona had thought of his notice was that the great man, much admired among the young lady students, was sorry for her in her comparative loneliness and wanted to be kind to her; she appreciated his effort, and smiled a little sadly when she saw that he had grown weary of the kindness, but consoled herself with the thought that he had not been the help to her that she had hoped, and then she dismissed him from her mind altogether.

Mrs. Ordway could not so easily conform herself to the situation.

"I don't know why they are so soon ready to set her aside," she said to her husband, half indignantly. "That is just the way Jack Leeson did; one doesn't expect stability from him, of course, but I should think she must be quite as intelligent a girl as most of those whom Mr. Selling notices. Why do you suppose he dropped her so soon?"

But Mr. Ordway went off into shouts of laughter over his wife's "delicious inconsistency." First she was vexed with the young men for showing her protégé any attentions, and then she was vexed with them for ceasing to show it. "My dear, you are hard to suit," he said, and laughed.

Meanwhile, over the little Electa was coming a subtle change. She was weaker and quieter and sweeter than she had been. The restless complainings that at times had almost worn out her nurses, as well as herself, almost entirely ceased. Was this because her weakness was increasing so rapidly? Or was there another cause?

She was still deeply interested in her Bible; certain stories had been read to her until she knew them by heart and could, as she told Weewona, "read them over to herself in the dark." Chief among her favorites was the little maid who was not dead, but sleeping.

Yet there were times when she turned from all the stories and demanded strong, quiet words.

"I don't want that tonight," she said one evening when Weewona was beginning to read the next narrative in course, as had been planned the night before. "I have found something new. I read a little of it today by myself, but it tired me, and I want it again. I marked the place. I'll show you. There; it begins 'Let not your heart—'"

And she lay back among the pillows while Weewona read the immortal words:

"Let not your heart be troubled; ye believe in God, believe also in me. In my Father's house are many mansions; if it were not so, I would have told you. I go to prepare a place for you. And if I go and prepare a place for you, I will come again, and receive you unto myself, that where I am, there ye may be also. And whither I go ye know, and the way ye know."

"Isn't that beautiful," said Electa, "and wonderful? Do you know when it was? It was just the night before they killed him; and he knew all about it, knew he was going to be killed, and told them so; and he said he was going to prepare a place for them and would come back and get them. O Weewee, mustn't they have been happy! What if I had been living then! Or what if he were living here now and had said that to me! Do you possibly suppose that he could have meant that place for anybody beside those people he loved when he was here?"

"I don't know," said Weewona. The words were almost a wail. Oh, to *know!*

It was on the following evening that Electa greeted her with shining eyes.

"I've found something," she said. "Something wonderful and grand. It was on that same night, and Jesus was praying for them the beau-ti-ful-est prayer! And right into the midst of it comes this verse; read it."

Weewona read: "Neither pray I for these alone, but for them also which shall believe on me through their word."

"Think!" said the child. "At first I didn't see what it meant; I said it over and over, and thought a long time; then it came to me that it must mean that he was praying for the people who would believe on him because those disciples of his told them about him. Mustn't it mean that, Weewee, don't you think? And if it does, can't you and I belong to them, and have the prayer for us?"

That evening Weewona summoned all her courage and asked Mrs. Ordway if she did not think Electa would like to have their minister come and see her.

The response was startled eyes, and a series of frightened questions:

"Why? What has happened? Have there been any bad symptoms? You cannot think she is worse! The doctor told me only yesterday that he thought her better. My dear girl, I *hope* you have not been talking to her about dying, or putting any such ideas into her mind? You know the directions were to keep her as happy as possible."

"I have tried to obey directions," Weewona said simply. "It is because she is interested in subjects that I do not understand, and asking questions that I cannot answer, that I thought of the minister. Does he call only on people who are about to die?"

"Of course not!" said the shocked Mrs. Ordway.

"What an idea! But I think I know what you mean. The dear little girl is inclined to be morbid sometimes, and to brood over subjects too old for her; but she is really distinctly better, the doctor says, and I am sure you must have noticed it yourself; the nervous restlessness which has disturbed her so much is very greatly relieved, and he considers that a good symptom. Don't imagine that I am finding fault with you, Wona; we all know how much you have done and are doing for our darling; only don't let your love for her make you morbid, that is all."

And Weewona went away sorrowful to wonder what she could do to help Electa, and who would open the eyes of her mother to the truth.

22

AT LAST HE WAS READY

WHEN Kendall Fletcher finally counted out in gold fifty dollars that he felt did not belong to him, and carefully computed the interest to be added thereto, it was more than a year and a half away from the Sabbath afternoon in which he had sat on Mrs. Carver's side porch and talked with Weewona.

At last he was ready to discharge his debt to her. Innumerable and disheartening had been the delays and disappointments through which he had arrived at this goal. A dozen times he had seen success just ahead of him only to have his hopes dashed at the last moment by the unexpected. His mother's financial affairs did not improve with time, and more than once when he was all but ready to discharge the debt that so pressed upon his conscience, decency compelled him to come to her rescue from a dilemma perilously near disgrace.

Nor was this his only trouble. A serious illness in the midst of term time taxed his resources to their utmost, compelling him to draw upon the sacred hoard. Then, a few months later, to save a friend from temporary embarrassment, he loaned what had accumulated once more, in the expectation of having it returned in three weeks at the latest. In less than that time, his friend was dead and buried; his poor affairs had passed into the hands of indifferent and not overscrupulous strangers, with not the dash of a pen to prove the dead man's obligation to his friend. There were times when young Fletcher, moodily reviewing his experiences, felt convinced that a perverse fate was at his elbow bent on frustrating his return to honor and self-respect. In his secret thoughts he had long ceased to call his transaction with Weewona a matter of business. The utmost that he permitted himself to say for himself was that he had not meant to steal her money, but his soliloquy always closed with the statement that, nevertheless, he should feel like a thief until every penny was paid.

Meantime, he worked hard; habits of study formed while he was trying to hide from himself were continued because he was interested; and his mother, who had always been vain of his handsome person and grace of manner, grew uncomfortably vain of his reputation as a student.

He graduated the honor man of his class, and, without waiting for the vacation that his mother was sure he needed, entered the famous law firm where his father had been a partner and gave himself to what he called getting ready for the law school in the fall.

"I always knew that you would be a scholar," his mother said, plaintively, "because you are your father's son, but I never believed that you would be so devoted to study as to forget your mother; your father never did that."

He reassured her, and made certain promises with regard to society, which he laboriously fulfilled. Whatever interest another sort of society might have for him in the future, it was certain that he did not enjoy the social functions which his mother called by that name. Yet he was loyal to her. It did not even occur to him that there was another kind of social life. The nearest that he approached to criticism was to wonder within himself why women were so different from men in their choice of entertainment.

And now, at last, the hour had arrived when, by making a hurried visit to his uncle and discharging the obligation that had galled, he believed he should be able once more to respect himself.

During all this time he had held no communication with his uncle's family. His mother, who was at all times an indifferent letter writer, had long ago ceased to correspond with her brother; she wrote to him only when in dire need of his financial help, or, rather, when the emergency was such that she had hope of persuading him of the need. In her own opinion it always existed; but, as she plaintively explained to Kendall:

"My poor brother's impossible wife has him under such complete subjection that she has stifled all his generous impulses and made a different being of him."

For these, and other reasons, Kendall had remained in ignorance of any changes in his uncle's family.

It was on the evening following his careful computation of compound interest that he sprang from the platform of the way train at his uncle's station and, without waiting for the slow-moving omnibus, swung off with rapid stride toward the house on the hill. In his pocket, securely packed in a rosewood box, almost as dainty as the three-cornered one in which those gold pieces had reposed, lay the result of his computation.

He vaulted a fence and crossed an unused field to cut off part of the walk. Freedom was so near that he could afford to be complacent, and as he made long strides over the stubbly ground, he conferred with himself after this fashion:

"Well, chappie, the thing is about over. Tonight when you go to bed you can look in the glass and behold a decent fellow once more. And, old fellow, if you haven't learned a lesson in common honesty that will last for a lifetime, then nothing will ever teach you. No more borrowed money for you, my lad, nor business transactions that won't bear daylight. Kendall Morse Fletcher, you and I have got to call things by their right names after this, and don't you forget it."

And then he was at his uncle's door, receiving his hearty handshake and his astonished "Well, I never! This can't be you!" touching his lips as lightly as possible to his aunt Sarah's offered cheek, and giving heed as much as might be to his cousin Clara's volley of questions; his eyes the while roving eagerly about the large old-fashioned dining room in search of another face.

They rested doubtfully enough at last on Weewona's successor, a girl whose yellow-brown hair was done in a caricature of the modern style, and whose not overclean dress was adorned with cheap lace and gilt jewelry. The girl would have changed, of course, but never into this!

Having settled it by the time they were being served at supper, he waited until the maid disappeared, then boldly asked his question:

"What has become of the help who reigned when I was here before?"

His cousin Clara laughed. "How are we expected to know?" she asked. "That was ages ago, and we have had legions of them since. You have been most devoted to your relatives, haven't you! We might all have died and been buried for all that you knew about us."

"Or married," said Kendall, good-humoredly. "I've been expecting an invitation down here to a wedding: Waiting for it, I may say; you see I knew you would never be married or buried without having me in at the ceremony."

"You two have begun just where you left off," his aunt said, with a kind of grim humor. "Clara is right enough, though, about your staying away. I should think your mother would want you to visit your uncle occasionally, although she doesn't care anything about the rest of us."

"My mother would have been more willing; but I have been very busy indeed, on a regular grind, in fact; Mother complains that I have not had time even for her. I have run away now from work that was crowding, just to have a look at you all before term time. Now, enlighten my curiosity about that queer little girl with an Indian name and original ideas."

"Mother," said Clara, "do relieve his suspense. Don't you remember that Kendall was awfully interested in that girl?"

"You needn't ask me," said his aunt, ignoring her daughter. "I don't know a thing about the girl; haven't the least knowledge as to what has become of her, though of course I can surmise. She found that she couldn't manage me, and left without an hour's notice; and I haven't laid eyes on her since."

Then Mr. Carver interposed in his mild, quiet voice.

"Well, you know, Mother, she spoke to you about

it a whole month beforehand; I guess she thought she was doing right."

"Father always stands up for Wona," laughed his daughter. "He would, all the same, if she had taken the best spoons and forks away with her."

"She has really left you, then? I fancied, someway, that she was a fixture. Wasn't she as satisfactory as any of them, Aunt Sarah? I remember telling my mother that you thought so."

"Oh, she did well enough at first; after she got over some of her wild ways. I thought that she might work into decent help, in time; but something upset her. She grew restless and dissatisfied; wanted ridiculous things, and when she found she couldn't have them, she left."

"I'm surprised that Ken doesn't know where she is," said Clara. "You seemed so deeply interested in her when you went away that I thought you would certainly correspond."

The young man felt his face redden over this thrust, and was vexed that it should. He told himself that his cousin grew disagreeable as she grew older. He knew, and was tried with the knowledge, that this sort of talk had power over him because he had something to conceal.

On this occasion his aunt saved him the necessity for reply.

"I have always been afraid, Kendall, that it was you who turned the head of that foolish girl.

"I don't mean, of course, in any silly sense," she made haste to add, noting the look on her nephew's face, "but you were the one who gave her the fancy that she could study, and make something extra of herself; that is really what upset her; she spent every spare minute poring over books."

"Yes, and a good many that weren't 'spare,' if the

truth were known. Mother was awfully indulgent to her; let her burn an electric light in her room every night until ten o'clock, and have nearly all of Saturday afternoon. She was spoiled, if ever a girl was."

"I certainly tried to treat her well," said Mrs. Carver, with the air of a martyr, "and got my usual thanks for doing so; but we don't do good in this world for the sake of the thanks we will get; that is one comfort."

Mr. Carver was not one who could let this inference go unchallenged.

"I don't think she meant to be ungrateful, Mother; she thanked me as nice as a girl ever did for being kind to her, though, land knows, I didn't do anything for her; I hadn't a chance."

"It's no use, Mother; you might as well give up and consider that girl perfection. Father and Kendall will persist in investing her with all the virtues, in spite of facts."

Clara's ever-ready laugh tried to soften the disagreeableness of her words.

"What interests me is what has become of her," said Kendall, sturdily.

"And me, too," said his uncle, both of them ignoring Clara's question, put in curious tone:

"What on earth do you care?"

"I'd give a good deal," added Mr. Carver, "to know that she found a nice home, and was doing well."

"As to that," said his wife, "I think we can know only too well. Girls like her, who chafe under wholesome restraint and practically run away from it, never come to any good. It is my opinion that she ran away from the place where she was living when she came to us. I never took any stock in that mountain yarn of hers. And it stands to reason that we should have heard something of her if she had not been ashamed to let herself be known. Clara and I both took the trouble to inquire about her at Center every time we went there, and never heard a word."

"I should say we did!" exclaimed Clara. "I tramped the length and breadth of the town and talked with everybody I knew, and lots of people that I didn't know, just out of curiosity to see what had become of her. She pretended to want to go to school at Center; said she had heard of the schools. I presume she got that knowledge from you, Ken, but she never went near any of the schools. I knew she wouldn't; she just wanted to tramp about like a gypsy. I shouldn't wonder if she were part gypsy."

Kendall Fletcher was very much disturbed. He sat long in his room that evening staring into darkness and thinking over the whole perplexing situation. He was sure of only one thing: that he must find that girl. No thought of not being able to do so had before this evening entered his mind. He told himself that he was a fool for supposing that anyone who could get away would stay long in the same house with his cousin Clara; but evidently he had calculated on finding her there. She must be hunted for, but how? His eagerness to get rid of the money he had for her increased with the difficulties in the way. He knew why he had not been willing to wait even twenty-four hours after the last penny of it was secured, and felt increasingly sure that it would be impossible to look upon himself as better than a thief so long as he had it in his possession. What was the next step for him? Should he go to Center and institute a search for a girl named Weewona? He told himself, with an annoyed smile, that he was too young a man for such a search, and that it would be difficult to hunt for a girl who had not even a name! Clearly, what his aunt and cousin, with such high motives as they had brought to the search, could not accomplish, he need not hope to do.

Should he confide in his uncle and secure his help? He could feel the blood surge into his face at the thought.

His cousin Clara, he believed, would look upon the money episode as a huge joke, and his aunt Sarah, with her sharp tongue and keen outlook for personal interests, would feel only amazement that a girl "without a decent rag to her back" should have had money to lend; that she had, would only be another proof of her general badness. But his uncle, quiet, patient, honest to a halfpenny, and clear-eyed to the honesty of others, would be kind, would help him to the utmost, but he would call the transaction by the name that it deserved. He shrank intolerably from the quiet man's disapproval. He could not tell the story to him, not yet—not until other efforts had failed.

23

◆━◆≡◆━◆

"IT IS EXPERIMENTAL KNOWLEDGE
THAT A FELLOW NEEDS"

IT ended in his making what excuses he could for the brevity of his visit, and returning to town the next afternoon.

But on the Saturday following, he came down to Center and spent the day in that ambitious little town, making his investigations and inquiries with such skill that by evening he felt convinced that no girl answering to Weewona's description had spent any time there, and that no undue curiosity had been aroused by his efforts.

When he reached home he wrote to his uncle; a brief, carefully worded letter. It was quite important that he get on the track of that little girl named Weewona. He had something in charge that belonged to her, and that he had promised to take care of. He had done so until now, but there were reasons why he was anxious to return it to its owner. Would his uncle help him in trying to find her?

Over this letter the Carver family argued and wondered for many days. It is not certain that Mr. Carver would have held counsel with his wife and daughter, had not the former availed herself of a wife's privilege and opened the letter in his absence.

Clara, especially, was agape with wonder, and fertile in surmises.

"What on earth *can* it be? Oh, I wonder—do you think it could have been a ring? How would that set to which she belonged get a *ring* of any account? Still, it might have been her mother's. I suppose people of that kind have wedding rings, sometimes. Or it might—Ken better look out; perhaps he will get mixed in with a theft of some kind. The idea of her giving it to him to take care of! The minx! I should think we would have been much better guardians for it."

What Mr. Carver thought is not discovered. It is only known that he made a quiet, but very thorough search, not only through Center, but surrounding towns, and failed to find the slightest trace of the missing girl.

Then was Kendall Fletcher almost in despair. He lay awake the greater part of an entire night devising plans for continuing the search. He composed and rejected dozens of ads designed for her eye, smiling sarcastically at himself the while over the idea of that girl reading the daily papers! He could imagine her only as she was when she sat on the side porch that Sunday afternoon; very grave and a trifle—should he call it stupid?

One bit of information his uncle had given him privately that he felt ought to help in the search for the lost girl. She had taken to herself a name.

"I don't take much stock in its being spelled out of a handkerchief," his uncle wrote. "She tried it on me, and I couldn't make head nor tail of the writing; something had been written there, but whether it began with a *W* or an *M* or an *L,* and whether the

next letter was an *e* or an *a* or a *u,* I couldn't tell, and
I don't believe anybody else could; writing on cloth
isn't very plain at the best, and this was more than half
washed out, so that one thing could be made of it as
easy as another; but I didn't tell her so. The poor girl
was so glad over it and it seemed so kind of hard not
to have even a name, that I didn't let on but that I saw
it as plain as she did, and that's the name she will go
by, all right; *Westervel,* Weewona Westervel."

This was certainly a clue. But Kendall Fletcher, after
considering the matter for one entire night, abandoned any attempt at advertising, and, determining to
search steadily and systematically as opportunity afforded, opened a special bank account in favor of one
Weewona Westervel; the money to be held at compound interest until it could be paid to the person
herself, or her accredited heirs.

As the young man turned away from the bank he
assured himself for the dozenth time that he would
give his life to a hunt for that girl and restore to her
her own.

Certainly the experience, humiliating as it had
been, had helped to steady his life. He worked even
harder in the law school than he had during his last
year in college; and found, greatly to his surprise, that
the study of law interested, even fascinated, him.

"In spite of my being 'all Carver,'" he told himself,
"I must have inherited a small section of the legal
mind I have always been told that my father possessed."

But he was careful not to let the law absorb all his
attention. As systematically as he had promised, he
gave himself to the search for Weewona. Wherever he
had correspondents, on such terms as to make inquiries of the kind possible, he fell into the habit of

adding a carefully worded paragraph to the effect that business reasons made it desirable to locate the address of a girl calling herself Weewona Westervel, who probably worked as an ordinary servant, though she might be for part of the day a schoolgirl. Would his correspondent, should he chance to hear of such a person or have any knowledge that would throw light on her present whereabouts, kindly communicate with him?

In time, he grew interested in this part of his correspondence; he became skillful in weaving inquiries in a businesslike way; quite, he believed, as a fully developed lawyer might have done. He grew stronger also in the conviction that he would find that girl if he had to travel to the ends of the earth to do it. It was preposterous to suppose that in so short a time a girl, even if she had wanted to hide, could drop out of the knowledge of everybody! Of course, she could be found, unless, indeed, she had dropped out of life. The thought startled him. What if she were dead, and had died without any knowledge of that sunset gate which had so deeply interested her? This made him think again of his friend Templeton, who had gone his long journey without the knowledge for which he had questioned. Gone without it because his friend, Kendall Fletcher, could not give it to him!

Neither yet was he able. Given a like opportunity he would be in exactly the same dilemma. This did not seem exactly like the workings of a legal mind! The law student knew that an acknowledged inability to answer any legal question that he might reasonably be supposed to know would have sent him at once to his textbooks; and he would not have slept nights until he had learned all that he was capable of learning about that particular matter. Why did he not set about acquiring the necessary knowledge of that other subject?

But he tried to excuse himself. "It is different," he said. "A fellow doesn't know how to set about this." Yet he had spasms of trying to set about it. He went to church with a regularity that was a constant source of gratification to his mother; and he read, at intervals, in his Bible. But he knew in his inmost soul that something more than these things was needed.

"It is experimental knowledge that a fellow needs," he confessed, and his ideas about how to secure that were vague indeed.

It was on a midsummer Sunday afternoon that he found himself in an insignificant little town on a branch of the main line of railroad. He had been sent out by the law firm of which he expected one day to be a member, and which sent him here and there during vacation to look up evidence or follow possible trails of information.

This was a phase of business that keenly interested the young man, who never forgot that he had important business of his own in this line, and was always trying to find a trail to follow connected with it. But it seemed to him very like a waste of time to be stranded in this unimportant town for over Sunday. A broken rail and a many-hours-delayed train had accomplished this result, and he was impatient of the delay and tired of his own company. He had taken a long walk from the station in search of what was reported as the best hotel, and had found it, viewed from his standpoint, very second-rate, indeed. He had turned with an impatient shudder from the general waiting room, with its highly colored, old-fashioned ingrain carpet, its haircloth sofa and impossible chairs; but in sheer desperation as the day waned and his own small room grew warm and stuffy, he went down to it. On the way down he reflected with satisfaction that at dinnertime he had seemed to be the sole guest who would be likely to seek that room; at least, he would not be bored by others. But he was mistaken. A stranger, a man of perhaps middle age, was pacing up and down the long room humming softly the bars of a familiar tune. It required but a single glance at the well-shaped head and shoulders, the clear-cut features and the general makeup to tell an observer that he was a gentleman, and a man of affairs. The humming ceased as Kendall entered the room, and the stranger bowed courteously. A few minutes of desultory conversation followed, then Kendall inquired if the man was also a victim to the broken rail of the branch road.

"Yes and no," he said, smiling. "I was on the train that got no farther, but I intended to stop off here for Sunday. I am in search of an old friend whom I had reason to hope that I would find in this part of the world."

This struck Kendall as an interesting coincidence. Here was another searcher. He felt a curious desire to know for whom the man was searching, and whether he had been successful. A whimsical inclination to ask if he had seen anything of Weewona floated through the young man's mind, which, of course, he resisted, and murmured something about its being a misfortune he should think to be found in such a place as this. Wasn't it the most forlorn, dingy, altogether disreputable town he had ever seen? And as for the hotel!

"They told me at the station that I would find better accommodations uptown," he said. "But if I have, I certainly hope there were no victims corralled in that downtown house; still, it can't be worse than this."

"It is," said the stranger, significantly, "and there are many victims. I was one until an hour or two ago, when I came out to see what other accommodations I could find. They are evidently not used to entertaining strangers, but it is a pretty little town up on the hills; there are some very pleasant homes, with lawns and flourishing gardens."

Kendall replied that he was glad to hear it, although it was difficult to think of anything but dirt and disorder flourishing there.

"Oh, they have a very neat little church," the other said, "and a good man in the pulpit. Am I mistaken in thinking I saw you in the audience this morning?"

Yes, he was there, Kendall said; he went for the want of anything better to do. He wondered how it would sound to explain that he went to find a girl of whom he had been in active search for months, and visited the Bible class also for the same reason. Instead, he asked a question.

"Did the pulpit incumbent strike you as a good man for that place?"

"Yes, on the whole. He is a very good man, I believe. I am told that he has the confidence of his people, and is accomplishing an important work here."

Oh, Kendall said he was glad to hear it, of course; but he was thinking of the pulpit. The man's work was evidently not to preach.

"Well, as to that, I think he helped the people this morning."

"Were you helped, sir?" Kendall's smile was significant. The whole appearance of this man, as well as his manner of speech and choice of language, indicated a person of culture and wide experience. He thought his question would be embarrassing.

"I was, indeed," the stranger said, earnestly. "As he talked of my Master and my future home, I felt my faith strengthened and my desires quickened. The truth is, I rarely hear a sermon even from an illiterate preacher, which this man was not, that I do not get something helpful for the day's living."

The slightly superior smile faded from Kendall's face, an almost wistful look taking its place. Here was a man who apparently *knew!* If he also knew how to impart his knowledge to others, and they should get to talking in that line—but this young man, born in a Christian home, among churches and Bible schools and professing Christians, felt that he did not know how to ask questions about the facts or theories that he wanted to understand. He did not even know how to lead up naturally and without embarrassment to the subject upon which he desired information.

He therefore left the little church and the poor preacher abruptly and asked about the special industries of that valley. In the course of conversation it developed that the stranger's name was Kendall.

Kendall Fletcher repeated the name with interest and asked, smiling:

"Could we claim kinship, do you suppose? My given name is Kendall; I was named for my father, and he for his maternal grandfather; away back somewhere our forefathers may have been brothers."

Whereupon this stranger opened the way to the very heart of the subject that he thought he wanted to understand.

"Perhaps we are brothers by a nearer route. If we can claim kinship through the Elder Brother, isn't it the closest tie of all?"

But this young man, living all his life on the trail of Christianity, was not sufficiently at home in the language of the Christian family to feel the significance of the phrase. It came to him that he might be intruding on an older man's desire for quiet, and turning aside he picked up a newspaper from the table and made a pretense of interesting himself in its columns. He gave a sarcastic smile to the date of the daily paper, for it was three days old, but he told himself that it matched its surroundings. Then his eye fell on a comment about a matter of public interest that had escaped his notice, and he really began to read.

Mr. Kendall strolled toward the old-fashioned battered and bruised piano that occupied a place of honor in an alcove and seated himself on the shaky piano stool.

Thin of tone and much out of tune as the instrument undoubtedly was, there nevertheless issued from it presently some very sweet strains.

The reader, instead of giving heed to the editorial that he had resolved to read through, found himself listening. It was unusual, he thought, to see a man of gray hairs at home with a piano, unless, indeed, he was a professional player. This man was evidently at home. Kendall noticed his skillful avoidance of the most jarring keys, and wondered at the harmony that he succeeded in producing. Snatches of well-known tunes, bits from a favorite oratorio, scraps of hymns that had been familiar to the boy's childhood each took its turn, and flowed out with remarkable sweetness. Sometimes the player accompanied the instrument for a bar or two with a fine bass voice. When the music ran too high for him, he broke into a soft, clear whistle.

He is a musician, all right, decided the listener. *I wonder if that can be his business?* He lowered his paper and gave careful attention to the fine, erect form, the clear-cut profile, the strongly defined forehead and the keen, grave eyes. Music, as a profession, did not seem to fit the face. He looked more like a lawyer, and it came to the young law student that he would like to study law with such a man. Then he smiled to think how much he, an embryo lawyer, was taking for granted. Why should he jump to the conclusion that this stranger with whom he had exchanged a dozen sentences was a man to be trusted? Even to be leaned on?

Suddenly all his senses were on the alert. He abandoned his editorial entirely, and rising quickly walked toward the distant corner where the piano stood. What was that the man was singing?

24

EVENING BELLS

CLEAR and sweet the melody flowed out; the words as distinct as reading.

> *"I am traveling toward life's sunset gate,*
> *I'm a pilgrim going home;*
> *For the glow of eventide I wait,*
> *I'm a pilgrim going home.*
> *Evening bells I seem to hear—*
> *As the sunset gate draws near."*

Then followed an indescribable effect; a low humming sound from the closed lips of the singer, and a piano accompaniment that was strangely like the tender chiming of distant bells.

"It is a peculiar effect, isn't it?" the musician said, glancing up with a smile at his absorbed audience. "Do you sing?"

"No; that is, yes, sometimes. What is that you are singing?"

"A peculiar little melody that I heard at a mountain summer camp, where we had a Bible school and music school and several other pleasant things. The effect of this particular song echoing among the hills and fading away in the distance was peculiarly impressive."

"I should think so. Is there more of it?"

"Oh, yes, several verses. I don't recall the intervening ones, but this is the closing," and he sang again:

> *"I shall rise again at morning dawn,*
> *I shall put on glory then.*
> *With the shadowy veil of death withdrawn,*
> *I shall put on glory then.*
> *Evening bells I seem to hear,*
> *As the sunset gate draws near."*

It was all there! The glory and the bells, and the sunset gate that Weewona had so eagerly described. Kendall Fletcher was strangely moved. He was back on his uncle's porch beside the desolate girl, noting the gleam of powerful interest in her eyes, and the flash of hope that faded so quickly.

"Where is this mountain camp?" he asked. "And when did you hear this song? I wonder if my poor little girl could possibly have heard it at the same time?"

"What little girl is that?" Mr. Kendall's voice was vibrant with the kind of interest and sympathy that invites confidence; before Kendall Fletcher realized it he was telling what little he knew of Weewona's pitiful story.

"Poor girl!" the other said, infinite pity in his voice. "Poor little girl! So young, and yet so eager for the sunset gate! It might have been the very singer to whom I listened that reached her heart. We were up among the northern hills near the loveliest pine plateau that the country affords. I do not wonder that she was moved. I hope you pointed out the way so plainly that she was able to enter at once upon the journey?"

Fletcher's face flushed almost painfully. "I did not," he said, quickly. "I could do nothing for her; I should have been the blindest of blind guides. Besides, she did not understand that the language was figurative; she was the strangest of literalists. She was bent on finding a real 'sunset gate,' and 'glory' was a veritable garment that one put on, like a robe."

Mr. Kendall gave a thoughtful sigh. "Poor lamb!" he said; "lost, right on the line of the trail; Christian people, I suppose, all about her? What has become of her?"

"I would give all I am worth to know!" Fletcher spoke with an energy that was almost fierce. The desire to see that lonesome girl again, to help her, to lead her to this man who knew the sunset gate, and knew the way, took hold of him with a kind of strength that he felt would be satisfied with nothing less.

Mr. Kendall regarded him with an interest so genuine that the young man felt himself yielding utterly to the spell of his influence, and wishing keenly that he might have such help as this in the prosecution of his search. While he was hesitating whether or not to tell the story of the borrowed coins, Mr. Kendall spoke again:

"I fancy I can understand why you are anxious to find this particular lost one. Is it not because you failed to help her before, and now would be able to do so?"

The flush on Kendall's face deepened perceptibly; he spoke with quick energy. "No, I couldn't help her in that; not one whit better than before; I do not know anything about these matters; but there are reasons why I need to find her; business reasons," he added quickly, meeting the gaze of the keen gray eyes. They were very grave eyes, indeed; and now he knew that, for his own self-respect, he must tell the entire story. He could not have that man—of all men—think what he might think by this time. Nor did it seem so strange as might have been supposed, this making a confidant of a man whom he had known but an hour, telling him what he had believed he could not tell his most intimate friend; he felt impelled to the confidence by some force that seemed to be outside of himself.

Mr. Kendall was a flattering listener. From time to time he asked clear-cut questions, such as showed his careful grasp of the situation; for Fletcher began at the very beginning, explaining in almost painful detail the new and embarrassing position in which he found himself the summer that he visited his uncle, and the necessity that seemed to be upon him of securing fifty dollars from somewhere immediately.

"But no such idea as borrowing from this girl possessed me, sir, when I went out that Sunday afternoon and talked with her on the side porch; my motive was to make the long, warm day seem a little less lonesome to her; and—well, yes, I had another motive, perhaps, to pass a little time that was hanging stupidly on my hands, and get away from my own thoughts. She seemed original, or, at least, a trifle queer; unlike others, and I thought I might find her amusing."

"Was she a foreigner?" interpolated Mr. Kendall.

"No, that is—at least I do not think so; my aunt believed that she had a mixture of Indian blood, but that, I fancy, was more on account of her Indian name than for any other reason. I found her interesting in a different way from what I had expected; intensely, even pathetically interesting, as I have already explained. She was so tremendously in earnest about that sunset gate, and the putting on of glory, that it seemed almost uncanny, although I must admit that her eagerness seemed to have more to do with the interests of the one she called Pete, dead though he was, than with herself; but that, too, was pathetic, you see. I tried to turn her thoughts away from it into a more wholesome channel, but I had no more intention of trying to borrow money of her than I had of the turkey strutting about my uncle's barnyard."

"But you borrowed it?" This was another keen, incisive question.

"I borrowed it." Again the blood surged hotly over Fletcher's face. "It will seem incredible to you, I know; it would to any decent man. I don't excuse myself in the least; it was simply an ingenious method of stealing, that is all; taking advantage of a girl's indifference to money because ignorant of its uses. And yet, I declare to you that at the time I meant no wrong to the girl, and thought no wrong. Instead, I thought that in the end it would be helping her. That is the way I argued it out with myself; and as a matter of fact, the sum, with interest, of course, was long ago placed in the bank to her credit; but still I know—"

He paused abruptly, choked with a sense of shame. The idea of a son of Morse K. Fletcher having to explain and excuse his actions! Why should he have told this humiliating story to a perfect stranger? One who did not know and could not know his inheritance of honor, and the fact that this was his first and only lapse from the spotless integrity for which the name of Fletcher had always stood?

He had seated himself early in their talk in the large, old-fashioned armchair that stood nearby, while Mr. Kendall had kept his station at the piano. At this moment the man arose from his seat and, bending his tall form a little, laid a kind, strong hand on the young man's shoulder.

"I understand," he said. "I think I understand it as fully as though I had been reading your thought. You believed that you could repay the loan at any hour, if it were needed, and that in the meantime you could put the money in the way of adding to itself a little, for the girl's benefit. No thought of changes, or possible difficulties in reaching her as soon as you were ready to report, entered your mind; young people do not think of those things."

It is not likely that Mr. Kendall will ever forget the look that a pair of young eyes gave him at that moment, eloquent as they were, with relief, gratitude and resolve. It is certain that Kendall Fletcher will never forget the moment when he felt the strong, kind hand and heard the firm, kind voice putting his mistake into words that gave him a hint of returning self-respect. It was like a touch of healing balm upon a throbbing wound. How well this man understood! This stranger. He had *not* meant to steal! Not for a moment! It was a blessed thing to have it understood, to be spoken to as though the man had known generations of Fletchers.

"Thank you," he said, his voice breaking in spite of his tremendous effort at self-control. "I did not think anyone could be made to understand, but I see you do." In his inmost soul at that moment sprang up the determination never to be guilty by so much as a thought of anything that could shadow this good man's trust in him; and to be to young men, so far as he could, what this man was being to him this day. After a moment he spoke again: "Still, I know now, and, in fact, I knew less than twenty-four hours afterward, that I had done wrong. I had traded on innocence and ignorance, and I have suffered for it, as I ought. I am suffering now, because—how am I ever to get that money back to its rightful owner?"

"We must find her," Mr. Kendall said, with a kind of calm assurance that someway increased one's courage.

Then, with an evident intention of covering the young man's emotion and letting him down to the commonplace, he said:

"One cannot help wondering how a girl in such circumstances as you have described had money to lend. Did you learn at all how she became possessed of it, and why it had not been invested for her? By the way, what did you say her name was?" He drew a small notebook from his pocket. "I must get the name accurately, so that I may help you in your search. I travel about a great deal."

"The name is Westervel," said Fletcher. "Weewona Westervel; at least, that is the name she adopted. Did you speak, sir?" For the older man had made a sound that might be the beginning of a sentence, but that sounded like an exclamation.

"No," he said; "I beg your pardon. It was another coincidence in names that struck me. 'Westervel,' do you say? It is very like a name I used to know well; only that had a final *t*, Westervel*t*. What were you about to say?"

And Fletcher told him the story of the handkerchief name, as reported by his uncle. The stranger seemed almost pathetically interested in it; once he covered his eyes from view.

"Poor, desolate child!" he murmured. "It wrings one's heart to think of one so young and utterly alone that she is not sure even of a name."

"As to her having money," said Fletcher, "it is a singular story. She seemed never to have come in contact with those who knew or cared more about money than she did herself. This Pete who absorbed her life, and who must himself have been a singular character, would not even have the little bank opened in which it was kept. He said it must be held until the child wanted to open it herself; so it was put away, and through the years forgotten."

"Did the child know how she had come by it? Did they question her?"

"Not very much, I fancy. You see, it was a strange, sad time. The mother died, as I told you, almost immediately, without a word; and the child mourned for her, of course. I suppose the man Pete's idea was to say as little to her as possible, and so help her forget everything the sooner. He seems to have been very kind to her; must have been, or he could not have dominated her life as he evidently did. Her feeling for him was nearer like worship than anything else."

"And the money was in a bank, you said?"

"Yes, a very curious one. Pete evidently did not discover its secret spring, and thought it would have to be smashed, the girl said, in order to get its contents. He believed them to be pennies, and insisted, Weewona said, that his mother let them alone until such time as the child should elect to smash the bank herself."

Had Kendall Fletcher been an ordinary storyteller he might certainly have been flattered by the keen interest which his listener manifested in his story. Each minute detail seemed to hold him; his questions were as keen and incisive as though he were examining a witness in an important trial. He seemed to feel the singularity of this himself, after a little.

"Pardon my curiosity," he said. "I have so long been accustomed to study into every detail of a story that it has become a habit."

This was Fletcher's opportunity to ask if he were a lawyer.

"Oh, no," he said, "I am only a businessman, a banker; but I have an object in life entirely apart from business. I, too, am on a search; a far more vital one than yours, and I have learned to look keenly into the most trivial incidents. Will you tell me about this bank; a child's toy bank, was it?"

"No, it was not a bank at all; not the usual kind, at least. It was a beautiful little box, velvet covered, gold bound and all that sort of thing; a triangular jewel box gotten up apparently by—I beg your pardon, what did you say? My dear sir, you are ill! Are you faint? What can I do for you?" He sprang up eagerly, looking about him for water, for air, above all for a bell; there was nothing. The stranger, who had grown ghastly pale, waved his hand in protest and tried to smile.

"It is nothing, my friend; don't be alarmed; a passing faintness. No, don't summon anyone, please; I am better already; I shall be quite myself in a moment." He wiped the moisture in great drops from his face.

"This room is like an oven!" muttered Fletcher, standing irresolute and anxious. But Mr. Kendall had recovered himself.

"Be seated, please," he said. "I am quite over the attack, and I want very much to talk to you."

At that moment they were interrupted. An influx of grumbling travelers, evidently from the other hotel, swarmed into the room. Old women and young, children and middle-aged men, all talking, all setting down bags and grips and shawl straps and lunch baskets on chair or floor.

"Nothing can be worse than what we have escaped from!" one woman was asserting. "I would rather sit up all night in this room, or slip off of that horror of a haircloth sofa over there, than try to endure what I did last night."

Mr. Kendall bent over young Fletcher, who had seated himself again, and spoke low:

"Will you come up to my room? I have a story to tell you."

25

"I Lost Them Both"

KENDALL Fletcher followed his new friend in wondering silence; his sudden illness and equally sudden recovery seemed strange; and what story could he have to tell to him?

"Between amazement and hope and fear I am almost bewildered," Mr. Kendall said as soon as they were alone.

"I hardly know how to begin an explanation; but in order for you to understand, I must tell you my story. Will you listen to a long one from a stranger?

"What seems like a lifetime ago to me, but is in reality only a few years, I had an ideal home, a wife who was as good as she was beautiful, and her beauty was marked by all who saw her, and a little daughter so like her mother in eyes and features, in every way, indeed, that she would have been recognized anywhere as her child. I loved those two with a greater love than a man ought to give to human beings. I idolized them; I felt that life had nothing more to give to me, that I needed nothing more, and that heaven could furnish nothing better. I lost them both in a single day."

"Oh!" said Kendall Fletcher, putting a volume of pity and sympathy into that monosyllable. "They died?"

"It was worse than death, infinitely worse. A thousand times I have told myself that if I could have held them in my arms, and watched the life go out, and closed their eyes and laid them in the grave, I could have thanked God for his mercy. But to have to think of them as all alone, in suffering, in terror, in mortal peril—it is a wonder to me that I kept my senses! If Jesus Christ had not found me I could not."

"Can you tell me about it?" asked Fletcher, presently, feeling that for the older man's sake he must break the silence into which he had fallen, "or is it too hard for you?"

"No, oh, no; I must tell you the whole of it, you of all men! I was young and positive and fierce of temper and altogether in the wrong. We quarreled, my wife and I. She had a friend who had been her playmate in her childhood, and she persisted in keeping friendship with him after he went wrong; after he disgraced himself and the honored name he bore as only a man can. I do not mean that she sought him unduly, or did anything in the least unwomanly, but I thought that she ought not to recognize him on the street, and she believed that by treating him with kindness she could keep her influence over him and save him. She persisted in this course, not violently, but with a gentle dignity, assuring me that she could not do as I wished without violating her conscience.

"He took advantage of her goodness; her name was whispered about by certain malicious gossips in connection with his. They were envious of her, and delighted in the chance of smirching the name of one far above them. It drove me wild. I knew that her motive for all that she did was as pure as an angel's could have been; but the thought that her name was being bandied about, on the lips of those who would not dare to address her, got hold of my reason and common sense. The climax came one evening when I was rushing home from the train after a two-days' absence. Two street loafers at that moment under the influence of liquor were just ahead of me, and as I was about to pass, one of them uttered my wife's name, coupling it with that fellow's in such a way that I could not help knocking him down, half intoxicated though he was. Then I went home to my wife in a fury. I accused her of being indifferent to my honor, of disgracing the name I had given her, and that had been above reproach. I trusted her utterly, and yet in my insane rage I believe I made her feel that I had lost faith even in her! It was monstrous! It seems beyond belief. I have never had a clear idea of what I really did say on that awful night, but I think I must have driven her into actual insanity. I know I left her in fierce anger, and spent the remainder of the night in my library. I knew that I must take a very early train on the following morning, but she did not know it, and I left without a word for her. I expected to return by the afternoon train, but when I missed it I wired her at once, but received no answer. This kept me away overnight; long before that I had come to my senses, and I made my second wire so lengthy, and so worded that I felt sure she would reply, but she did not. That, and the fact that she did not meet me at the train as I had asked her to, alarmed me; I knew that she was incapable of petty revenge. Have I told you that all this happened away from home? Business had called me to another town for the season and we had taken rooms at a hotel well uptown. The fellow who was the cause of all my misery was employed in the same town, and it was here that gossip had dared touch her. Of course we were comparative strangers, else her position and well-known reputation would have saved her even from professional gossips. During the short ride to my hotel I filled the space with images of illness and suffering that tortured me, but that were only as a pleasant dream compared with the reality. I could not find her! All that they could tell me at the hotel was that she had gone out early on the afternoon before, dressed as for a walk, taking the child with her. She had left no word, but her key was in the office as our custom was when we went out for a few hours. When she did not return for dinner, all they thought was that she had decided to dine elsewhere. Both of my telegrams were in the office awaiting her return, but they had not known where to look for her, nor had they felt that there was any cause for alarm; supposing that she had chosen to spend the time of my absence with friends. I searched, of course, in every reasonable and unreasonable place for a message, a penciled word, anything that would give me a hint as to where to look for her. I found nothing; *nothing!* And I never saw her or my child again."

"Oh," said Fletcher, "that is awful! Do you mean— you *cannot* mean that you never heard anything from them, or of them? Oh, God help you!"

Mr. Kendall became almost instantly calm, and spoke in his ordinary tone.

"God did help me, my friend. There is nothing in all the world of which I am so sure. But for the realization of him in the face of Jesus Christ, mercifully revealed to me at that time, my reason must have deserted me. It was awful, as you say. No words, of course, will ever describe it. I have never before tried to tell it in detail; I find that I cannot. But I came to know Jesus Christ in a way that I had not dreamed he could be known, in the flesh, at least; and I have been able all these years to look into his face, and live."

There was a silence then that Fletcher did not dare nor want to break. He felt as though he was on holy ground.

"Of course you know what I did," Mr. Kendall began again. "I went everywhere and did everything; I have given my life to the unavailing search. I constructed theories innumerable, and called to my aid all the public and private facilities for following them out. My wife's father was living then; he was a rich man and spent his years and his fortune in vain. I buried him five years ago, and since then have been alone."

"And you have never found the slightest clue to the mystery! What was your theory?"

"Never that she had voluntarily left me and kept intentional silence. She would never have done it. She must have wandered away. We were in the foothills, and she was given to long walks, venturesome walks. I have known her to go miles, without fatigue. She was teaching the little one to walk, to climb the hills, and delighted in the power to resist fatigue which the child showed. My belief has always been that she lost herself in some of the almost impenetrable forests of the region, wandering on and on until all trails were lost and all sense of direction, and—"

His voice sank into silence again. He could not put the rest of his imagined horrors into words.

After a little, he began once more, this time in a changed and energetic tone.

"But my reason for shadowing your young life with this awful story is a tremendous one; it almost overwhelms me. My friend, my little girl, my Winifred, had a jewel box exactly like the one you have described to me! I had it cut for her to use as her own little bank, and I gave her gold pieces to drop into it. There was a ten for every birthday—she was five, not six—and there were also tens for two birthdays of her mother's that had been especially memorable ones to the child."

Fletcher, who had risen in strong excitement, now interrupted.

"Seventy dollars! Mr. Kendall, there were just seventy dollars in gold in that box I told you of."

"And I guided the fingers that placed them there. My friend, your lost Weewona is my lost daughter."

"I believe it, sir, from my soul. She told me little things that make for proof. She dimly remembered her father; he held the box for her while she put in the money, and there were flowers in the room and pretty things. And her—"

Fletcher stopped abruptly. It would be the refinement of cruelty to tell this man that the mother had cried and cried, and then that they "walked and walked and *walked* and were lost!" He would not tell these things just yet; at least he might wait until the first almost awful excitement was past. Mr. Kendall had dropped into silence again, a strange, solemn silence.

Suddenly he asked a question.

"Did you tell me, I think you said she told you that her mother died?"

"Yes," said Fletcher, a wave of almost intolerable pity rolling over him for this poor man. "Weewona remembered her mother's death and burial. They were very good to her," he made haste to add, "Pete and his mother; they must have been very good sort of people indeed; she was bound up in them. Undoubtedly they did all they could from the first."

"Her mother's maiden name was Westervelt," Mr. Kendall said, with apparent irrelevance, "Winifred Westervelt."

"Then 'Westervelt' must have been the name on the handkerchief," Fletcher said, eagerly.

"Yes, that was what gave me the first shock while you were talking. She wrote it so; Winifred Westervelt Kendall."

He started up and began to pace the room so far as its meager limits would allow; he was evidently putting a strong check upon himself to keep his emotions within bounds. Suddenly he stopped beside Fletcher and laid a trembling hand upon his arm.

"You saw my daughter," he said solemnly; "saw her in her young maidenhood, and heard her voice. She had come so far on her lonely journey in safety; poor, deserted, desolate lamb, needing a father so much and lost to him through his own fault! Father in heaven, how can I bear it!"

Fletcher had never been so moved in his life; it was with difficulty that he kept back tears; but there were no tears in the other's eyes, they were dry and bright.

"We must find her," said Fletcher, at last. "We have settled it, sir, that now she *must* be found."

Mr. Kendall did not speak, but he gave to the young man one of his rare smiles, rich with a grateful appreciation of the effort to comfort him.

Well into the night the two sat talking.

When the old-fashioned supper bell resounded through this primitive house, they went down together and went through the pretense of eating the warm, greasy supper, talking only in a few general commonplaces, because of the presence of the crowd of grumblers who were still vigorously grumbling. As soon as possible they escaped, and returned as if by previous arrangement to Mr. Kendall's room, where they began again, quite as though it had not all been said before, and went over every minutest detail of the story as known to each, finding small corroborations as of their theory that had been unnoticed before.

Then they began to map out the future, and to learn accurately just where each had already been in his fruitless search, and just what he had done, or left undone. Both had new hope, the one because he had now a clue and a name to follow up, the other because a methodical, skillful, and determined man had put his powerful shoulder to the task of finding this girl. As for motive, it would have been hard to find stronger ones than each possessed. The young man told himself that with him it was a matter of common honesty; for the other, every nerve in his body throbbed with the wonderful thought: *She is my child, and he saw her in the flesh only a little while ago! The earth is small, and God is good, I shall find her.*

In the early morning they parted: Kendall Fletcher to take the long-waited-for train back to the city where he was expected, and Mr. Kendall to satisfy them both that no such person as one calling herself Weewona Westervel was to be found in the length and breadth of that small town; then to take the next train back to his own city.

Each of them had carefully made out duplicates of the places they meant to visit, and the persons they meant to consult in the course of the next few weeks. Each of them came to the Monday morning with renewed courage. The one because he was young and strong and there was a new day and all his pulses were aglow with energy; the other because he had spent the morning hours alone with God, and received the fulfillment of the promise that his strength should be renewed.

"We must keep in constant communication with each other," was Mr. Kendall's parting word. "I will write you each week; oftener if there is occasion, and will wire you, of course, if I have any light; and you will do the same for me?"

"Yes indeed," said Kendall with great earnestness; wondering the while how it was possible for him to feel such a sense of loneliness at parting from a man whom he had not yet known for twenty-four hours. Did sons feel something like this when they said good-bye to fathers? What a thing it would be to have a man like this one for a father! And what a sore deprivation for a girl who had a right to claim him to live her life without him! She must be found.

But along with the decision ran a sharp feeling of apprehension over the complications of success. What sort of a daughter would the girl who sat on his uncle's side porch that Sunday afternoon be for a father like Mr. Kendall? Yet, even so, if she were really his daughter he would wish to find and care for her, no matter what she was.

26

"The 'Mostest' Thing"

FROM this time on was conducted so truly systematic and vigorous a search for the missing girl that it did not seem as though failure would be possible. Even if the girl had died, reflected Fletcher, there would surely be some persons living who would know of it. "Or had married," he added, stopping aghast over the complications that such a possibility would entail upon his new friend. Of course it was a possibility; girls of that class were given to early marriages. Then he shivered again over the thought of her "class." Environment for a dozen years or more had outwitted heredity; was it within the realm of hope that the girl could catch up in the race?

Other topics besides the one central in their thoughts were discussed in the letters that were frequently exchanged between Mr. Kendall and his new ally. Kendall Fletcher's conscience did not get away from the very last word his friend had spoken with a kind hand resting on his arm:

"And remember, my young brother, there is One seeking you; you think it is the other way, that you have been seeking him, but let me assure you on the authority of one who knows by experience, that when you 'search for him with all your heart, he will be found of you'; it is his own word."

The young man set the seal to his real honesty of intention by taking hold with resolute will of the subject on the edge of which his thoughts had so long hovered. Under Mr. Kendall's guidance he became an intelligent and earnest student of the Bible. Doubts that had arisen in the course of his contact with skeptical minds were frankly expressed and as frankly discussed. Mr. Kendall met him fully and kindly at every point. He wrote once:

> You are fighting over my old battleground. It is like reviewing my own life to read your letters. I believe I have not told you that it was not until I had lost all that I thought made life worth living that I began to give heed to these matters. My wife was a lover of the Lord, but I merely tolerated in a superior way what I considered her superstitions. It was what we have an irreverent way of calling an accident that finally drew my attention sharply to the subject of the Christian religion. I know now that it was a merciful Providence. Someday, if you care to hear it, I will tell you the whole story; it is peculiar. But I have to confess that it was my longing to be in touch on all possible points with my wife, after I had lost her, that held me steadily to an exhaustive study of these topics. Perhaps you will think the statement extreme, but I hold to the belief that no sane man can give honest continued study to the subject of the Christian religion as set forth in the Bible without reaching the conclusions

that I reached. Try it, my brother, and prove me mistaken if you can.

At another time, in reply to Fletcher's questions, he wrote:

You are putting the mystery in the wrong place. There is mystery in the doctrine of the changed life. "Ye must be born again" is as bewildering a statement today to the merely human intellect as it was in the days of Nicodemus. But the human part is simple enough and as clear as sunlight. With you and me, my friend, it is simply a question of the human will. "Ye *will* not come unto me," the Lord said, and the one insurmountable obstacle to the changed life is still just there. When the honest soul says, "I will," his part is accomplished; that opens the door to the divine One who has promised to come in and abide. He takes hold of the mystery, and works the transformation that we cannot. Don't burden your thoughts about human impossibilities; just try God's way and see how simple it all is, from the human side, and how sure and far-reaching is the divine side.

Just why this simple statement of a world-old fact that must have been at least referred to in dozens of sermons to which this young man had listened, should have suddenly flashed its simplicity and its common sense upon his mind as he read it in that letter, Kendall Fletcher could not have told; but he knew that his mind, at that moment for the very first time, grasped at the human side of the plan of salvation, and accepted it. There came an evening when he wrote the briefest of notes to Mr. Kendall from a full heart; it was, in fact, only two lines:

> My dear friend: I have this day signed the covenant between Jesus Christ and my soul, and for all days to come can say "My Lord and my God."

Only those who have helped to lead a soul into the light will be able to understand the joy that the message brought to that lover of the Lord.

To Kendall Fletcher, along with this experience, came renewed determination to find the girl who had sought help of him for this very way, and sought in vain. If he could but have a chance to help her discover the way to the sunset gate and the glory, what a joy it would be!

⇌ ⇋

"Weewee," said Electa, using the pet name that she had made, "what do you want most of anything in all this world?"

Weewona laughed brightly. "What a big question!" she said, "when there is a whole world full of wants."

"Yes, but they are not all *most* things; I want *the most* thing; that would be just one. Tell me what it is, please."

"Well, then, to go to college." Weewona hid the flash of longing in her eyes from the keen-sighted girl on the bed and made herself speak lightly. She must not let this darling desire of her heart show too plainly, lest it shadow the brightness of Electa's day; the little girl was always coveting the best things for her beloved Weewee. Moreover, Weewona was trying hard to stifle this unreasonable desire. Why should a girl who had begun so late in life even a common-school education, and had been exceptionally favored in reaching what had once been her highest ambition, dare to even think of anything more? Sometimes it almost overwhelmed her, the thought that she was really a high school graduate.

The swift-passing months had brought almost no outward changes to her life. She was to all intents and purposes a fixture in the Ordway household. Her special charge had become more than ever a *very* special charge. Electa had grown so fond of her nurse that the mere thought of separating them was cruelty. Mr. Ordway stood ready to make sacrifices if necessary in order to retain Weewona's services. Had she been so disposed, the girl could have commanded an exorbitant salary. No such thought even entered her mind. She accepted gratefully the voluntary raise of wages with which from time to time the family strove to anchor her, for she had long ago learned something of the power of money; but had she received no wages at all, she would not have left Electa unless forced to do so.

"Is that really the very mostest, Weewee, to go to college?" There was a wistful note in Electa's voice. Weewee hesitated; the want which she almost never put into speech flashed into her thought. Should she tell it to this sympathetic little girl? It was undoubtedly her "mostest."

"I have wanted one thing more than any other, for years," she said, gently, "but it is a foolish thing to want, because impossible to have."

"What is it, please?"

"Knowledge of my father, and a right to some name." The girl's voice was very low; sometimes a burning sense of shame possessed her in the thought that she had not even a *name* that she could rightly call her own.

"Oh, poor Weewee!" said the child, with instant appreciation of the pain of this confession. It was in ways like these that the little invalid was old beyond her years.

"You don't know your father's name, do you? I had not thought of that." Then, after a moment's silence: "Weewee, dear, I wish so much that you would take my Father for yours. I mean my Father in heaven; he is yours, too, if you want him. I'm real sure of it, Weewee; I've found it out by myself; and, besides, he says so. He says it in the Bible, did you know that? The reason why I asked you for the very biggest wish was because I wanted to talk to my Father about it. Do you know, Weewee, I've found out that it does do good to pray? You know we talked about that? Well, it does; he hears, and he answers. I don't mean that he always gives us just what we ask for, because we are silly people, you know, and might make dreadful mistakes, but he does the very best he can for us; and I mean to ask him about your two big things."

"I wouldn't, darling," said Weewona, with an almost hysterical little laugh. "You see they are both impossibles."

"God can do impossibles if he thinks it would be better," the child said calmly. "I shall ask him about it, anyhow; that won't do any hurt."

What strides the child had taken!

Contrary to their fears, the little invalid had for several months been steadily improving. Her improved mental condition, the doctors said, had undoubtedly contributed to this change for the better. Certainly she had gained in self-control; from being nervous and fretful, hard to please and rarely staying pleased more than a few minutes at a time, she had grown remarkably patient, and her pain-worn face had taken on a wonderfully pleasant look. Her mother was sure that she was getting well, and the entire family shared her sanguine predictions.

"You know what a sunny little creature the child was before she had that awful fall," Mrs. Ordway would say to any interested listener. "Why, she was just a little bundle of smiles! And now nature is reasserting itself; can't you all see that it is because she is getting well? I don't mean, of course, that I expect her to be walking about like other girls," she would add, with a patient little sigh, the remark being designed to prove her entire reasonableness, "but think what a blessing it will be to have her comparatively free from pain and able to enjoy home life again!

"Besides, if she should continue to improve as rapidly in the next six months as she has in the past, I have by no means given up the hope that she may get well enough to be taken abroad, to some of those wonderful doctors and baths that seem to work almost miracles."

But Electa herself made no such plans; and Weewona at least noticed that she was gently quiet whenever they talked before her about her getting well.

One evening when Mrs. Ordway had spent a longer time than usual in her daughter's room and been unusually happy over the marked improvements she had noted, and unusually voluble over her hope of foreign travel and foreign doctors, Electa lay quite silent for some minutes after she had gone. Weewona was moving about, making things ready for the night. Suddenly the child said cheerfully:

"I am going abroad, Weewona, but not where Mamma thinks; and I shall not come back. Did you know that?"

Weewona, who had been most carefully instructed to discourage anything like what Mrs. Ordway called "somber" talk, hardly knew how to reply; indeed, her own foreboding heart was too sore just then for answer of any kind. After a moment's silence, she said almost in a tone of reproach: "Why do you speak as though you were glad over a thought that hurts us all so much?"

Electa turned her face into fuller view; there was a tender smile on it, and her voice was very sweet.

"Dear Weewee, think; if you knew you could never take a single step in this world, and couldn't even raise yourself up in bed, or turn your head without making an ache somewhere, wouldn't you be glad over the thought of going away to a place where you could hop, and run, and never have a single ache anymore?

"Besides, Weewee, dear, this is the way it is to be; Mamma thinks I am getting well, and she cries if I try to tell her anything else; but you see I know how it is, because—well, you know what I told you about God being our Father and talking with us? He has talked to me a great deal, and I understand things ever so much better than I did. Weewee, if you knew Jesus Christ and talked with him, you would understand all about it."

In the heart of the older girl was a great longing to sit at the feet of this child whose angel surely beheld the Father's face, and learn of her; but she dare not encourage her to talk in this strain; it was directly contrary to orders; there seemed to be nothing for her but silence.

When Electa spoke again it was on an entirely different subject.

"We are going to have company this week. Do you know? Did Mamma tell you? Yes, he is our cousin; at least he is Mamma's cousin; but Mamma never saw him. His name is Halford Averill; isn't that a pretty name? But it isn't so pretty as his father's. Mamma knew his father; he is her uncle, but he was only a little bit older than she; isn't that funny! His name is Lawrence; I think that is such a pretty name; if I had a brother I should want him named Lawrence; but Mamma says they always called this boy Lance. Don't you think that spoils the name?"

The brush which was making gentle passes over Electa's abundant hair was suddenly arrested.

Among this girl's vivid memories standing out in bold relief amid a network of commonplaces was that name: Lance Averill. That was the man whom Pete had killed! Could there be another man with exactly the same name? Or was it possibly the same family, with a son coming as a guest to the very house in which she lived! There was a single moment of unreasoning terror, then an instant sense of relief. What if it were? Pete was beyond all harm now.

"Is he dead?" she asked, with an eagerness that was startling.

Electa looked puzzled. "Is who dead, Weewee?"

"The father of this young man who is coming?"

"His father? Oh, no, he isn't dead; but Mamma hasn't seen him since he was almost a little boy. Mamma didn't like him very well, I think, if he was her uncle; he was queer. He went away when he was real young and didn't have anything to do with his family.

"Mamma never knew the lady he married, and she

says she thinks they are none of them our kind of people. But this young man is nice, I guess. He has been to college, Weewee, so you will like him."

Weewona's smile over this queer little conceit was somewhat strained; she had not yet recovered from the shock of the name: Lance Averill; but, of course, it was not the same family; that Lance Averill was dead; Pete had killed him.

27

"An Everlasting Gump!"

THE cousin came, a handsome young man, having an assured man-of-the-world air about him, and an easy way of making comrades of everybody who gave him the slightest opportunity. He patronized his little cousin Electa in every possible way, offering to sit with her at any time, to read to her, to sing to her, to tell her stories; in short, to do anything in the world that would help to amuse the child.

"It shows that he has a good heart," Mrs. Ordway remarked. "All young men would not be so willing to spend hours in amusing a little invalid cousin." But the daughter Edith said she was afraid it showed that he had an eye for a pretty face wherever he found it. Her tone was significant, and Mrs. Ordway, shocked, said:

"Why, you don't mean—just what do you mean, Edith?"

"Oh, I don't mean anything very serious; only Halford looks at Weewona, not Electa, the most of the time when he is up there; and whenever he can get a chance elsewhere to look at her or speak to her he seizes it. Didn't you notice him yesterday noon when she took Norah's place and waited on table? His eyes followed every movement she made. And she is a graceful, pretty girl, Mamma."

"Of course she is," Mrs. Ordway said, greatly disturbed, "but I should not want her to have anything to do with the Averills; it is distressing to think of her even meeting one of them in my house. Weewona is too pretty, Edith. I don't know what is to become of her in this wicked world with no father or mother to help her."

But Weewona had reasons all her own for being anxious to meet Mr. Averill. It was barely possible that he might be connected with the family with whose life tragedy she had been so strangely associated. He might even have heard of Pete; he might possibly be able to tell her something that he had heard about Pete's young manhood, before his life was shadowed by that awful experience. The bare possibility of hearing some word about him set this lonely girl's heart to throbbing.

It was on the fourth day of Mr. Averill's visit that she had her opportunity. It was early evening and she was hurrying home from the library, Mrs. Ordway having agreed to sit with Electa until she went for an important book.

As she turned into her home street Mr. Averill suddenly appeared from the shadows somewhere and walked beside her.

"I'm just in time," he said, gaily. "I hate walking alone; I hope you do."

And then Weewona seized her chance.

"I am glad to have a chance to ask you a question. I used to know about some people of your name, and I have been wondering if you were possibly of the same family. Did you ever hear of a man named Walsh?"

"I should say I did! One Pete Walsh is a person likely to be remembered in our family. I hope he wasn't a friend of yours?"

She was glad that he could not see the color flame into her face, nor hear the beating of her heart. It required great effort to ask quietly what he knew about him.

"I know a great deal about Pete Walsh, but it is not at all likely that your acquaintance is the same one; the name is common enough. This one tried to kill my father."

"Didn't he kill him?"

It was an extraordinary question, viewed from Averill's standpoint; it emphasized his belief that this was an unusual sort of girl.

"Well, hardly!" he said, with a light laugh. "He was very much alive when I left home. Oh, it happened a long time ago when I was a little chap. Quite a romance it was; if you were a novel writer I would give it to you for a plot. I heard all about it, of course, and was just young enough to have it make a deep impression. They thought at first that my father was dead; then they thought for several days that he would die. But Pete Walsh didn't wait to see; he and his mother ran away that very night; they knew enough to understand that the country about there wouldn't be safe for them. He was a queer chap, anyhow. Reckless, I suppose, in all sorts of ways, and so jealous of his wife that a man couldn't bow to her without making him crazy mad. That was what made the trouble about my father; he was kind to her, of course, and I guess she thought it was fine for him to notice her; they belonged to a lower class than our family, you understand, and Pete got jealous, poor fool! He had to run away without his wife, though; she was ill, and she died that night. So you see it is quite a tragedy; it would make a splendid plot for a novel. Do you ever write stories? Your eyes look as though you could."

So here was the other version of the poor wrecked life; and it had all been for naught!

She had heard all that she wanted to know, except, perhaps—Did he possibly know something about Pete's mother?

She ventured a carefully put question. "What became of them? Did you ever hear anything more about them?"

"Not a word. They must have gone to another part of the world, another country, probably. I don't believe they ever went back to the old place; my father said Pete wouldn't dare to, and that he hoped he would never hear of him as alive and well; that it was good punishment for him to think of the gallows as waiting for him. People wouldn't have waited for any gallows, though, if my father had died; Pete knew that, I guess. It was a wild kind of a place, a bit lawless from all I have heard. I know nothing about it personally. My father moved a couple of thousand miles from there the year following this trouble, and never went back. What about the Mr. Walsh that you know? Is he your sweetheart? I hope he isn't related to the one whose story I have been telling."

"The man I used to know is dead," Weewona said, coldly.

Not for the world would she have told him anything more. She felt that he was the kind of man it would be easy to hate. She ran up the steps of the Ordway porch without heeding his remonstrance about her being in such towering haste. Then came a dismayed exclamation. She had forgotten her latchkey, and she knew that the entire family, even the cook, were gone out. Mrs. Ordway, in Electa's room, would not be likely to hear the bell.

"Never mind," said Mr. Averill, cheerfully, when she explained the embarrassing situation. "We can sit here and wait until some of them come; it is pleasanter than in the house, anyway."

"But I ought to be in the house. Electa will need me. Do you know the time, Mr. Averill? Mr. Ordway will be on the seven forty-five train."

"Then there are only about ten minutes to wait," he said, holding his watch out to a streetlight; "it is almost twenty-five of eight now. Sit down and let us have a sociable time."

Weewona, with an anxious sigh, dropped to a porch seat; there seemed to be nothing else that she could do.

To her annoyance, Mr. Averill seated himself as near to her as he could.

"This is cozy," he said. "I've been wanting a chance to have a visit with you. Do you know I think you are a mighty nice girl? Quite superior to your position."

She felt only annoyance, and answered coldly that her position at Mrs. Ordway's was entirely satisfactory; but the colder her tone the more friendly his became. He lavished fulsome compliments upon her and kept drawing so close to her that she began to feel positive alarm.

"I think I will ring," she said, trying to rise. "Mrs. Ordway might possibly hear the bell." But he caught her arm and held her down.

"No, don't; don't be so foolish. There is the whistle of the train; Mr. Ordway will be here in less than five minutes; do be sensible and let us have a little visit.

Don't you understand by what I have been saying to you that I really like you very much? I don't believe you have the least idea what a pretty girl you are. I thought so the first time I saw you. If you choose to be friendly, you and I can have no end of larks if I stay here this summer. I'm thinking of doing so, and I may as well own that you are my chief reason; now give me one kiss while there is time, and say you are glad."

She tried to spring away, to free herself, but he held her as in a vise with his face close to hers.

"Don't squirm so," he said. "I'm only going to kiss you; that can't be a heavy trial, and you mustn't pretend it is; such a pretty girl as you must be used to it."

"Mr. Averill," she said, pushing his face away from her with all the strength of her free hand, "if you do not let me go this instant, I will scream for help, and I shall tell Mr. Ordway that you insulted me."

The fellow kept his hold and gazed at the angry and frightened girl with increasing admiration.

"Why, you charming little spitfire!" he began, "I am only—"

"What does this mean?" said a stern voice at his elbow, and Mr. Ordway, who had dropped from the last car of a long train and shortened his walk by taking a back street, stepped on the porch. Averill loosed his hold on Weewona and tried to laugh.

"By Jove!" he said. "It looks awkward, doesn't it? But upon my honor it is a tempest about nothing. I merely offered to give a pretty girl with whom I had been out walking a good-night kiss, and she seemed to suddenly lose her head and mistake me for a highway robber."

Meantime Weewona gasped out a single sentence: "I haven't my key!"

As Mr. Ordway applied his own key, and the girl

vanished, he made a single remark to the man who was a guest in his house:

"The trouble is, sir, the girl is used to gentlemen!" with marked emphasis on the last word. He was not an admirer of this young man who was claiming hospitality on the ground of relationship.

Weewona, instead of going at once to her charge, flew up two flights of stairs to her own room, closed and locked her door and threw herself on her bed in a passion of weeping.

What was the matter with her? How was she different from other girls, that young men thought they could treat her as they would not dare to treat those who were sheltered by their own homes? It was not the first time that she had been made to feel the bitterness of her unprotected state. If only she had a father or a brother or anyone whose right it was to protect her.

Then softly, like a bit of harmony from another world, seemed to come to her the sound of Electa's voice:

"Listen to this, Weewee: 'And they shall be my sons and daughters.' It is God speaking! Oh, Weewee, dear, you said you wanted a father so much, why don't you take him?"

Why, indeed? Oh, if she only knew how! She sank sobbing to her knees, and perhaps the first real prayer of her life was voiced in that low cry:

"O God, be my Father; take care of me."

One gleam of comfort the girl had in the darkness of her pain and shame. Mr. Ordway, as he came up the walk, must have heard her passionate words; he would know that she was not staying there willingly to be insulted.

As for Mr. Halford Averill, he decided in the night

that he would cut his visit short and shake the dust of this stupid city from his feet without delay. No fun to be had here; the little idiot had probably before this time spread her woes before that very proper cousin of his, who would look upon him with holy horror. He gave the chair near his bed a vicious kick as he thought of it all, and said aloud: "The girl is a fool, in spite of her eyes; who would have supposed that she could be such an everlasting gump!"

He took the first westbound train in the early morning, the same train that two hours later Kendall Fletcher boarded, grip in hand, taking a seat directly behind his old-time acquaintance. Averill, meantime, had found an acquaintance to talk to, and had not noticed Fletcher's entrance. That young man had no desire to renew his friendship with Averill; they had not met for months, and although the old feud between them had been long since smoothed over, they were now only civilly polite to each other when they chanced to meet, neither having the least desire to seek each other's society.

Fletcher was in no mood this morning to try to talk with Averill, and would have retreated to another car had he noticed him in time. As it was he crouched in a corner of his seat and drew his hat well over his face as if for a nap.

In truth he was in no mood for conversation of any sort; he had just parted from the man who was now his best earthly friend; and for the first time since their acquaintance began, Mr. Kendall had seemed almost depressed.

It was now many months since the most systematic and vigorous search had been carried on without the slightest result.

"Do you think it can be," Mr. Kendall had said with

a smile that was pathetic, "that I am never to find my daughter? I deserve it all. I was cold and hard to the sweetest woman God ever gave to man; but I did not know *him* then; I could never be hard with my daughter. Still, I do not deserve to be trusted. There are times when it drives me almost into a frenzy to feel that she may be in bitter need, and I powerless to help her. But at other times I realize that I can trust my Father."

After a moment's silence he began again.

"Even though she were dead, it seems as though we might find her grave. But perhaps I have thought too much about graves; I had a hope that she would know where to find her mother's. Of course, you have no sort of idea as to the whereabouts of that mountain cabin she told you of?"

And Fletcher had been compelled to admit that he had not the faintest clue, and felt disgusted with himself because he had not called out from the girl every minutest detail of her story.

They had parted with renewed pledges of faithfulness and energy.

"We will act exactly as though we had not lost an ounce of courage," the elder man had said, again with that pathetic smile. Then he had added with the touch of a tender hand upon the other's arm:

"We have each other, thank God." Fletcher's voice had failed him. He had been compelled to put his good-bye into that last handclasp.

As he shaded his eyes in the corner of the car and seemed to be sleeping, he told himself again that he would never give up the search as long as he lived. He did not believe that the girl was dead; *she should be found.* Then he thought of Averill, and wondered if it would be possible to avoid him. He could not seem to be sleeping all the while, yet it would be hardly possible to bring himself to the level of a conversation with him. Perhaps he could slip away unnoticed into the next car.

Then, just as he was meditating this attempt, Averill's voice, being raised to overcome the roar of a passing train, became distinct to him.

28

"What Has Happened?"

NO, I had a beastly time; stupidest old town I have struck, this trip."

This was the beginning of the story from Averill's lips that arrested Kendall Fletcher's attention.

"I've been doing some cousins that I never saw before, and never want to again; awfully respectable people, you understand, of the prune and prism sort; keep their lips always ready for such words.

"There was one awfully pretty girl in the house, though, real stunning pretty; just your kind, too, big-eyed, you know, and all the rest.

"No, she wasn't a cousin, not much! Wasn't their kind, at all; she is in service, nurse to a sick child, or something of that sort. Not at all the ordinary kind of servant; I tell you she is *extra*ordinary, in every way; has Indian blood in her, I guess; at all events she has an Indian name, 'Weewona.' Isn't that musical enough?"

The hat of the supposed sleeper behind Averill was pushed suddenly back, and Kendall Fletcher sat erect with every nerve on the alert. He could seem to hear a clear, incisive voice saying: "No, there isn't; there is only one girl in the whole world named Weewona; Pete said so."

It was an unusual name; could this possibly be— Wait! What was that fellow saying?

"She is a smart enough girl for work, and they trust her entirely with the child, but she is a perfect fool, for all that. I tried to show her a little kindness in a good-natured way; I saw that she was by herself, as you may say, and rather forlorn; I even went so far as to take a walk with her one evening, and when I attempted to kiss her good-night, what did the creature do but make a fuss!

"Oh, you may laugh, but it was no laughing matter I assure you; I was never in such a mess in my life, nor so disgusted. Catch me attempting kindness to pretty nurse girls again! Hello! This your station? Sorry to lose you. Well, so so, until we meet again."

Two minutes more, and Averill was expressing his surprise over the appearance at his side of Kendall Fletcher.

"Got on at the junction, did you say? Queer I didn't see you. I was busy talking with Holmes, I suppose. Know Holmes? Well, no great loss. Oh, he's a good sort of a chap, but don't amount to much. Where are you bound?"

"On a short business trip," said Fletcher. "By the way, did I hear you mention Monta Sacra to your friend?"

"Shouldn't wonder. I just came from there; beastly name for a town, isn't it? Stupid town, too.

"Oh, yes, a city; a little one; fifty or sixty thousand, perhaps, but slow."

"Are you acquainted there, Averill? I wonder if you could perhaps put me in the way of finding a man named Baldwin, a retired fruit dealer, who may possibly live there? Our firm has occasion to confer with him and I am looking him up."

"You lawyers are always hunting people up! Is it a legacy left him? I wish you'd raise one for me. I'd agree to give you no trouble in finding me. No, I have no acquaintances in Monta Sacra; never was there before, and hope never to be again. Hold on, though; there's my cousin, where I was staying; he's an old resident, and knows everybody. Ordway, the name is. Like his address?"

While it was being written, Fletcher studied ways of putting a question that should enlighten him as to whether the pretty nurse girl was named Weewona Westervel; and abandoned them all as unsafe. He must take his chances; if there was a girl in the world named Weewona, he meant to see her.

The train was slowing up for a station, and he seized his grip and hurried his thanks.

"Got to stop here?" said Averill. "Why, man alive! The place isn't larger than a teacup and has only one train a day! You can't go until tomorrow."

"Nevertheless," said Fletcher, with a smile and a parting bow. He had no idea where he was stopping. He only knew that a train must soon be due that would take him back over the route that he had just traveled; and that the city of Monta Sacra lay still beyond, in the same direction. The present aim of his life was to reach Monta Sacra with as little delay as possible.

Four hours later he was waiting for admittance at the door of the address that Averill had given him. He was sure of nothing, save that every possible clue was to be worked for all it was worth.

His plan was to ask boldly for Miss Westervel. Failing in this, he would fall back on the Mr. Baldwin whom he was looking up for the law firm, and see if Mr. Ordway could help him in this, and also advise him as to a member of his household named Weewona. In event of a Miss Westervel presenting herself who could not, by any stretch of imagination, be made into the Weewona of his search, he must simply explain that he was searching for a friend by that name, whose address he had lost. It was all easy enough; but he waited in the Ordway dining room with a strangely beating heart. He had taken his friend's cause so utterly to himself that this had ceased to be a matter only of money and honesty.

He had got as far as the dining room, at least. The servant who admitted him had owned, with some hesitation, that there was a girl by that name in the house, and she guessed she was at home; then she had stood before the open door of the reception room irresolute, and finally turned toward the dining room. He inferred that "Miss Westervel" was not in the habit of receiving formal calls, and that the maid had been at a loss what to do with him.

Could he have followed her to Electa's room he would have heard her voluble tongue.

"Is Weewona here, Miss Electa? Oh yes, you are; well, there's an awful handsome fellow waiting in the dining room to see you; you better take off your apron before you go down; I ain't seen such a handsome man since I came to this town."

Weewona laughed good-naturedly.

"He won't mind my apron," she said. "I will be back in a few minutes, Electa. I presume it is Professor Morrow with some papers that I am to copy for him; it won't take him but a minute to show me about them."

The dining room door opened, and a vision of

loveliness appeared to Kendall Fletcher. He knew her in an instant; he told himself afterward that he should have known those eyes anywhere.

The awkward, uncouth, hopelessly bewildered stranger who had sat with him on the side porch of his uncle's house, that Sunday afternoon, had possibilities that he dimly recognized even then, and had blossomed. The abundant brown hair, the unusually large eyes, the contour of the face were the same; but time and culture of the best kind had done their work; Weewona was beautiful.

"Weewona!" he said eagerly, and stopped, confused. By what authority did he address this lovely stranger by so familiar a name? Evidently she questioned his right, for the smile that had been on her face when the door opened, vanished, and she stood before him a very statue of dignity. There flashed upon him the thought of Averill trying to kiss this girl! But for his indignation at the thought of such a thing, he could have laughed at the fellow's folly.

"I beg pardon," she said. "Is there some mistake? I expected to meet Professor Morrow."

"Then you do not remember me?"

In spite of an effort not to have it so, he felt that there was a note of reproach in his voice, and he had also an absurd feeling that he hated Professor Morrow.

"I certainly do not," was the cold reply. "May I ask if you have business with me, or is it a mistake?"

"Yes," he said, recklessly, stung unreasonably by her cold dignity. "There is a mistake; I have spent years in hunting for a friend, and find that I have met only a stranger. But I have business with you, Miss Westervel. I am Kendall Fletcher, and I want to return the money I borrowed of you years ago."

A sudden lighting of her face gave him another

view of her beauty. Her extreme dignity was gone, and she held out a cordial hand.

"It seems strange that I did not recognize you," she said. "I have never forgotten you, Mr. Fletcher. You were almost the first friend I found in a strange world. But you have changed very much."

"I presume I have," he said. "Certainly you have! Yet I knew you on the instant. Will you tell me why you hid yourself away, so that a persistent search over the continent had to be made before I could have a chance to discharge my obligations to you?"

She looked astonished.

"I never thought of such a thing as hiding, Mr. Fletcher. I came here, to this home, as soon as I left your uncle's and have been here ever since. It is a long way from Mr. Carver's, it is true; I met Mrs. Ordway on the cars with a sick child and came home with her. I had not thought of there being anyone to care where I was.

"There was a misunderstanding, Mr. Fletcher, between Mrs. Carver and myself. I thought she wanted me to go away, and that I had given her proper notice, but she did not think so; and I felt sure that she would not care to hear anything about me."

"But how did you think I was ever to pay back the money I had taken?"

Her face flushed under his gaze, but she laughed a little musical laugh as she said:

"At the risk of being considered as ignorant as I was then, I shall have to confess to you that I never thought of that; of not being easily found, I mean, whenever anybody wanted to find me."

"Then you did not think that I intended to cheat you out of that money, to steal it?" He spoke with an eagerness that he could not conceal.

"Of course not! You said you would place it where it would earn more, and I had perfect confidence in your word."

She laughed again, softly, as she added:

"Before I had got very far in arithmetic I used to fancy that it might, in time, earn enough to pay for an education! But I gave that up as soon as I learned to calculate interest!"

He joined in her laugh, and began to feel at ease. The mystery about her seemed to fade away in her presence; it was all so simple and commonplace from her standpoint. She had not meant anything unusual in any way.

There was a movement just then on the stairs, at which she seemed to listen; then, this unconventional girl cut short the interview.

"Do you know, Mr. Fletcher, I shall have to ask you to excuse me? I have a dear little charge here, a helpless invalid; and it is time that I do for her what only I can do to her satisfaction."

And then the tremendous thing that he had yet to say, rushed upon Kendall Fletcher's consciousness and he spoke with headlong haste.

"But I must see you again, at once. There is something of great importance; something that I want to tell you, and that you will want to hear."

"Yes," she said, looking pleased. "Thank you. Could you possibly come again this evening? I shall be at liberty at seven, for an hour."

After that, he got himself away, he hardly knew how, save that he found himself in the street and felt that he had been dismissed. Whatever her duties were, this girl evidently had a realizing sense of their importance. But wasn't she wonderful! And wasn't it all wonderful! Could it all *be,* possibly, or was he dreaming? What should he do with the afternoon? How manage to exist until—wait! He stopped short in the street, looked at his watch and his timetable; then hailed a passing cab and gave the man an extra quarter to get him to the telegraph office in three minutes. He had suddenly remembered that it was but that morning he had parted from Mr. Kendall, and that he was now probably within fifty miles of Monta Sacra; then had discovered a train that in another half hour would leave the town where he expected to spend the night. If a telegram was promptly delivered, he could be at Monta Sacra by five that evening.

There was no time in which to study the careful composition of a telegram; a brief message, imperative enough to bring Mr. Kendall at once, was all that could be managed.

Mr. Kendall was just leaving his hotel with a view to seeking an interview with a man of whom he had come in search, when the clerk came to him with a telegram that read:

> Take 2:14 train for Monta Sacra. Important. Don't fail.
>
> Kendall Fletcher.

Being a man of business, after the first glance Mr. Kendall looked at his watch: It was ten minutes after two!

Fortunately, he was across the road from the station, and at five o'clock he was shaking hands with the young man from whom he had parted in the morning with the probability of not meeting him again for several months.

"This is a day of surprises!" he said. "I thought that

by this time you would be two hundred miles away in another direction. What has happened?"

"Wait," said Fletcher. "Wait until we get to my room; it is not far away; I have something very important to talk over with you."

He had seen this man grow deathly white under the vaguest possibility of news of his long-lost daughter; he had no mind to risk, on the street, the effect of the full flood of certainty that he had to pour out upon him.

29

"The Sunset Gate"

AS the city hall clock rang seven, two men were waiting admittance to the Ordway home. Both had lived through a strenuous hour. Mr. Kendall, having waited for many years, had found it almost impossible to add another hour to the long ordeal; yet had been the first to suggest that the girl who had so long counted herself fatherless ought not to be taken by too sudden a surprise. Fletcher must see her first, and make what preparation he could.

"It is not all self-restraint," he said. "I cannot help a feeling that it is a delicious dream from which I shall awaken to the reaction. Talk with her, my boy, and if you find some fact in her history that shatters our hopes, I know you will spare me all that you can."

But Kendall was jubilant; he had not a shadow of doubt; and all his fears about environment and "class" had been laid forever to rest by that one brief interview.

The preliminary difficulties had been lessened considerably by Mr. Kendall's announcement that Mr. Ordway was a business friend of long standing, and that he would be glad to take him into confidence and explain as much as was necessary of his story, while Fletcher was preparing the girl for the coming of her father.

It was Mrs. Ordway who was anxious. "What, again!" she said with lifted eyebrows in response to Weewona's request for the use of the sewing room to receive a call from her friend.

"Did you say he was the one who was here this noon? Why, Weewona, is he a very particular friend? It is unusual in ordinary friendship to call on the same person twice a day."

Then Weewona with heightened color explained the unusual circumstances as best she could.

When at seven o'clock two gentlemen appeared instead of one, Mrs. Ordway's anxieties were relieved for a moment, until she learned that one of the cards was for her husband.

"Mr. Tracy Kendall," Mr. Ordway said, studying the card. "Good for Kendall. I did not know he was in this part of the world. There isn't a man of my acquaintance whom I respect, and indeed heartily like better than he. Is Weewona's friend with him, do you suppose, or did they just happen here at the same hour? If he is a friend of Kendall's, you needn't worry over the call; that is introduction enough for him."

Mrs. Ordway did not care to explain the cause of her worry, nor to own that if the young man were above reproach it would worry her still more. Men never saw an inch ahead, but she had Electa to think of.

In the sewing room, a small, homelike place opening from the dining room, Kendall Fletcher waited with emotions scarcely less pronounced than Mr. Kendall's own. He realized to the full the strangeness of his story, and wondered if he would be equal to his part in this drama.

For the first few minutes after Weewona's coming she fairly dazzled him. She was in the simplest of evening dresses, but it was pure white, and the bib apron that had adorned her neat gingham of the morning was gone. The single dark red rose that Electa had slipped into her belt as she bent to kiss her seemed to belong there and be a part of the girl herself. Fletcher found himself deciding that she ought always to wear white with just a touch of crimson. Then he pulled himself together and went to his task.

He had brought a checkbook with him and was ready, he told her, to take up that note. She laughed as she admitted that she had kept it safely, and was not sure that she cared to surrender it. She had discovered that it was well to have money at interest, she told him; and he insisted upon discharging his debt.

"I will invest it again for you tomorrow, if you wish," he told her gaily, "but I have been struggling all these years to get free from debt, and I must be encouraged. Now for the full name."

He held his fountain pen ready for writing and watched the flush deepen on her face as she asked if he remembered that she had had to guess her name. He remembered, but he questioned, and heard the story of the name on the handkerchief from her, and assured her that he believed it was spelled with a final *t*. Then, unable to pave the way, he plunged headlong into the momentous question.

"Did you make that effort you were resolved upon, to find your father?" Her face saddened a little as she told him that she had realized the folly of that idea long ago.

"Oh, but I do not think it is folly," he said eagerly. "Do you know, I believe your father is living, and that you will find him; and I believe part of your name is Westervelt, spelled with a *t*. Weewona Westervelt Kendall."

He spoke the name slowly, as if trying its effect; he had even forgotten that his own given name was Kendall. She had not. She did not understand what he meant, but it sounded like an insult, or at best a heartless attempt to play with her desolate, nameless condition. She had not been prepared for this, from him.

"Mr. Fletcher!" she said, and rose from her chair. Then he understood his blunder.

I'm making a mess of it! was his mental exclamation. Aloud he said:

"Weewona, wait!" For she was moving toward the door.

"Do let me tell you what I came to say! I am not using idle words; won't you trust me? I have a wonderful story to tell; one that deeply concerns you.

"Weewona, I know the man who guided your hand when you dropped the gold pieces into that box. I know him well; his name is Kendall. That is what I meant, although I said it bunglingly; I believe in my soul that you are that man's daughter!

"There! I've done it now!"

For in place of the scarlet, Weewona grew suddenly as white as her gown, and the room seemed to float about her. She would have fallen if Fletcher had not caught her. But she rallied almost instantly and struggled to free herself from his help.

"I shall not faint," she said; "I never do; you said such a strange, wild thing! What did you mean? Why did you say it, Mr. Fletcher?"

"Because it is true," he said, throwing caution aside. "I tell you I know your father! I am sure of it. Are you really better? Well enough to hear all about it?"

He made her sit down, and told his tale; not attempting to condense it, but planning to give her time to recover herself, and get used to the strangeness.

It was not an easy task; at first she was keenly alive to every word he said, and questioned him with the skill of a lawyer, bent on finding a flaw in his logic; then, as the marvelous possibility dawned upon her she seemed fairly dazed with its brightness. Even when he finally left her and went across the hall to the library to summon Mr. Kendall he almost doubted if she fully understood that the man who claimed to be her father was in the same house with her at that moment.

He carried with him afterward a vision of the girl as she looked when he returned. She had risen, and was standing almost in the center of the room, one hand resting on the table for support; her whole face seemed luminous. The look it wore could not be described, but he remembered thinking that if he were an artist and could catch it on canvas he could make his name immortal.

Mr. Kendall was by nature a quiet man, and he was one who for years had cultivated, with regard to this life sorrow of his, a rigid self-control. He had replied to Fletcher's caution, that he would take great care to hold himself in check, but he had not been prepared for the vision that the opening door revealed. It was not of his daughter that he thought then; suddenly, the years rolled backward and he was young again; what he said was, "Oh, Winifred!" and he had her in his arms.

The little Electa was radiant. She could not hear the wonderful story too often.

"It is all beautiful," she said at last, clapping her hands in an ecstatic way she had. "It couldn't have been better, Weewee, could it? I did not know just how it would be, but I expected something; because, don't you know I told you I meant to pray about it, and our Father in heaven said he could make everything nice for you. He did, truly, Weewee. Oh, I don't mean he spoke *words,* but he told me in my heart.

"Now, by and by, you will go away with your father, and I will go away to my Father, and it will all be beautiful! But I wonder—Weewee dear, do you think it would be very selfish in me to ask Jesus to make your father willing to wait until my heavenly Father sends for me?"

And Weewona, in a voice choked with unshed tears, held the child in a close embrace and promised that she would not leave her. Well she knew that the waiting would be short.

It was left for Mrs. Ordway to be dismayed. Of course, it was lovely for Weewona to have found her father, and to have him such a splendid man; she had always thought that the girl was very unusual, and came of royal blood; she deserved it all, but—It did not seem as though they *could* have Electa grieved by parting from her. Wasn't it really too bad! If the man were only poor, so that he could be bought to allow his daughter to remain, she would not care what it cost; but, as it was, she did not know what to do.

Like many another, she was borrowing trouble that could have been avoided. Poor lady! To the heavy trouble waiting at her door they thought her eyes were blinded. She made her plea that evening. Could Weewona be happy away from the child who would be missing her and grieving for her? Then Weewona, who had resolved upon frankness at any cost, said tenderly that she did not mean to leave Electa even for a single day; that her father was glad to have her stay a little while; and looking with tear-filled eyes straight into the mother's eyes, she saw that she was understood. Then the mistress laid her hand on the shoulder of her maid and their tears fell together.

The door of the little log cabin on the mountain was wide open, and on the old log doorstep sat Weewona. But this time she was not alone—Kendall Fletcher sat beside her.

It was an evening not unlike that other one in which Weewona had sat there in utter desolation while Pete's mother slept inside; yet a whole lifetime of change swept between that time and this.

There had been few changes on this isolated and hidden portion of the mountain, and inside the little cabin—save for the inroads of dust and rust and decay—things were just as Weewona had left them, the poor little table being still spread in its sorrowful attempt at family life.

A little way from the doorstep the rude board still swayed back and forth in the evening breeze. Its crude lettering had been worn and blackened by dust and wind and rain, but Weewona had cut the letters deep in the wood and they were still plain.

Here Lies Peter Walsh.
The Sunset Gate.

Only a few feet away from Pete's grave could be seen the stake that Pete had set up long ago to mark that other grave; it was on that and the bowed figure near it that Weewona's eyes were fixed. It smote the girl's heart sorely to realize that her grief for Pete had swallowed up all memory of that other grave, her mother's. It seemed strangely heartless to her now, but she had never thought of marking it. Why had she not planted lovely ferns and beautiful creeping vines all about it, and cared for it tenderly through the years? Pete had not taught her to do so was the only explanation she had. Pete must have believed that entire silence was the best way to aid the natural forgetfulness of childhood; for Pete had always done what was his best for her; more and more as the years passed she had come to feel and be grateful to him for this. Tears dimmed her eyes and fell slowly, as she thought of it all, and of the blighted life. He had never understood about the sunset gate; if he had he would surely have told her. Whose fault was it that Pete, who had lived in the world until grown to manhood, surrounded, probably, by those who could have explained to him the beautiful earthly ending planned for all lives, and the beautiful blessed road through this world to its very gateway, had gone the journey to its bitter end on the wrong trail? Ought such mistakes as that to be possible? She knew all about the trail now, but how long, how *long* she had been in finding it! How nearly she had missed it, when all the while there had been but a single step to take, and she had been surrounded by people who had taken it!

But oh, her father's poor head had no need to be bowed that night in a grief like hers, for her mother had known the way home! Still, she could feel that his grief was bitter as he stood beside that lonely grave paying his tardy tribute to its memory.

"Poor father!" she said at last, feeling that Kendall was waiting for her to speak.

"Yes," he said, in quick sympathy. "Poor father, this is a hard hour. Yet I know he remembers that he has you."

"And you," she added significantly, as her hand sought his. "My father says that you were a son to him from the hour that he first met you."

Those three, father and daughter, and son, had crowded much living into the years just behind them. With the autumn leaves that followed that eventful summer in which Weewona came to her own, the little Electa's Father in heaven had sent for her, and she went joyfully away; she, at least, had found the trail that led home.

Soon after that, Weewona bade good-bye to the place that had so long sheltered her, and accompanied her father to his home in a distant state. Early in the winter that followed, the two went journeying in search of Pete's mother. They had no difficulty in finding her, for Halford Averill, who had already been of such signal service to them, was able to give the needed directions.

She had become an old, old woman, which, somehow, astonished Weewona; for, although she had always thought of Pete's mother as old, and as steadily growing older, yet she had never realized that she would find her greatly changed.

Still, the change seemed only outward; when they tried to talk with her she was still the grave, reticent woman of the girl's childish memory. She was decently clothed and cared for, and made no complaint of her surroundings. She lived with a granddaughter, she explained; yes, her children were gone; but the grandchildren were as good as could be expected. She received Mr. Kendall's earnest attempts at gratitude for all that she had done for his wife and daughter with a stolid gravity that bordered on indifference. Her only gleam of something like interest being when she looked intently at Weewona, once, and said, addressing Mr. Kendall:

"She looks like her. I didn't think she would, but she does. It's the clothes, partly. She had on fine clothes. Pete set out to have me keep 'em—Pete was always—kind of curious about the girl, but I cut 'em up; I had to; we couldn't get along without it; Pete saw it himself after a while."

It was the only remark she volunteered, although she answered readily, and as fully as she could Mr. Kendall's eager questions about that awful day when his wife had appeared suddenly from out of the tangle of forest, and with the single pitiful cry: "We are lost!" had sunk down and died.

They stayed long, and made earnest efforts, but the old woman had no confidences to offer, and apparently no wishes to gratify. She expressed no surprise over the change in Weewona, but said, after looking at her intently: "I knew you'd get on, I told you so." Then, suddenly: "You didn't ever go back, after Pete, did you?"

"Not yet," said Weewona, looking at her father with wistful eagerness; and then they had the comfort of seeing the stolid old face light up with something like joy. It was when Mr. Kendall explained that it was his intention to have Pete's body sent to rest beside his father and to mark the spot with a marble shaft bearing both names. But a moment before the old woman had said, in response to inquiries, that she didn't want anything, she was too old to care for things; all she needed was something to eat, and a grave pretty soon beside Pete's father; she had the one now, and the other was waiting for her. What more was there?

But her eyes shone at that word, and her lips quivered with feeling as she said:

"I thank you for that. Nobody knows how I have wanted it ever since Pete's father died; and I never expected to have it, for either of 'em, and now to have 'em both!" Her voice broke in a real sob. But she controlled it and added eagerly:

"I s'pose my name couldn't be cut on it, too, could it? You see I'll go soon."

When told that a blank should be left, and the name and date cut, when the time came, her satisfaction seemed complete.

Weewona, sitting in the little cabin doorway, had gone over the scene in detail; she had added some of the particulars to Kendall, speaking softly, as they sat there waiting for that watcher beside the grave.

"She is watching her graves tonight, perhaps," the girl said, gently. "She can see them both from her doorway. I can fancy just how she gloats over the gleaming shaft and traces the names in the moonlight. Poor old woman."

There was a later memory over which the girl loved to linger. It was when her father, bending over the shriveled woman, holding her wrinkled bony hand in his, had said:

"Good-bye, Grandmother. Will you try to remember that the Lord Jesus Christ loves you, and wants you to take him for your Savior? Won't you give what is left of your life to him? He wants to take you home to rest forever."

"She really seemed to understand," said the girl, recalling the scene, "and Father thought that she followed intelligently when he prayed. O Kendall, do you think she really may have found the way?"

"We will hope so, dearest," he said. "And pray God to reveal himself to her as only God can do."

Then they had dropped into silence. There were so many memories for these two, and the night and the scene wooed them to look backward.

For Weewona, she was making her way again down and down and *down* that unknown trail, alone, and with the night deepening around her. She was peeping into the great empty tent with a sense of desolation striking into her very soul. She was flying down the ravine away from that dreadful man who had seized her and accused her of evil. She was leaping fences and wading brooks and making for the open road to get away from *people;* and she knew not that one of the two men who had looked after her and frightened her anew, and had questioned one another as to who she could be, was her very own father; and that he had sat in the tent that first evening and helped to swell the harmony of the bells that had thrilled her poor hungry soul. If she had but known! And yet, if she had—would she ever have sat on Mrs. Carver's side porch, and would Kendall Fletcher ever have come and sat beside her?

"Weewee," said Kendall Fletcher, breaking the stillness, speaking softly—he had appropriated the little Electa's pet name for occasional use, and he was the only one that Weewona cared to have use it—"do you remember, I wonder, that on that first Sunday of our acquaintance, I offered to share my name with you and you refused it?"

She looked up wondering, a soft flush mantling her face. How strange it was that he too should be thinking of that Sunday, at just that moment!

"What sent your thoughts there just now?" she asked.

"I don't know. That porch scene came back to me vividly. It often has, as I think I have told you before. Suppose we had foreseen all that we two have been through since? It is good to be like little children, isn't it, and be led, without any foreknowing? But my darling, I am glad that you did not continue to be so indifferent to my offer as you were that day. Dear heart, do you know I am glad for everything tonight? All the shame and the pain were good for me; I can see it plainly. I had to learn through discipline. And while I think now that I would have shielded both you and your father from it all if I could, perhaps if I had been God, I would have led through just the same trials. What is that verse, 'I will refine them as silver is refined, and will try them as gold is tried, they shall call upon my name and I will hear them; I will say: It is my people! and they shall say: The Lord is my God!'"

Then the silence fell again; until suddenly Kendall Fletcher spoke in a changed tone.

"Do you know, dearest, we ought to go at once? We shall be late. I think I must tell you of something I have planned. I thought to surprise you, but perhaps it will be better to speak of it. They have arranged to sing your song for us tonight at the tabernacle at exactly eight o'clock. We shall just have time to make it."

"Oh!" said Weewona. "Do you mean 'The Sunset Gate'? How lovely! Father dear!" She arose as she spoke, moving toward the watcher beside the grave. "Do you know, we are to have our song tonight, at the tabernacle? Kendall says they have promised it for eight o'clock, and we shall have to hasten to be in time."

Mr. Kendall turned at once, and without speaking bent and kissed his daughter, drawing her hand through his arm, and they three went down the trail. Single file presently, down and down and down, until by and by they came to the wider, smoother pathway where they could walk together, father and daughter and son.

It was just as they reached the great tabernacle on the pine plateau that the lovely harmony so dear to them all, so vividly remembered by one of them, burst in full glory on the evening air:

> *"I am traveling toward life's sunset gate,*
> *I'm a pilgrim going home;*
> *For the glow of eventide I wait,*
> *I'm a pilgrim going home.*
> *Evening bells I seem to hear—*
> *As the sunset gate draws near.*
>
> *"I shall rise again at morning dawn,*
> *I shall put on glory then;*
> *With the shadowy veil of death withdrawn,*
> *I shall put on glory then."*

Then, from a choir of three hundred trained voices whose harmony the marvelous echoes caught up and repeated and prolonged until it seemed that the angels of the celestial city itself were joining in the refrain, came that indescribable effect produced by humming in imitation of bells; louder and louder, swelling upward—while with infinite pathos the soloist voiced the word, soft and softer still, and farther away, as he seemed to near the gate:

> *"Evening bells I seem to hear,*
> *As the sunset gate draws near."*

The End

Other Living Books Best-sellers

400 CREATIVE WAYS TO SAY I LOVE YOU by Alice Chapin. Perhaps the flame of love has almost died in your marriage, or you have a good marriage that just needs a little spark. Here is a book of creative, practical ideas for the woman who wants to show the man in her life that she cares. 07-0919-5

ANSWERS by Josh McDowell and Don Stewart. In a question-and-answer format, the authors tackle sixty-five of the most-asked questions about the Bible, God, Jesus Christ, miracles, other religions, and Creation. 07-0021-X

BUILDING YOUR SELF-IMAGE by Josh McDowell and Don Stewart. Here are practical answers to help you overcome your fears, anxieties, and lack of self-confidence. Learn how God's higher image of who you are can take root in your heart and mind. 07-1395-8

COME BEFORE WINTER AND SHARE MY HOPE by Charles R. Swindoll. A collection of brief vignettes offering hope and the assurance that adversity and despair are temporary setbacks we can overcome! 07-0477-0

DR. DOBSON ANSWERS YOUR QUESTIONS by Dr. James Dobson. In this convenient reference book, renowned author Dr. James Dobson addresses heartfelt concerns on many topics, including questions on marital relationships, infant care, child discipline, home management, and others. 07-0580-7

THE EFFECTIVE FATHER by Gordon MacDonald. A practical study of effective fatherhood based on biblical principles. 07-0669-2

FOR MEN ONLY edited by J. Allan Petersen. This book deals with topics of concern to every man: the business world, marriage, fathering, spiritual goals, and problems of living as a Christian in a secular world. 07-0892-X

FOR WOMEN ONLY by Evelyn R. and J. Allan Petersen. This balanced, entertaining, and diversified treatment covers all the aspects of womanhood. 07-0897-0

GIVERS, TAKERS, AND OTHER KINDS OF LOVERS by Josh McDowell and Paul Lewis. Bypassing generalities about love and sex, this book answers the basics: Whatever happened to sexual freedom? Do men respond differently than women? Here are straight answers about God's plan for love and sexuality. 07-1031-2

Other Living Books Best-sellers

HINDS' FEET ON HIGH PLACES by Hannah Hurnard. A classic allegory of a journey toward faith that has sold more than a million copies! 07-1429-6 *Also on Tyndale Living Audio 15-7426-4*

HOW TO BE HAPPY THOUGH MARRIED by Tim LaHaye. A valuable resource that tells how to develop physical, mental, and spiritual harmony in marriage. 07-1499-7

JOHN, SON OF THUNDER by Ellen Gunderson Traylor. In this saga of adventure, romance, and discovery, travel with John—the disciple whom Jesus loved—down desert paths, through the courts of the Holy City, and to the foot of the cross as he leaves his luxury as a privileged son of Israel for the bitter hardship of his exile on Patmos. 07-1903-4

LET ME BE A WOMAN by Elisabeth Elliot. This best-selling author shares her observations and experiences of male-female relationships in a collection of insightful essays. 07-2162-4

LIFE IS TREMENDOUS! by Charlie "Tremendous" Jones. Believing that enthusiasm makes the difference, Jones shows how anyone can be happy, involved, relevant, productive, healthy, and secure in the midst of a high-pressure, commercialized society. 07-2184-5

MORE THAN A CARPENTER by Josh McDowell. A hard-hitting book for people who are skeptical about Jesus' deity, his resurrection, and his claim on their lives. 07-4552-3 *Also on Tyndale Living Audio 15-7427-2*

QUICK TO LISTEN, SLOW TO SPEAK by Robert E. Fisher. Families are shown how to express love to one another by developing better listening skills, finding ways to disagree without arguing, and using constructive criticism. 07-5111-6

REASONS by Josh McDowell and Don Stewart. In a convenient question-and-answer format, the authors address many of the commonly asked questions about the Bible and evolution. 07-5287-2

THE SECRET OF LOVING by Josh McDowell. McDowell explores the values and qualities that will help both the single and married reader to be the right person for someone else. He offers a fresh perspective for evaluating and improving the reader's love life. 07-5845-5

Other Living Books Best-sellers

THE STORY FROM THE BOOK. From Adam to Armageddon, this book captures the full sweep of the Bible's content in abridged, chronological form. Based on *The Book,* the best-selling, popular edition of *The Living Bible.* 07-6677-6

STRIKE THE ORIGINAL MATCH by Charles Swindoll. Swindoll draws on the best marriage survival guide–the Bible–and his 35 years of marriage to show couples how to survive, flex, grow, forgive, and keep romance alive in their marriage. 07-6445-5

THE STRONG-WILLED CHILD by Dr. James Dobson. Through these practical solutions and humorous anecdotes, parents will learn to discipline an assertive child without breaking his spirit and to overcome feelings of defeat or frustration. 07-5924-9 *Also on Tyndale Living Audio 15-7431-0*

SUCCESS! THE GLENN BLAND METHOD by Glenn Bland. The author shows how to set goals and make plans that really work. His ingredients of success include spiritual, financial, educational, and recreational balances. 07-6689-X

THROUGH GATES OF SPLENDOR by Elisabeth Elliot. This unforgettable story of five men who braved the Auca Indians has become one of the most famous missionary books of all time. 07-7151-6

TRANSFORMED TEMPERAMENTS by Tim LaHaye. An analysis of Abraham, Moses, Peter, and Paul, whose strengths and weaknesses were made effective when transformed by God. 07-7304-7

WHAT WIVES WISH THEIR HUSBANDS KNEW ABOUT WOMEN by Dr. James Dobson. A best-selling author brings us this vital book that speaks to the unique emotional needs and aspirations of today's woman. An immensely practical, interesting guide. 07-7896-0

WHAT'S IN A NAME? Linda Francis, John Hartzel, and Al Palmquist, Editors. This fascinating name dictionary features the literal meaning of hundreds of first names, character qualities implied by the names, and an applicable Scripture verse for each name. 07-7935-5

WHY YOU ACT THE WAY YOU DO by Tim LaHaye. Discover how your temperament affects your work, emotions, spiritual life, and relationships, and learn how to make improvements. 07-8212-7